Once Haunted, Twice Shy

THE PEYTON CLARK SERIES

Also by H.P. Mallory

The *New York Times* and *USA Today* Bestselling
Jolie Wilkins Series:
Fire Burn and Cauldron Bubble
Toil and Trouble
Witchful Thinking
The Witch Is Back
Something Witchy This Way Comes

The Dulcie O'Neil Series:
To Kill a Warlock
A Tale of Two Goblins
Great Hexpectations
Wuthering Frights
Malice in Wonderland
For Whom the Spell Tolls

The Lily Harper Series:
Better Off Dead
The Underground City

The Peyton Clark Series:
Ghouls Rush In

Once Haunted, Twice Shy

THE PEYTON CLARK SERIES

H.P. MALLORY

Montlake Romance

This is a work of fiction. Names, characters, organizations, places, events, and incidents are either products of the author's imagination or are used fictitiously.

Published by Montlake Romance, Seattle

www.apub.com

ISBN-13: 9781477824061
ISBN-10: 1477824065

Cover design by Eileen Carey

Library of Congress Control Number: 2014903118

Printed in the United States of America

Chapter 1

Being possessed isn't exactly a walk in the park.

Granted, I've only been possessed for a few days, but they've been a very long and exhausting few days. As to how I became possessed and who is taking up residency in my body? Well, luckily for me, it wasn't like I was taken against my will. It was nothing like the Hollywood histrionics you see in movies like *The Exorcist*. Instead, I actually permitted the ghost of Drake Montague, a twentieth-century French Creole policeman, who also happens to be the biggest Casanova I've ever encountered, to share my body.

"*Ma minette*," Drake's voice sounded in my head. "*Please tell me we will venture outside the confines of our home today? I believe this ceaseless imprisonment shall cost me my sanity!*"

Oh, and one other thing: Drake has a flare for the dramatic.

"*Really, Drake?*" I mentally replied as I busied myself with painting my toenails "Feelin' Hot-Hot-Hot!" pink by OPI. "*You've been stuck inside this house for, oh, the last ninety-five years and you haven't lost your sanity yet. What difference could another three days possibly make?*"

Our conversations usually went exactly like that—like two voices in my head, only one of them wasn't mine. At first, it was sort of weird—having a random, disembodied, masculine voice periodically spouting off in my head. But, after a day or so, the novelty wore off and I was left mentally arguing my viewpoint with a very obstinate, stubborn man who seems set on nothing more than getting his own way.

If I close my eyes and concentrate, I can actually see Drake, and that makes our conversations a little more normal because then he isn't just an ethereal voice. As for the rules on how all of this ghostly stuff works? I'm not really sure. I wouldn't exactly call myself an expert when it comes to things that go bump in the night—or getting possessed by things that go bump in the night, as the case may be. Basically, whatever visual I get of Drake is whatever visual he chooses to send me. That is to say, when I close my eyes, Drake is the one who creates the scene that unfolds behind my eyelids. One thing I can say, though, is that it usually involves him in some state of undress; he's oftentimes missing a shirt or appears in his chonies. One time, he even had the gall to appear completely naked, causing me to immediately open my eyes, thereby shattering the visual. And, of course, he got an earful for that one. Drake, in general, is pretty self-impressed; but what's even more frustrating is that I can't deny that seeing him in the near buff makes my breath catch and my heart race . . . at least a little.

Although I don't know much about how the possession ritual worked, what I have learned is that despite Drake's spirit sharing my body with me, my spirit predominates. Even though I'm possessed, I ultimately have control, because it's my body. So when there are times that I'd prefer he not see and hear what I see and hear (like when I'm getting dressed or using the facilities), I can shut him out just by thinking those exact words.

"*This is quite different, ma minette,*" Drake continued, calling me by my pet name, which means "my pussycat" in French.

"*How is this any different?*" I railed back at him, pausing from painting the little toe on my right foot. I leaned back to admire my paint job, while trying to maintain my balance and keep from falling off the bathtub lip. As to Drake, it was difficult not to get irritated with his constant complaining. Sure, I wasn't exactly providing for his needs. I mean, he *had* been shut up in my house (well, what once had been his house) for nearly one hundred years, haunting it. And now he had the chance to experience life through me, so of course he was eager to get on with the adventure. But, on the other hand, it *had* only been a few days since Christopher, the warlock, and Lovie, the voodoo witch, performed the ritual that allowed Drake to take possession of my body. And to say the whole ritual exhausted me was an understatement—I'd basically had to sleep off the fatigue for at least a day or so. Even now, I felt as if I were just getting over a terrible flu.

"*How is this different?*" Drake repeated, obviously put out. "*Quelle audace! The nerve! Prior to my taking residence within you, I was stuck within the confines of these walls. I had no gateway to the world outside this house.*" He cleared his throat. "*But now I do—in you. Yet, you actively impair me from experiencing a world I have missed these many years.*"

"*Drake,*" I started as he huffed, as if to say he would not be swayed on this point. I took a deep breath as I prepared myself for the continued lecture that was sure to come.

"*You have kept me from experiencing the joy of sunshine on my back; of inhaling the exquisite aroma of the rose; of tasting the richness of crawfish étouffée, and the sweetness of a woman's lips, and the taste of her skin . . .*"

"*Stop there, Rico Suave,*" I said with a laugh as I shook my head and carefully placed my foot with the painted nails on the ground. I pulled my other foot out of the tub and positioned it on the lip of the bathtub. "*I won't be kissing or touching any women for your benefit anytime soon, Don Juan, so wipe that thought right out of your, er, my head.*"

"*Ah,*" he replied with a dramatic sigh. "Vous me blessez, *you wound me, ma minette.*"

"*Then consider yourself wounded,*" I continued, my tone of voice conveying my lack of empathy. Leaning down, I unscrewed the cap on the nail polish and started on my big toe.

"Quelle horrible odeur*!*" Drake said, giving me the distinct impression that he was turning up his nose and making a funny face. "*Whatever it is you are painting your toenails with, the odor is quite potent!*"

"*Zip it!*" I thought back as I started in on the next toe. "*For a supposedly manly man, you sure act like a whiny little girl sometimes.*"

"*Humph,*" was his response.

As to why I'd willingly allowed Drake's spirit to possess me? Well, at the time it seemed like a good idea because Drake had taken it upon himself to act as my protector of sorts. What that means is there was an even bigger and badder spirit in my house. This bigger and badder entity sought to take possession of my soul, and Drake, ever the dedicated police officer and protector, guarded me from said spirit. In the process, the malevolent entity latched onto Drake like a parasite and, little by little, weakened him until he was in danger of being engulfed by it. By allowing Drake to possess me, not only did I save his spirit from certain doom, but I buffered my spiritual protective forces as well. Two spirits in one body are apparently better than two in the bush . . . or something to that effect.

After painting my little toe, I screwed the cap back onto the nail polish, closed my eyes, and decided to try to have this conversation with Drake as much in the flesh as possible. Otherwise, it just felt like I was arguing with myself. It didn't take much concentration before I found myself looking at Drake, who was standing in "our" living room. Except the living room appeared as it would have back in 1919, when Drake had been very much alive and my house had belonged to him.

He was leaning against the large, black marble fireplace centered against the wall in the living room, five floor-to-ceiling picture windows flanking either side of the fireplace. The windows were trimmed in cornflower-blue silk drapes that danced in the Louisiana breeze coming through the windows.

I couldn't help but smile as I took in Drake's frown, his furrowed brows, and his arms, which were crossed against his expansive chest. With his thick neck, broad shoulders, long legs, and considerable height, he had an admirable physique. He was dressed in his police uniform, probably because he knew I found him incredibly handsome in it.

As to the subject of Drake and handsomeness, the two go together like peas in a pod. He appears to be right around my age, in his early thirties. His thick, dark hair recalls what would have been in fashion in the early twenties for men: long on the top and short on the sides. With his tanned skin, square jaw, high cheekbones, strong but symmetrical nose, and large, penetrating dark-brown eyes, the guy is handsome and then some. But the kicker is that he knows it . . .

"Do you really expect me to believe that back when you were alive, you just hung around your house in your police uniform all day?" I asked, sounding obviously put out. Sometimes the visuals in the mindscapes I shared with Drake were so detailed, I got confused between what was real and what wasn't. It was like experiencing an incredibly realistic dream while sound asleep.

Still picturing Drake's living room in my mind's eye, I figuratively threw myself into one of the two French bergère oak chairs in front of the fireplace. The chairs looked as if they were from the early 1900s and were upholstered in a light blue to match the drapes. One thing I could say for Drake was he had very good decorating sense. Well, that is, if he had been the one who decorated the place—which was highly questionable given the number of women I felt sure he must have "entertained" in his time.

It was an odd thought that all I had to do was open my eyes to shatter the image of Drake's living room as it existed nearly one hundred years ago. Even stranger to grasp was the fact that everything I was experiencing was a mere hallucination of my mind, just images created by Drake's memories. None of it was real.

Drake dropped his arms from where he'd been clasping them tightly against his chest. The three metal buttons on the lapel of his jacket and his badge reflected in the sunlight streaming through the windows. I frowned and cocked an unimpressed eyebrow at him while he smiled and eyed me like I was Little Red Riding Hood and he was the Big Bad Wolf.

"Why do you bear prejudice against my uniform?" he asked, shrugging his large shoulders as if he was purely innocent in this game of cat and mouse.

I leaned forward and rested my elbows on my knees as I glanced up at him and smiled, all the while shaking my head. I had to admit that even though conversations with Drake tested the limits of my patience, he was amusing. "So, did this whole innocent, 'woe is me' shtick work with women in your era?" I asked, continuing to shake my head. "'Cause, I gotta admit, it's not working with me."

Drake dropped his smile and cleared his throat, before offering me a frown. "If you must know, ma minette, my wooing skills rarely failed me . . . if ever." Then he grew silent as he glanced toward the ceiling, as if trying to remember an incident when his "wooing skills" were anything but successful.

"Let me guess," I started with a laugh. "Can't think of any examples of when they failed?"

Drake laughed, a deeply resonant and pleasing sound. "*Non*, ma minette, I cannot think of one." Then the laugh died on his lips, leaving a boyish smirk, which he aimed in my direction. "Save one, and I happen to be looking at her this very moment."

I rolled my eyes, wondering if it were possible for Drake to be anything but wildly flirtatious. *Yep, he can also be wildly complaining and, as such, wildly irritating*, I reminded myself. "So, anyway," I started, still amazed by the realism of this visionary world as I leaned into the slightly uncomfortable chair and stretched my long legs out before me.

Still in my mind's eye, I glanced down at myself, taking in my Victoria's Secret light-gray, stretch yoga pants that clung to my curves like a second skin. On top, I wore a baby-pink sweatshirt and my platinum-blond hair was pulled into a short ponytail, but most of my shoulder-length hair escaped the rubber band. Yes, I could have probably imagined myself wearing something more exciting, but there it was.

"I do not understand," Drake started as he shook his head and sighed, while studying me intently. "I do not understand how it is that I find you so attractive when your appearance is quite . . . slovenly."

I laughed, not taking offense because sometimes Drake was pretty funny. Thinking I should defend myself, though, I started to tell him to go find a short plank on which to take a long walk when I began to feel exhausted again. In response, I opened my mouth into a wide yawn.

"*Bonté!* Goodness!" Drake said as he shook his head and chuckled while I remembered to cover my mouth. "Your manners!"

"Ugh," I grumbled. "You sound just like Ryan."

"Ah, le barbare, the barbarian," Drake responded, his lips turning down in distaste. "Or perhaps, I should refer to him as your boyfriend?"

I cocked my head to the side as I considered whether or not the title of "boyfriend" fit Ryan. The last time I'd seen Ryan, we'd had the whole "maybe we should take this friendship up a notch into romantic-relationship territory" conversation, so I guessed he was my boyfriend. But the road to boyfriendom hadn't been an easy one, by any stretch of the imagination.

Ryan Kelly was the general contractor on my house, which was currently undergoing a remodel. Even though I'd only been living in my house for about a month, Ryan and I had gotten pretty close. I had to wonder to whom I was closer: Ryan or Drake? Technically, I'd met Ryan first since he'd basically shown up on my doorstep the first night I'd spent in my house while Drake had made his presence known after a week or so. Not that it really mattered whom I was closer to . . .

For as handsome as Drake was, Ryan was just as good-looking, only in a different sort of way. While Drake was tall, I'd guess he was maybe six one or six two, Ryan had to be about six six with the overall build of a football player. With incredibly broad shoulders and a barrel chest, he had a chuckle that rumbled through him like thunder. His hair was the color of honey and his dimples were enough to melt a girl's heart. His eyes were the same shade of amber as his hair, which, paired with his deep Southern accent, made me wobbly in the knees whenever I saw him.

But, going back to the road to boyfriendom with Ryan, it was a road that was paved with obstacles, a road that was both bumpy and painful for me because it was basically impossible to know Ryan and not love him. And loving Ryan wasn't something I did willingly. Ryan was a definite gamble because he was almost incapable of falling in love, since he was completely overwhelmed with grief. Ryan had lost his wife in a freak accident five or so years earlier and, as such, was living the life of a sequestered hermit where his emotions were concerned.

"At any rate," Drake continued, clearing his throat and frowning at me again, clearly irritated by the thought of Ryan, "I am tired of staying indoors and subsisting on your Kellogg's breakfast cereals for all our meals of the day."

"What do you have against Frosted Flakes?" I asked, throwing my hands in the air with mock exasperation.

Drake cocked a brow in my direction and appeared apathetic. "Perhaps if this cereal comprised only one of our meals instead of all three, I would not be so biased against it." Then he frowned. "Do not forget, ma minette, that I have not tasted real food in nearly a century."

"How could I forget when you do nothing but constantly tell me?" I railed back, while reminding myself that everything I experienced, he experienced. I could only wonder how he'd deal with period cramps . . .

As far as the Frosted Flakes that we'd been subsisting on for the last day . . . I hadn't ventured to the grocery store since Drake took up residence in my body. That was mainly because I didn't have the wherewithal or the energy to explain modern conveniences to him. Consequently, we'd survived on peanut butter and jelly sandwiches until the jelly ran out, then popcorn, and then Frosted Flakes. And I think we were on our last box . . .

Hmm, maybe I wasn't exactly being the best host.

As fate would have it, I was spared from further consternation regarding Drake's cabin fever when my cell phone rang. I immediately opened my eyes, shattering Drake's dreamscape, and reached for my cell phone, which was currently in my pocket.

"*Who is calling us?*" Drake demanded, irritably.

"Ryan," I answered with a smile after I glanced at the caller ID. I added, "And he's calling me, not us." The truth was I hadn't exactly spilled the beans about Drake to Ryan. Well, not as far as Drake's taking domicile in my body, anyway. Yes, this was information that Ryan absolutely had the right to know, especially after the intimate moments he and I had shared; and I was more than sure he wouldn't think three was company. Yes, Ryan for sure needed to know about Drake, and it was just a matter of time before I told him.

"Pey?" Ryan's voice sounded on the other line as soon as I clicked the phone icon. "You there?"

"Yep, I'm here," I answered quickly, inhaling deeply and then exhaling as I tried to calm my nerves. Somehow, they always went on high alert whenever I talked to Ryan. "Hi."

"Hi." He chuckled and I felt my lips break into a smile of their own accord. There was nothing I loved listening to more than Ryan's thick Southern drawl. "What are you doin'?"

Arguing with Drake, I thought, but knew I couldn't say that out loud. Well, not yet, anyway. I really *did* plan on telling Ryan about Drake soon though. Maybe even today . . . that is, if the opportunity presented itself. "Um, I'm not doing anything, why?" I asked.

"*Oui, that is the problem*," Drake grumbled in my mind. "*And we shall continue not to do anything for the foreseeable future, it appears.*"

"*Shut it, you!*" I thought back at him.

"Then let me swing by an' pick you up and we'll go to Commander's for lunch," Ryan said. "I'm just a couple streets over."

"Where are you?" I asked.

"Chestnut an' Fourth," he answered before muttering something underneath his breath, apparently directed at whatever car had just cut him off.

"What are you doing over there?"

"I'll tell you when I see you," he answered quickly. "I'm turnin' on Prytania now. Commander's—yes? No?"

"Commander's is fine," I answered as I shook my head, wondering what Ryan could possibly be up to that he'd have to wait to tell me about it when he saw me. As to Commander's Palace, it was my favorite restaurant in the area where Ryan and I lived, the Garden District of New Orleans. Luckily for me, Ryan lived just five houses down the street from me.

"Alright, doll, I'll see you in a minute," Ryan said before hanging up.

"*Am I to understand that this means we will be venturing out today?*" Drake sounded from inside my head, his tone of voice audibly excited.

"Yep, guess this is your lucky day," I answered out loud as I glanced down at myself and decided I should look more presentable. My gray sweatpants had been doubling as my pajama bottoms for the last two nights. The top I wore made my ample breasts look pretty good, although the ketchup smudge above the right one was pretty unsexy.

Taking a deep breath, I jumped up from the tub and launched myself into my bedroom, which was also one of a few guest bedrooms in my house. The master bedroom still wasn't finished. Ryan had agreed to tackle the remodeling of the first floor of my three-story house, and so far, he'd managed to finish the guest bedroom and bathroom, the foyer, and the hallway. The kitchen was completely gutted, although the plumbing was the only item able to be checked off at this point.

Throwing my closet doors open, I hemmed and hawed until my eyes settled on my tight-fitting, white spandex turtleneck sweater, which just happened to look phenomenal when paired with my equally tight 7 For All Mankind jeans. The butt cheeks of the jeans were nicely accented with rhinestone detailing. A little bling really did go a long way. I reached for the sweater and the jeans and threw both onto my bed. Wiggling out of my sweatpants, I had to be careful to focus on the wall across from me because my view was Drake's view.

"Quelle honte," Drake's voice sounded in my head. "*What a shame.*"

Yanking the dark-blue jeans up my thighs, I stared at the ceiling as I pulled my sweatshirt over my head, being careful not to glance down at my bra, which was lacy and see-through. Yes, I could have just thought the words to prevent Drake from sharing my view, but that was just another step I'd have to take. And another step meant more time I didn't have. (I had to concentrate like an SOB in order for my words to work.)

"*What are you going on about?*" I thought, only half paying attention to our silent conversation. I found it somewhat difficult to push my arms into my sweater and pull it over my head without allowing my breasts to come into view.

"*I am always eager to view your lovely body, ma minette, whenever you are in the act of disrobing, and yet you thwart me at every turn,*" Drake grumbled. "*If that is not a great shame, I do not know what is.*"

"*You know what blows my mind?*" I asked.

"Non, *I do not, ma minette, please enlighten me.*"

Once dressed, I glanced at the mirror and frowned at my reflection. My hair was pulled back into a high ponytail, but it was so short, it looked more like a Doberman Pinscher's cropped tail. Pieces of platinum-blond hair stuck out this way and that, looking exactly like what it was—hair that hadn't been brushed in a day or more. I sighed as I realized it was a job that would call for more time than I actually had. Eyeing my black baseball cap where it sat on the chair just beside my bed, I reached for it and covered my head.

"*You are exceedingly attractive, mon chaton,*" Drake continued, calling me his other pet name of choice: my kitten.

After brushing my teeth and washing my face, I grabbed my favorite lipstick at the moment, a Lip Tar called "Annika," which was lying on my bedside table. I painted the highly pigmented pink gloss onto my lips before making a pouty sort of face and wishing I could Botox out the line that appeared between my eyebrows.

"*As I was saying,*" I continued. "*It blows my mind that after one hundred years of being dead, you are still so horny.*"

Drake chuckled a deep, rumbling laugh that seemed to sound throughout my entire body. I even felt myself smiling in response. "*Ah, is that not more reason for me to be so 'horny' as you phrase it? It has been a lifetime since I have experienced a woman.*" He paused for a few moments while I dusted my cheeks with blush. "*I wonder what the experience would be like for me if you were to . . . pleasure yourself?*"

"*Oh my God!*" I sounded exasperated and shocked at the same time. "*Drake!*"

He chuckled again and as I was about to lambaste him, my front doorbell rang. I glanced at myself one more time and figured I looked as good as I was going to for the time being. With a sigh, I started for the hallway.

"*I do hope you will enlighten le barbare about me at lunch today,*" Drake said.

"*That's what I was planning.*"

Without waiting for his response, I pulled open the front door and felt my heartbeat start to race when I found Ryan standing there, wearing that lopsided, dimpled, boyish smile of his. Along with his adorable smile, he wore navy Dockers-type pants with a button-down, short-sleeved shirt, which failed to hide the expanse of his shoulders or the generous swells of his biceps and muscled forearms.

"Hi," I said almost shyly as I smiled up at him and wished my heart would slow down. One of these days, he would give me a heart attack.

Saying nothing, he took a few steps toward me and before I knew it, I was airborne as he lifted me by my waist until we were face-to-face. Then he offered me a quick smile before his lips were on mine. I felt like I might choke on all the butterflies that were now making their way out of my stomach and up my throat.

"*Ma minette!*" Drake yelled from within me. "*I do not appreciate this!*"

I instantly pulled away from Ryan and felt the heat of my embarrassment claim my cheeks. I ran my hand across my face as I took a deep breath, smiling up at Ryan as he put me back on my feet.

"I'm sorry," he said with a large smile. "I can't seem to control myself whenever I'm around you."

I laughed. "It's okay; I like it." Then I remembered I was the one who pulled away from him. "I was just worried that one of our neighbors might see us."

Ryan waved away my concern with his large hand. "Who cares?" He smiled down at me again, taking stock of my outfit. "I like that ensemble," he said, his eyes twinkling. "Legs go on forever and your breasts are just beggin' for some attention."

"Ryan!" I said with feigned surprise and a nervous giggle.

"*If I were in the flesh, I do believe this man's overtures would cause me to vomit*," Drake said from deep within me. I, however, decided to ignore him.

"Shall we?" Ryan asked as he grinned down at me. "I'm eager to parade you around on my arm." Then his smile broadened. "That is, of course, if you'll oblige me?"

I cocked a brow at him and pretended to consider it before I felt a smile surfacing on my lips. "I'll oblige you."

Chapter 2

As soon as I stepped into Ryan's white Ford F-350 truck, Drake's questions started. I couldn't say I was surprised, but I also could barely muster the energy to deal with him.

"Incroyable! *What form of automobile is this?*" Drake started. "*Is it powered by steam? I have never seen anything so grand! Not even our patrol wagon could compete with the scale of this . . . monstrosity!*"

"*This is called a truck,*" I responded, immediately feeling exhausted. "*And no, it's not powered by steam. It's powered by gasoline . . . maybe it's diesel, I'm not sure.*"

"Il est énorme! *It is enormous! Please turn your head so I can behold the entirety of this . . . colossal beast.*"

I glanced from left to right, taking in the interior passenger cab, then over to the center console seat between Ryan and me, and finally, the driver's cab.

"*And the rear?*" Drake continued. "*I would like to see what is behind us.*"

I rolled my eyes, figuring Drake would nag me until I acquiesced, I glanced at Ryan where he sat behind the wheel and smiled, trying to appear as normal as possible, given the circumstances. And the circumstances were way beyond normal—chiefly, there was a ghost inside me, barking out orders left and right.

"Hi, Pey," Ryan said with that stunner of a smile. "How're you holdin' up in that house of yours?"

He was referring to the exorcism that had been conducted in my house only days prior. Christopher, the warlock, and his companion, Lovie, had (hopefully) ousted a malevolent entity that had resided in my house and had not only physically assaulted me, but had also tried its damndest to completely wipe Drake out.

I shook my head, instantly feeling my stomach flip-flop when I recalled the ritual, which had reduced the temperature inside my house to such a degree that I could see my breath. Then there were the gusty winds blowing through the rooms even though none of the windows were open, followed by what felt like an earthquake originating at the center of the house. The climax of the whole ordeal had come when all the windows in the house exploded as the entity was forcibly extricated. Luckily for me, that same day Ryan had managed to get his construction crew over to the house and they'd replaced all the windows. What he told them by way of explanation, I had no clue. As to the construction on my house, I'd asked Ryan to take a break this week and last. I wasn't in the proper emotional state to deal with much more than what was already on my plate.

"I'm okay, so far," I said. "I haven't noticed anything out of the ordinary, which is good."

"That is good," he answered as he nodded thoughtfully before shaking his head. "I have never experienced anythin' like that." He glanced over at me and chuckled. "An' I hope never to experience it again!"

"You and me both!" I laughed as I reached for his hand and squeezed it. "I'm just so happy you were there with me. I don't know what I would have done without you. Thank you."

"We're in this together, Peyton, don't forget that," Ryan replied as he turned from the red light in front of us and faced me, kissing the top of my hand.

"Assez de balivernes!" Drake interrupted. "*Enough of this drivel! I need to understand this machine, this truck. How does it operate? What are all these gadgets along the dashboard? Ma minette, please show me the remainder of this brute! I am in awe!*"

"*You are so obnoxious!*" I replied, shaking my head before thinking better of it. Even though Drake's demands were driving me nuts, I'd expected them. It made sense that he was awestruck by everything he was experiencing through me, so I figured I'd just throw him a bone and give in to his demands.

I released Ryan's hand just as the light went green and allowed my eyes to travel to the dashboard, where the CD player dominated the square area of the center dash. I heard Drake's gasp as I focused on the two circular air vents flanking either side of the CD player.

"*What are they?*" he asked.

"*Air conditioning and heating vents. They push out either hot or cold air, depending on which you want.*"

"Stupéfiant! *Astonishing!*" Drake replied. "*And those buttons below the vents?*"

"*Those are the controls that regulate the air temperature,*" I answered as I glanced farther down at the climate controls, one set for the driver and one for the passenger. "*The ones just beside the blue and red buttons heat up the seats.*"

"*The seats can be heated?*" Drake repeated in a tone of utter disbelief. He grew quiet for a few seconds before he spoke again. "*I am amazed at the advancements society has made in just shy of one hundred years. I am struck dumb, ma minette, struck dumb.*"

I figured Drake would still be interested in seeing the backseat of Ryan's truck so I checked behind his seat and then turned my body so I could take in the length of the backseat and the extended cab behind that. I hummed something, trying to maintain the guise of casual interest as I studied the area just behind my seat before facing forward again.

"Lookin' for somethin'?" Ryan asked as he peered over at me curiously.

"I was just wondering why your truck is so clean? Aren't men supposed to be pack rats or, at the very least, cluttery?" I shot back, impressed with my off-the-cuff response.

He chuckled. "Not this man."

"So, uh, why were you over at Chestnut and Fourth?" I asked, attempting to start up a conversation to detract from the conversation going on between Drake and myself in my head. "Remember, you said you'd tell me in the car?"

"Ah right," Ryan answered with a nod. "An old client of mine, Ms. Wilson, is interested in expandin' her front porch so she asked me to stop over an' I did."

"Really?" I asked with a genuine smile. "Are you going to do it for her?"

He glanced over at me and chuckled. "If I can ever finish your job—maybe."

Even though it might not have seemed monumental that Ryan was considering work at Ms. Wilson's, it was huge in my book. Ryan had spent the majority of his adult years working for himself in construction, when his wife had died suddenly on one of his jobs. He'd sworn off construction work altogether; that is, until I forced him to take on the renovation of my house . . .

"C'est incroyable! *It is unbelievable,*" Drake interrupted as I settled my attention on my passenger door, resting my arm against the window. "*What are those buttons on the panel of the door there?*"

I pushed the button and rolled down the window, then pulled up on it to roll it back up again.

"*Ah!*" Drake sounded thrilled. "*And the button just beside it?*"

I locked and unlocked the door while answering, "*Door locks.*"

"You all right, Pey?" Ryan asked as he glanced at me with furrowed brows, apparently finding it odd for me to roll my window up and down while locking and unlocking my door. "You seem a little restless, like you can't sit still."

"I'm fine," I answered immediately, realizing how neurotic I must've appeared. "I'm just hungry, that's all."

Ryan laughed and we pulled into the parking lot of Commander's Palace. "Well, luckily for you, we're here." He shifted the truck into park and turned off the engine, but made no motion to open his door.

I glanced up from where I was intently studying the center console, figuring I'd end up explaining all the buttons and gadgets there for Drake as well. Lifting my eyes up to look out the windshield, I spotted Commander's Palace, the striped awning of the turquoise Victorian building hard to miss. My stomach grumbled in response. Apparently, Drake wasn't the only one who was sick of Frosted Flakes.

"Are you sure you're okay, Peyton?" Ryan asked as I turned to face him. "You don't seem like yourself."

I waved him away with an unconcerned hand, all the while scolding myself for not doing a better job of acting normal. "I'm fine." But I knew he wouldn't go for my brief explanation because my actions weren't those of a person who feels "fine." "I've just had a lot on my mind lately . . . We've gone through hell and back. You know that."

He nodded. "Yes, I do." Then he smiled his boyish, adorable smile and made me feel all giddy inside. "Everything that happened is behind us now, Peyton. We need to focus on movin' forward."

I was sure it was a statement he'd repeated to himself many times. In his case, though, he was moving on after the death of his wife. "You're right," I said softly with a grin before returning my attention to the beautiful building in front of us.

"*Commander's Palace . . .*" Drake piped up from inside my head.

"*Yep,*" I answered. Commander's Palace had always been a Garden District go-to since the late 1800s, so I wasn't exactly surprised that Drake recognized it.

"*The building is as it was in my day!*" Drake exclaimed as I studied it for him. "*But the color!* Mon Dieu! *The color!*"

"*What color was it before?*" I prodded, finding the conversation interesting, given my fascination with everything historical. I'd studied history in college, even though I hadn't earned my degree. Unfortunately, I'd put my dreams on hold and gotten married instead. It was a mistake I tried not to focus on. Instead, I attempted to live my life with no regrets.

When I noticed Ryan stepping down from his seat, I followed suit, jumping down from the truck as the New Orleans air engulfed me with a warm, moist hug. Ryan beeped the truck locked behind us and I was surprised that Drake didn't mention the noise. Apparently, he was still too taken with Commander's to observe much else.

"*Last I saw this place, it was painted beige or brown, perhaps,*" Drake responded before chuckling. I could just imagine him shaking his head in wonder. "*I never expected to step foot into Commander's again.*"

"*Well, technically, you aren't. I'm stepping foot . . .*"

As I felt Ryan taking my hand, I glanced over at him and he beamed down at me. "Turtle soup for you again, Pey?" he asked with a chuckle.

I shook my head, but couldn't hide my smirk. He had to coax me into trying the turtle soup the last time we were there and it wasn't an easy sell. As it was, I only had a tiny spoonful of the creamy stuff before deciding I preferred having turtles in their natural environment or in a tank. "Thanks, but I'm going to pass."

He chuckled and shook his head. "You can take the girl out of California, but you can't take California out of the girl . . ."

I laughed. "Something like that." Then I cleared my throat and thought about what I was in the mood for. "I'm thinking maybe some comfort food."

"As in Southern Comfort?" Ryan continued with a chuckle, pulling me into his hard body as he wrapped his arms around me and kissed the side of my neck. I immediately leaned into him, relishing his smell—something between the scent of clean skin and the spiciness of deodorant. And there was also a factor I never could put my finger on—whatever it was, though, it was uniquely Ryan.

"La souffrance!" Drake chimed in, which I took to mean: the suffering!

I immediately pulled away from Ryan as soon as I remembered my bodily guest. Then, feeling a twinge of anger flow through me, I decided to scold him. "*If you keep that up, I'm going to permanently shut you out of seeing or hearing or tasting anything!*" I yelled at him. I reached down and gripped Ryan's hand, not wanting to alert him by pulling away. There were times that I definitely wasn't comfortable with Drake's persistent eavesdropping.

"*Very well, ma minette, I will behave,*" he immediately answered before going silent as Ryan opened the door for me and I entered the stately building. The main dining room of Commander's featured tables with white linen tablecloths. White napkins were folded into fans and stood proudly on top of the circular, white plates. The white theme continued with the floral arrangements standing in the middle of each table—eight white roses amid plentiful greenery. The ceiling was dominated by golden chandeliers bedecked with strings of pearls that hung from their boughs. The chandeliers paled, though, in comparison to the light streaming through the multiple windows on every wall. Some windows were partially obscured by grayish-purple shades featuring gold-scroll designs, which matched the hue of the darker purple carpeting. It too featured the same gold-scroll design as the shades.

"*This looks nothing similar to what it did in my time,*" Drake piped up.

"*Well, did you really expect it to?*" I inquired.

"J'espère que non!" Drake chuckled. "*I should hope not! I am not certain of its reputation now, but it was certainly known for its ill repute in my day.*"

"*Ill repute? What do you mean?*"

"Comment dois-je dire . . ." His voice trailed off. "*How do I say . . . I do not want to offend your delicate feminine sensibilities, ma minette . . .*"

"*Oh please!*" I guffawed. "*You've already offended my delicate feminine sensibilities more times than I can count!*"

"*Very well,*" he responded, sounding much more uptight. *It was previously run as a brothel of sorts.* "*Many a lonely ship captain found himself entranced by a beautiful woman in the upstairs lounge, ma minette.*"

"*Wow,*" I said, surprised as I tried to imagine Commander's as a house of prostitution. I looked around myself, observing the blatant tourists, clad in their faded jeans, college football T-shirts, and grimy baseball caps as they tried to read through the menu. A few shrieking kids completed the picture, which didn't exactly lend itself to being a house of ill repute.

"*Shall I describe for you the acts that took place here?*" Drake continued, his tone becoming carnal and suggestive.

"*That's okay,*" I responded. "*I have a good imagination so please spare me the details.*"

"Two for lunch?" the hostess, a short, but lean and pretty girl, asked as soon as we walked into the reception area.

"Yes, please," Ryan answered. "We prefer to sit in the garden."

"Of course," the girl answered.

For as lovely as the inside of Commander's was, we never ate inside. Instead, Ryan and I liked the garden seating outside, which was, in one word . . . enchanting. The hostess grabbed two lunch menus and led us outside into the warmth of the New Orleans day. The hunter-green wrought-iron tables and matching green umbrellas perfectly blended with the lushness of the dense canopy and foliage above. The sun's rays filtered through the natural arbor with pockets of dappled light.

"How about that one over there?" Ryan asked, pointing to a single table surrounded by the fronds of a palm tree. The woman nodded and led us to the table, and Ryan pulled out my chair for me. She handed each of us a menu.

"Your server will be with you shortly," she announced with a sweet voice before disappearing into the greenery.

I waited for Ryan to seat himself before flipping up my menu and scanning through the various mouthwatering dishes. It was difficult to decide what to gorge myself on. It was not an easy task choosing from a cornucopia of entrées, complete with Creole Gumbo, Seared Gulf Fish, Honey Lacquered Quail, Hickory Grilled Pork, and a whole slew of desserts (dessert being my favorite meal of the day).

"*I would like to try one of each, please,*" Drake said.

"*What?*" I scoffed back at him. "*I'm not ordering one of every entrée! Choose one and be happy with it.*"

"Très bien," he grumbled in response. "*Very well. I am most eager to revel in the taste of the beef, ma minette, if you would so oblige me.*"

"*Okay . . .*" I started.

"*And, perhaps a slice of pecan pie for our second course? I have so missed the taste of Southern pecans, ma minette. Of course, that bread pudding soufflé looks quite appealing and . . . ah! Grits!* Bien sûr! *We must sample the grits, ma minette!*"

"*Ugh, I don't like grits, they taste like Cream of Wheat,*" I ground out even though it was more than obvious that Drake didn't care.

"Are you ready to order?" the waiter asked, suddenly appearing from around the grove of trees, and obscuring us from the rest of the outdoor area. He was maybe in his thirties, with a boyish face. A stray lock of blond hair intersected his forehead, which, when paired with his large, dark eyes, button nose, and smallish mouth, gave him the look of a Kewpie doll.

"Pey?" Ryan asked, deferring to me to order first.

"I'd like the Tournedos of Black Angus Beef," I started, handing my menu back to the waiter. "And a side of grits, please."

"*Ah,* merci, *ma minette!*"

I frowned inwardly and cleared my throat, facing the waiter again. "I'd also like the pecan pie for dessert and, uh, some bread pudding."

"Is that all?" Ryan asked, chuckling as he studied me with an amused expression.

"No," I answered with a sigh. "I also need three of the twenty-five-cent martinis." And, yes, I definitely "needed" them—they'd make dealing with Drake a lot easier.

"Three?" Ryan scoffed at me, his eyebrows reaching for the sky as the waiter chuckled.

"They're twenty-five cents each, Ryan! I'd try for four, but the cap is three," I said with a pouty face at the waiter. He just shrugged as if to say there wasn't anything he could do about the policy.

"Okay," Ryan continued. "Why not wait 'til you've finished one before orderin' another?" he asked with a grin.

"A couple of reasons," I answered nonchalantly. I flipped up my index finger to let it be known reason number one was about to be delivered. "They might change their mind and start charging full price for each drink." Ryan laughed but I tried not to smile as I flicked up finger number two. "And secondly, if I don't order all three at once, that means I have to wait in between drinks and I've never been any good at being patient."

Ryan laughed and shook his head as he faced the waiter. "You heard the lady . . ."

The waiter responded with a chuckle. "And for you, sir?"

"I'd like the Gumbo, the Heirloom Tomato Salad, an' a sweet tea."

"And a dessert for you, sir?" the waiter asked.

Ryan glanced at me with a smile. "I think I'll sample the smorgasbord my lovely girlfriend ordered."

I couldn't help blushing at his term of endearment. Although I was not yet completely accustomed to being Ryan's girlfriend, I had to admit that I liked the idea . . . a lot.

"*Do you plan on updating your barbarian about my existence during our luncheon?*" Drake, the voice of doom, suddenly sounded from inside me.

"*Yes!*" I yelled at him. "*Stop pushing me about it! It will take care of itself.*"

"*I am afraid that is what you always say, ma minette,*" Drake answered with a practiced sigh.

"Pey?" Ryan asked and I glanced up at him from where I'd been zoning out on my place setting while arguing with Drake.

"Yep?"

He cleared his throat and studied me for a few moments. "Would you be interested in comin' over tonight?" he started before clearing his throat again. "And, uh, spendin' the night?"

Butterflies immediately swarmed my stomach as my heartbeat sped up. Even though it wasn't exactly phrased as an open invitation to have sex, it was *an open invitation to have sex*. The reason for my sudden wave of anxiety was that Ryan and I had never had sex before. Yes, we'd come close, but never sealed the figurative deal. To say I was sexually frustrated would be an understatement.

I wanted to scream, cry, and yell "Yes!" but instantly remembered the little issue still plaguing me by the name of Drake Montague.

"I mean, you don't have to spend the night," Ryan started, obviously sensing my reservation, "if you don't want to . . ."

"No, I do want to," I interrupted him. He had no idea how badly I wanted to, but I certainly didn't want Drake eavesdropping. True, I could disallow him to see or hear anything, but that wasn't good enough . . . not when I felt I owed Ryan the truth and had to tell him that Drake was possessing me. I could never feel comfortable having sex with Ryan if he didn't know the truth about Drake.

"You want to but . . ."

"Um," I said, my tongue suddenly seeming to swell up and choke me.

"Peyton," Ryan started as he leaned forward, gripping my hand in his, "I know it's got to be tough for you . . . to be with another man since divorcin' your husband."

That wasn't it. That wasn't it at all. I was sooooo completely over my ex, Jonathon. In fact, he had become only a distant memory that hadn't resurfaced since meeting Ryan . . . until now.

"It has nothing to do with my ex-husband," I started, then swallowed hard, wishing I could summon up the nerve to just spit the words out.

I had to tell Ryan about Drake. And I had to do it now because the opportunity had definitely presented itself.

"We can go slowly," Ryan continued. "We don't have to do anything you don't want to do."

I shook my head. "No, that's not it," I said, sounding frustrated.

"*Come out with it, ma minette!*" Drake demanded.

"*Mind your own business!*" I railed back at him.

"I don't want to rush you into anythin'," Ryan continued, leaning forward and looking at me with compassion in his eyes. "I just have to be honest with you, Peyton. Seein' you just . . . does somethin' to me." My nerves started up again and I felt that telltale stinging in the pit of my belly. It was proof that Ryan caused the same reaction on my libido as I apparently did to his. "I don't know how much longer I can go without feelin' your body, without knowin' you . . . more intimately," he finished as I about melted into my chair.

I took a deep breath and forced my knee to stop bouncing up and down. I had to tell him about Drake, and I intended to tell him right then and there.

"Oh. My. Gawd! I couldn't believe it!" A heavy New York accent belonging to a woman exclaimed from right behind me. I turned around to find a very handsome African American waiter leading two women to a table opposite ours. One of the women, heavyset with flame-red hair, was probably in her forties, and the other woman was shorter and could've been in her seventies. Her hair looked as if it were striving for red, but got lost somewhere along the way and was now relegated to pastel pink. "I swear we musta gotten forty orbs in this one picture," the woman continued.

"Yes, Mabel, I think it was when you held the camera over the fence at the Beauregard-Keyes House," the older woman said, her accent just as heavily Brooklynese as the younger woman's. She glanced up at the waiter who seemed interested in their story, or maybe he was just interested in a good tip . . . it was hard to tell.

"Yeah, that's right, Mama," Mabel answered, glancing back at the waiter again as he pulled her seat out for her, only after seating her mother. "But every photo we took had at least ten orbs in it! The guide on our ghost tour said she'd never seen this much activity before an' she's been doin' these ghost tours for ten yee-ars."

"Oh. My. Gawd. Ten yee-ars? Is that what she said?" Mabel's mom double-checked.

Mabel nodded emphatically. "I know. I couldn't believe it!"

The waiter nodded as he handed each of them a menu. "That's interestin' yer guide said that 'cause one ah my coworkers tole me Emile has been at it agin for the last two nights, and no one heard a peep outta him in ova a year or somethin'."

"Emile?" Mabel repeated curiously.

The waiter turned toward her and nodded insistently, obviously intent on telling the story. "Emile Commander was the o-riginal proprietah of Commander's Palace back in 1880."

"And he haunts it now?" Mabel Senior asked as the waiter nodded repeatedly.

"He sho'nuff does," the waiter responded.

"Oh. My. Gawd," Mabel commented.

Ryan leaned in toward me, gripping my thigh under the table in a lame attempt to scare me. All it did was turn me on.

I faced him with a smile, placing my hand on top of his. "I was totally eavesdropping," I admitted, concerned that I still hadn't come out with the whole Drake thing. But I also couldn't deny my interest in this new subject matter.

"Hard not to eavesdrop when their table is so close," Ryan said with a laugh as we both faced our neighbors again.

"Stories go back ta 1970 when Commander's interior was redesigned," the waiter continued. "I guess that's when ghost stories about Emile first started poppin' up."

"What did he do?" Mabel Senior asked just as our waiter appeared with Ryan's salad. After he delicately placed the salad in front of Ryan, he offered to sprinkle some freshly ground pepper on it, but Ryan refused.

"Hey, Harry," the other waiter called over as Harry, aka Kewpie Doll, turned to face him. "What d'ya know 'bout Emile the ghost?"

Harry chuckled and took a few steps toward the other table, but kept facing us, as if including us in the conversation. Maybe it was that obvious we were already listening. "I dunno all the stories offhan', but I do know that lotsa our staff has noticed silverware an' dishes goin' missin'. Other times, stuff'll show up in different places than where someone left it."

The other waiter nodded before facing his guests again. "Lights turn off an' on fer no reason an' there've been lotsa reports o' footsteps upstairs when we're closin' up fer the night an' no one should be up there."

"Oh. My. Gawd," Mabel said as she inhaled for a few seconds.

"But jist recently, Emile has been lots more active," Harry

continued. "Landon said that jist yesterday he had ta refill a guest's drink three times 'cause the wine kept disappearin' right outta his glass!"

"That's a good way to get free refills," Ryan said with a laugh and everyone followed suit.

"F'sho it's true!" Harry said. "Emile is known for his love o' wine and it's not uncommon for lots o' wine bottles to jist go missin'. There were 'bout four bottles that disappeared last night an' dey still ain't accounted fer."

"Sounds like Emile needs to check in to Alcoholics Anonymous," Ryan continued, shaking his head as he laughed.

I laughed too, but there was something about that story and the women's story that bothered me. "So you were saying that Emile has only recently started up his antics again?" I asked Harry.

He nodded. "Yeah, it's sorta strange actually, but all o' the sudden both staff an' guests have noticed things goin' on that don't make no sense . . . So we just say it's Emile."

"An' did y'all read that article that came out yestaday in the *Advocate*?" A waitress appeared from directly behind Harry as if she'd just materialized from thin air. She was youngish—probably in her early twenties, with a long, lean, and willowy body. Her face was plain but would still be considered pretty. She glanced first at Harry, then at me, before her eyes settled on Ryan and continued to settle on him just like I figured they would.

"No, ma'am, can't say I have read the article," Ryan started and shook his head, offering her a lopsided smile, which caused her cheeks to color. "I'm a *Times-Picayune* man, mahself."

The waitress smiled submissively at him, batting her eyelashes as she dropped her chin and gazed at him with wide, brown eyes. Apparently I suddenly had lots in common with the invisible man for all the interest she paid me . . .

"What'd the article say, Sadie Rose?" Harry asked, obviously prodding her to continue with her story since the only task currently occupying her was making cow eyes at my boyfriend.

"Oh," she said with a little giggle, and then tossed her longish blond hair over her shoulder flirtatiously. "Well, jist that people are sayin' paranormal activity is up in N'awlins citywide."

"Really?" I asked, frowning because I couldn't say this information pleased me at all. In general, I didn't do well with anything ghostly given the fact that the haunt who had taken residence in my house better resembled the demon from *The Amityville Horror* than it did Casper.

The pretty waitress nodded but didn't divert her attention from the Adonis sitting across the table from me. "Yeah, really. The maître d' at Le Pavilion Hotel said he's gotten more accounts o' ghostly activity from his employees this week than he had all last year. An' apparently Count Arnaud has been causin' trouble at Arnaud's restaurant these past few days as well." She tapped her fingers against her lips as she appeared to attempt to remember more incidences. "The manager at Hotel Monteleone was also interviewed but I plum forgot what it was he had ta say 'bout it."

"Un-be-lee-va-ble!" Mabel piped up eagerly. "And on the ghost tour that Mama and I just took, everyone on the tour got oo-rbs in their photos an' about half of them said they could see a face in one of the windows."

"Really—?" I started before "Mama" interrupted me.

"Real-ley. Our guide said she'd never seen so much activity before." Then she faced Harry, nodding. "She also said that all the activity just started up a couple of nights ago."

"Jist like the article in the *Advocate* said," Sadie Rose added, nodding as she continued to gaze at Ryan. I glanced over at him and found him studying me with an expression that said he was hoping

I'd taken notice of the attention Sadie was paying him. I cocked an unamused brow and frowned at him.

"Very strange," Harry concurred as he started for the inside of the restaurant again, presumably to check on his other tables. "Guess we'll nevah know why!"

"I tell you, Mama," Mabel continued, "there's a reason awl this ghostly stuff is goin' on."

"You might be right, Mabel, you might be right," her mother answered.

I desperately hoped Mabel was wrong.

Chapter 3

I didn't know why, but I just couldn't deny or shake my sense of foreboding. Instead, it began to build up so much that I actually started to feel sick. It just seemed incredibly strange that in the course of a couple of days, the spiritual activity in this city seemed to be at an all-time high. I tried to talk myself down from my current mental position of perilously perched on a ledge by focusing on the facts. Fact one: all the ghost talk could be sheer hearsay. Fact two: even if it wasn't hearsay, there was only a handful of incidents in question; The happenings at Emile's, the ghost tour the women mentioned, and the three or so examples discussed by the *Advocate* newspaper. A more plausible explanation was simply coincidence—that Emile's, Count Arnaud's, and whatever other ghosts' spectral energy just happened to coincide with all the orbs that appeared in the pictures on the ghost tour. However, my upset stomach refused to stop churning. Why? Because I didn't believe things occurred by mere happenstance. Not anymore, anyway.

To make matters worse, I still hadn't told Ryan about Drake, and in my present state of frazzlement, that was one conversation I didn't look forward to having. Well, not yet, anyway. I felt sure there would be a perfect time to bring it up, but that perfect time definitely wasn't now. And probably not tomorrow either, come to think of it.

"Did you get enough to eat?" Ryan asked me with a restrained smirk as he dropped his gaze to the empty plates in front of me. That was probably another reason for my upset stomach—Drake insisting that I consume every last bite of the entire meal I ordered.

Looking up at Ryan, I raised one brow as if to say I wasn't amused by his question. "Yes, I ate plenty. Thanks for asking."

He chuckled as he shook his head. "Ah girl, I was just givin' you a hard time!" Then the laugh died on his lips as he reached for my hand, running the pads of his fingers across my knuckles. His eyes smoldered as he looked at me. "I do love those ticked off expressions of yours though."

I gave him another one . . . since he liked them so much. "Let's get out of here," I said after a protracted silence. Groaning with the weight of my stomach, I stretched my arms above my head, hoping the plethora of food inside me could find a previously unoccupied section of my belly to fill. But no such luck—it remained uncomfortably lodged in my stomach like a boulder.

Ryan nodded and stood up, pulling my chair out for me as I momentarily defied gravity and hoisted my body to standing. I offered Harry a quick wave when he approached us to gather our paid bill from the table. Ryan threw his arm around me and hummed something I didn't recognize as we started for the front doors.

"Want to check out Lafayette?" He casually asked as he pulled me into him for a hug. He gave me an extra tight squeeze, and growled like he was pretending to be a bear.

"Watch it, Hulk, you don't know your own strength!" I said with a laugh before answering his question on the subject of visiting Lafayette Cemetery. It was our usual jaunt after meeting at Commander's for brunch or lunch. Lafayette Cemetery No. 1 was right across the street from Commander's Palace, bounded by Washington Avenue, Prytania Street, Sixth Street, and Coliseum Street.

"*Lafayette Cemetery?*" Drake piped up. "*Oui, oui! I should very much like to see it!*"

I could just imagine him jumping up and down with unconcealed excitement. "Yeah, sure," I answered, addressing both Ryan and Drake even though I didn't really feel like visiting the cemetery. 'Course after eating so much, there probably wasn't anything better for me to do than walk off my massively large, and now lingering, lunch.

Holding hands, we scurried across Washington Avenue. Once we reached the sidewalk, I was careful not to trip over the invasive tree roots that contorted the cement, making it an obstacle course just to get to the cemetery. I paused for a second or two at the entrance, taking in the black wrought-iron gate, and the words "Lafayette Cemetery No. 1" scrawled across the top in white, capital letters.

"I do love this cemetery," I said in a small voice as I spotted the multiple aboveground tombs that were so iconically New Orleans. They were arranged in such a way as to look like houses in a city, which was a fitting description, seeing how the cemetery was dubbed the "City of the Dead." The cemetery was one of my favorite places, owing to its rich history, the beauty of the tombs, and the serene quiet that somehow always managed to give me peace of mind.

I took a few steps into the grounds and glanced left to right, taking in row upon row of housing for the dead. Along the wall that paralleled Washington Avenue were hundreds of wall tombs, but I couldn't say they fascinated me as much as the aboveground tombs.

"*I believe Lafayette has not changed at all in one hundred years, ma minette,*" Drake said with reverence.

"*Somehow, I'm not surprised.*" If the truth be told, the cemetery looked like it was a page straight out of a history book, preserved through time, even though the tombs themselves were crumbling with their advanced years. The walkways all around the tombs were broken and uneven and I'd watched tourists trip on several occasions. The narrow inlets between some of the tombs were so congested with weeds, broken bricks, and mortar, they were barely traversable. Rundown as it was, though, to me it was beautiful.

As we made our way deeper into the cemetery, we were interrupted by the loud voice of a woman, her heavy drawl pointing to her obvious Southern descent. She stood amid a crowd of maybe twenty people, pointing various directions as she spouted out anecdotes and information regarding the cemetery.

"Well, I'll be!" she interrupted her soliloquy as soon as she spotted Ryan. A huge smile widened her mouth and she immediately waved for us to join her. She wasn't exactly an attractive woman—maybe she had been at one time, but that time had long since passed. Her hair was dark and stringy, dangling to her elbows. It looked like it hadn't seen a pair of scissors in at least ten years. Her face was round and jubilant with red cheeks and open, round, smiling eyes. She was wearing something that resembled an Old West saloon girl: a purple ostrich feather jutting out of her headband, and black, lacy ribbons that adorned her deeply plunging décolletage. Her puffed sleeves billowed like her brown skirts, which were edged with black lace and completed with a protruding petticoat underneath. Owing to her exceedingly large belly, the costume made her look more like a tree trunk than a sexy woman of the night.

"Le choc! *The shock! I believe we have spotted a specter! Albeit a poorly dressed one!*" Drake said with an amused chuckle. I decided to ignore him.

"Hello, Prudence," Ryan said with sincere affability, dropping my hand and waving to her in turn. He faced me with a quick smile and whispered, "Pru an' I went to school together from the time we were young'uns."

"This, ladies and gentlemen, is a good friend of mine, Mr. Ryan Kelly," Prudence said as everyone in the tour turned to face Ryan and me. We both smiled uneasily, obviously nowhere near as comfortable in the limelight as Prudence was. "Mr. Ryan Kelly is not only the most handsome man in N'awlins, but also a well-known face 'round these parts! Rye, you gonna join mah tour o' what?"

Ryan chuckled, looking down at me inquisitively, but Prudence answered for me. "'Course the doll ain't gonna mind! This here tour's the best for history facts and ghost facts and best o' all, I ain't gonna charge ya one cent!" Then she glanced at the crowd and added: "That's what we call a lagniappe round these parts, somethin' a little extra."

"Thanks, Pru—" Ryan started before she interrupted him.

"Yep, free tour for you an' your honey, Mr. Kelly, though tips are very much encouraged an' appreciated."

Everyone laughed at that while I mentally resigned myself to my unexpected fate. "How can we turn that down?" I answered in as loud a voice as I could muster.

"That there is one smart woman!" Prudence hollered before turning back to the crowd and resuming her act of information-touting tour guide.

"Imposteur!" Drake yelled from deep inside me. "*I know more about Lafayette's history than this trollop! You should abandon this tour at once and allow me to answer any of your questions!*"

"*Drake, quit it!*" I barked back at him. "*Either be quiet and enjoy the tour, or I'm going to turn you off!*"

"La souffrance!" he replied theatrically.

"*I don't know how anyone could put up with your drama!*"

"*I will have you know that neither my face nor my character ever left me wanting where females were concerned!*" Somehow I wasn't surprised, but decided to withhold my comment. "*Depending on the severity of the trollop's offenses, perhaps I shall* request *that you turn me off!*"

"*Ugh,*" I grumbled in response. "*Just shut up and listen, will you? You might learn something.*"

And while it wasn't lost on me that he didn't respond, I couldn't say I cared.

"Now, where was I?" Prudence bellowed out. "Ah, yes . . . Lafayette Cemetery Numero Uno, this one we're standin' in, is the oldest of the seven cemeteries in N'awlins. There're about eleven hundred family tombs and more than seven thousand people buried in Lafayette One, which is just one single city block."

"*I could have told you that,*" Drake grumbled.

"*But you didn't, so shut it!*"

"What's the oldest grave here?" a young woman asked from the front row.

"*Drake?*" I asked with a secret smile.

"*Hmm,*" he started, and I imagined him striking the pose of *The Thinker*. "*If I am not mistaken, I believe the correct answer is the late 1700s, ma minette.*"

From her stance on a precarious-looking two-foot-high brick wall, Prudence smiled down at the woman in the first row who'd asked the question. But her grin was impatient and said she didn't appreciate any interruptions. "The first burial records we've come across are dated from 1843, although we do know that the cemetery was in use prior to that date."

"*Well, someone isn't up on his New Orleans historical facts,*" I said snidely. "*Good thing* you *aren't leading this tour, Drake Montague, or we'd all be fed incorrect information!*"

"*She should check her facts, ma minette.* Elle n'est pas digne de confiance. *She is not trustworthy and neither is the guff she's feeding all of these people.*"

I didn't say anything more, but laughed inwardly as I turned my attention back to Prudence and her (apparently) inaccurate tour.

"So how did most of the people buried here die?" she continued, pulling up her lace gloves that ended at her swollen elbows. "I'm glad you asked!" There were a few rounds of snickers and one or two laughs. "There are numerous victims of the yellow fever buried here. If you read some of the inscriptions on the tombs, you'll find other folks died from apoplexy and even being struck by lightnin'. Also, if you look close enough, you'll find eight tombs that list certain ladies as consorts!"

Everyone laughed at that, including Ryan and me. "She's pretty good," I whispered to Ryan and he simply nodded.

"Je suis en désaccord. *I disagree*," Drake said in a decidedly irritated manner. I didn't respond—I knew better.

"She's always been like this," Ryan answered. "She's got a flare for storytellin'."

"Now, let me ask y'all this: Why do you suppose the majority of N'awlins cemeteries feature aboveground tombs?" Prudence continued, her voice quaking audibly as she started to lose it. She coughed, cleared her throat, and pulled a bottle of water from a hidden pocket in her multiple skirts. After downing it, she walked the ten steps to the entryway and plopped it into a trash can.

"Quelle question stupide! *What a foolish question!*" Drake lashed out. "*It is owing to the city's propensity for flooding, of course!*"

A few hands shot into the air as someone from the back yelled out, "Because of the flooding problems!"

Hmm, so maybe Drake finally managed to get one question correct. It was about time!

"Seems reasonable enough, right?" Prudence asked and started to nod. "Wrong!" she shouted as she immediately shook her head.

"Merde."

I couldn't help my laugh at hearing Drake curse because it was so rare. Luckily, my laugh was timed well because no one glanced back at me quizzically.

"Most people think that our aboveground burials are due to the city's water problems but that ain't so. This type of burial actually started in the Mediterranean thousands o' years ago and was introduced to N'awlins by the French and Spanish Creoles. It's actually a very smart way to maximize space since one o' these here tombs"—she patted the one directly behind her as if it were a loyal pet—"can and does have multiple people buried in it."

"Wow," I said, actually pleased that we got sucked into her tour since I'd never heard this before about New Orleans cemeteries, and it made total sense.

"You must be eatin' this up, Ms. History Buff," Ryan responded with a little chuckle as he looped his fingers through mine before bringing my hand to his lips and kissing it. I smiled up at him and felt my heart rate increase as our eyes met. I wondered if he'd kiss me, right here in public.

"*Please instruct le barbare to keep his distance. I do not appreciate being touched by a man!*" Drake ground out. "L'indécence!"

"*If you don't like it, you can always move out!*" I responded. "*Speaking of which, when is that day coming?*" It was a question that suddenly begged for an immediate response. I never considered exorcising Drake previously because I wanted to ensure my house was no longer haunted before I allowed Drake to re-haunt it . . . that is, unless of course, he chose to go toward the light or wherever it was that promised him a happy forever.

The idea of him leaving my life suddenly overwhelmingly and inexplicably depressed me. That, in itself, surprised me because I usually felt nothing besides irritation where Drake was concerned.

"*I have no answer for you to that question, ma minette. It is something you must answer for yourself,*" he responded.

"*Well, we can figure it out later,*" I replied, very aware that I had a tendency to sweep things under the proverbial rug. Well, Drake's exorcism date could now keep company with my need to tell Ryan about Drake's tenancy . . . unless, of course, I allowed Drake back into my house soon. In that case, maybe what Ryan didn't know wouldn't hurt him? Hmm, the plan was worth a second look . . .

"Curious as to how these tombs work?" Prudence continued. I noticed a few people yawning while others shifted their weight from one leg to the other, and still others leaned heavily against some of the tombs. "Once a coffin is placed into a tomb, the tomb is sealed with brick and mortar at the vault entrance. It takes one year and one day for the body to basically cook in this pseudo oven, at which time the tomb can be reused again."

"You reuse these things?" someone asked, his tone decidedly offended.

"Yep, sho'nuff!" Prudence responded, before addressing the entire crowd again. "To reuse the tomb, the seal must first be removed, then the human remains are separated from what's left of the coffin. The remains are either pushed to the rear of the vault, or dropped in the bottom of the tomb. Then the tomb is ready for its next occupant!" There was a round of oohs and aahs and I was among them. "You'll get some time in a bit to walk around and count how many people are buried in any one vault. The most we've ever come across is thirty-seven."

"Wow, that's a lot for a one-bedroom tomb!" I said as I smiled up at Ryan. He just glanced down at me and smiled back, pulling me into him as he kissed the top of my head. I allowed myself to melt into him, Drake be damned.

"Okay, so now we arrive at the portion of our tour where we talk 'bout ghosts!" Prudence continued, her voice suddenly wavering as if she were playing the part of an apparition. "I will start off by tellin' y'all that most cemeteries aren't as haunted as people like ta think. Other places like houses an' buildings usually have more haunts than a graveyard does. If you think 'bout it, it makes sense. Who dies in a cemetery?" Prudence might as well have been under a spotlight, considering how attentive her audience suddenly became.

"Usually ghosts want ta haunt the places that meant the most to them in life, or the places where they met their tragic ends. Now, that bein' said, keep in mind the sort o' deaths that this cemetery has seen—lots o' epidemics like yellow fever. In fact, there were so many deaths from yellow fever in the late eighteen hundreds that people would just pile their dead outside the cemetery gates. Now that seems a pretty bad way ta go if you ask me!" A few people laughed, ending the audience's stupor and illusion that Prudence was an actor performing before an audience of expressionless mannequins. She took a deep breath and reached into another hidden pocket in the folds of her skirts, producing what looked like a miniature tape recorder. "Now this is a recordin' I've compiled o' all the instances of EVP I've encountered ova the years." She took another breath. "Anyone know what EVP stands for?"

"Electronic voice phenomenon!" someone answered jubilantly.

Prudence nodded. "That's right! So here, ladies an' gentlemen, for yer listenin' pleasure are some o' the EVPs I've recorded with mah paranormal society right here in this cemetery." Everyone took a few steps closer when she clicked the recording on. I could see people straining to hear voices or whatever she captured on tape. The majority of blank faces told me no one could pick up whatever it was we were supposed to hear. As for me, all I heard was what sounded like static. "You hear that?" Prudence called out.

"No!" a man yelled. "I couldn't hear a thing!"

"I did!" the man's wife responded before she elbowed him in the ribs as if to say she didn't appreciate his outburst. "The voice clearly said 'We're stuck!'"

"That's right!" Prudence said while nodding emphatically. "If you listen real close, you'll hear the other voice answerin' yes when I asked if it was okay for us to be there. An' on the last recordin', you'll hear the voice say 'Where's my bed?'" She took another deep breath and I thought she'd actually hit "play" on her recorder so we could listen for ourselves, but she didn't. Instead, she smiled broadly. "Now, I have some very interestin' news for y'all. Ova the last couple o' days, I been hearin' all this crazy stuff from mah fellow tour guides 'bout the spirits o' N'awlins actin' up way more than usual . . . "

"What?" someone asked while Prudence suddenly nodded violently. My stomach was already beginning to flip-flop.

"That's right. My fellow ghost-guide friends have been talkin' 'bout seein' all sorts o' stuff an' hearin' stuff on almost every tour. That rarely ever happens, I'm tellin' ya."

"Oh my God," I whispered, as my entire stomach instantly plummeted down to my toes.

"What's wrong, Pey?" Ryan asked as he wrapped his arms around me.

"She noticed it too," I said, my eyes widening as fear began to penetrate my psyche. What did it mean? What could it mean to have the paranormal side of New Orleans suddenly seem as if it had sparked back to life? And why was I so freaked out about it? Just because New Orleans was in a cosmic tailspin didn't mean that the entity previously haunting my house would suddenly start up again . . . right?

Of course it didn't! The entity was long gone, having been successfully exorcised by Christopher and Lovie. It went "where the goblins go, below, below, below," to quote the refrain of a Munchkin song from The Wizard of Oz.

"*Ma minette, you must stop this constant worrying!*" Drake said. "S'il vous plaît! *You are making yourself nauseous; do not forget that I feel every wave of it as well!*"

"*I can't help it!*" I yelled back at him. "*Why, all of a sudden, does it seem like all the spirits in New Orleans are becoming activated?*"

"*I cannot say,*" Drake answered. "*But the only spirit you must concern yourself with no longer resides in our home. Therefore, you have nothing to fear or worry yourself about. It is all quite unnecessary.*"

I took a deep breath, but it didn't make me feel any better. Instead, I resigned myself to paying attention to Prudence.

"Now, the recordin's I'm about ta play for y'all only occurred within the last two evenings, right smack here in this cemetery. Again, I was with mah paranormal society an' along with the EVP recordin's we took, we used EMF meters, an' took loads o' digital photos, an' even a video. An', ladies an' gentlemen, we caught somethin' o' ghostly origin with every device we used!" There was a round of gasps in response. "There were more orbs in our photographs than I ever saw before an' we caught all sorts o' wispy white images on the video camera when we played the footage back real slow." Another round of more audible gasps. When Prudence clicked "play" on her recorder, I took a few steps forward, leaning inward with my right ear as I closed my eyes. I was trying to separate the ghostly voices from the static of white noise in the background. I didn't have to concentrate very hard though.

"It comes!" The voice sounded robotic and slightly muddled, but it was clear enough for me to easily make out the words. I felt like my enormous lunch was about to revisit me in a most unkind manner. I had no time to recover, however, before the static returned, increasing steadily before it dropped again.

"It said, 'It comes'!" someone yelled out.

Prudence nodded, wearing that now familiar irritated expression of impatience. "Please don't comment out loud. There are so many words that come through, one right after 'nother, an' I don't want you ta miss any o' them." She clicked "rewind" on her recorder and the thing made a scratchy, high-pitched, and most annoying noise. "What I've captured here is truly unbelievable!" she finished, clicking "play" again.

"Save us!" The next voice that came through sounded as if it could belong to a woman. It was immediately followed by a much scratchier, much harder to hear voice. I couldn't make out exactly what it said.

"That one was, 'Make it stop!'" Prudence said quietly with a quick glance down at the recorder, presumably anticipating the next voice.

"The second day" came across so clearly, I gulped loudly without even realizing it. More static, and then a huge thud that sounded like someone just dropped a piano off a four-story roof. Half the people listening intently jumped back, obviously in shock, which I found slightly humorous.

"I'm not sure what that was," Prudence admitted. "We didn't drop anythin' durin' the recordin' an' there weren't any other audible sounds that any o' us noticed. Now listen for this one." She grew silent as the static on the machine increased tenfold and a very weak voice called out, "Must hide, must hide!"

Prudence clicked the recorder off and sighed. "Now let me remind y'all that everythin' you just heard was ova the course o' the last two nights. I got more EVP recordin's just in the last two nights than I ever got here in years!"

"That's amazing!" someone said while the rest began talking amongst themselves. I was so astonished, I couldn't say anything.

"Was there more?" a woman asked while the man next to her, presumably her husband, muttered something about Prudence making the sounds on the tape herself just so she could use them for her tour. His wife elbowed him in the side and he was quiet after that.

Prudence nodded. "There was more, but we couldn't really make out what was said. Sounded like names possibly."

I couldn't shake the feeling that something was wrong in this city—terribly, horribly wrong.

Chapter 4

Later that afternoon, a cold and blistery wind raced through the streets of New Orleans, leaving whorls of windswept leaves and street debris in its wake. The sound of scraping branches against the windows in my house reminded me of nails on a chalkboard so, in response, I increased the volume way up on the television in my guestroom. However, I still couldn't focus on *True Blood*. Instead, my mind was assaulted by images of Lafayette Cemetery as stories about Emile and the newly awakened ghosts of New Orleans occupied my mind.

"La cacophonie!" Drake sounded in my mind; I imagined the French meant "the cacophony," but didn't bother checking. "*Ma minette, please turn the volume down on that infernal contraption!*"

The television seemed to be the only technological innovation that Drake wasn't impressed by. Most likely it was because he'd gotten used to seeing them in his house for the last fifty-plus years when the previous owner lived there. I sighed, grabbing the remote and turning the volume down. I felt my hair stand up on end as soon as the scratching of the tree limbs on the windows assaulted my ears again. As if that alone wasn't enough to make me claw my face off, a steady rain began to fall, the fat drops plopping against the windowpanes in between the screeches of grating branches. But despite the New Orleans wind and water torture, I could admit I was still happy I'd moved from Los Angeles, even if the Californians were experiencing seventy-degree weather at the moment.

Our little adventure today, first to Commander's and then to the graveyard, had managed to absolutely do me in. I was beyond exhausted and even a little bit nauseous, which I attributed to the anxiety that was now flowing through me, and set for full steam ahead. Earlier, Ryan had invited me over to his house for the evening, but I'd declined. I did so not only because I didn't feel right being alone with Ryan when he still didn't know about Drake, but also because I was too exhausted to want to go. All I wanted to do was crawl into my jammies and morph into a couch potato—or a bed potato, as the case may be.

"*Ma minette,*" Drake continued as I inwardly sighed, secretly wishing I could tune him out and tune *True Blood* back in. "*I would like to speak to you. Would you kindly oblige me?*"

Figuring Sookie Stackhouse and the gang were now a lost cause, and hoping a conversation with Drake would keep my mind off the reanimated ghosts of New Orleans, I closed my eyes. I attempted to drift into the dreamscape that exists between this plane and the next.

It took me a few seconds to get my bearings, but when I did, I found myself sitting in a plush leather chair the color of milk chocolate. I could smell the remnants of a cigar, the rich, sweet odor still lingering in the air. Its faintness suggested the cigar must have been put out a long time ago.

"I didn't know you smoked cigars," I said as soon as I saw Drake. He was leaning against a stunning baby grand piano in the style of Louis XIV. It looked like it was carved out of cherry or some other dark and exotic wood. The legs of the piano were striking—they were carved, sculpted, and finished in gold leaf. On the top of each of the three legs was the head of medusa, but the legs themselves were modeled after those of a lion.

"On occasion," the handsome man responded. He was dressed in what I imagined was casual dress for his time period: dark pants with a blue collared shirt and the sleeves rolled up to his elbows. I tried not to stare at his muscular, tanned forearms, dusted with a light covering of dark, wiry hair, because I found them incredibly sexy. Forcing my eyes upward, I took in his charcoal-gray vest, which made his whole ensemble a bit dressier than it otherwise seemed. Drake's hair was parted on the side and appeared glossy in the low lights of the music room. Sometimes I had to remind myself that he was a ghost because on occasions such as these, when he seemed so real, when the whole dreamscape seemed real, I had to prod myself to remember what was true in reality and what only existed in my head.

"Where are we?" I asked, glancing around myself as I tried to make sense of the space. Two matching leather club chairs sat in front of the exquisite piano, which stood before a bank of picture windows.

"My music room, ma minette," Drake replied with a little smirk that meant he thought the answer was pretty obvious. So we were still in my house, only I was seeing it in a different time period, as it would have appeared while Drake was still alive. He turned toward a side table that stood between the two club chairs and approached it, lifting up a decanter containing an amber-colored liquid. He reached for one of two square glasses that were sitting in a leather tray on top of the table and poured a glass of the decanter's contents. He glanced back at me and raised a brow in question. "Ma minette?"

"What is it?" I asked, narrowing my eyes on the glass as I watched him swirl the libation around.

"*Ne jamais faire confiance à une femme qui ne connaît pas son alcool*," he responded with a secretive smile.

I frowned. "And that means . . . what exactly?"

He smiled even wider, looking much younger than his thirty-some-odd years. His smile made me smile because it was so charming and boyish. "Never trust a woman who does not know her alcohol."

"Ha-ha," I answered while wondering what made me think Drake was charmingly boyish and, worse, why I couldn't seem to stop staring at his forearms. I shook my head and mentally berated myself, figuring I must be ovulating. "Luckily for you, prohibition happened after you died."

He nodded and clucked his tongue against the roof of his mouth, then sighed as he shook his head. "Perhaps that was one benefit to my untimely passing."

As a rule, Drake and I didn't really discuss his "passing." I sensed he wasn't fully comfortable with it, so I figured I wouldn't press him on the details and didn't mind not knowing the specifics. For all I knew, dying was probably a very personal experience. Maybe the deceased didn't enjoy sharing the details regarding their particular exit from the earthly realm with those who couldn't understand it: the living. "So will you tell me what you're drinking?" I pushed. "Or do you want me to guess?"

"Whiskey, mon amour," he responded with a slight chuckle. "And the offer still stands if you'd fancy one."

"No chaser?" I asked, sticking out my tongue as I shook my head. "A big no-can-do-but-thank-you to that one!"

"Very well," he answered, replacing the lid on the decanter and facing me again. He cleared his throat, his eyes on mine as he took a sip and licked his lower lip suggestively. I wasn't sure why, but I suddenly felt uncomfortable. Maybe it was the way he kept looking at me . . . There was something raw and primitive in his gaze, something totally unapologetic. Sometimes, Drake seemed capable of channeling sex itself.

"So if you have a music room, you must play?" I demanded as I glanced over at the exquisite piano and then raised my brows at him.

Drake grinned. "*Bien sûr*. Of course."

"Okay, then play me something."

He grinned even more broadly. He definitely enjoyed playing the part of impressive. "What do you fancy, mon chaton?"

I wouldn't consider myself a classical music connoisseur by any stretch of the imagination but I did appreciate it all the same. At the moment, though, I was drawing a blank. "I can't think of anything," I admitted.

"I have one in mind," he said immediately as he placed his glass of whiskey back on the table. "I do not know why, ma minette, but it reminds me of you." He sat down on the piano bench and closed his eyes for a few seconds before he started playing a tune that I somehow recognized. I didn't say anything as I tried to place the soft and haunting melody.

"I know this," I said finally. "But I can't remember the name of it."

"'Scarborough Fair,'" Drake answered, still facing the piano.

"That's right," I said as I started humming along with the notes coming from the piano. I shook my head as I watched his fingers pour over the keys in a flourish of sound. "You're such an enigma, Drake."

"*Comment cela*? How so?" he asked as he continued to play.

"Everything about you!" I answered as I shook my head again, completely floored as to how and why Drake was the way he was.

"Example, ma minette."

"Okay, I don't imagine most policemen know how to play the piano."

He nodded. "I became an officer because I felt the need to protect those who cannot protect themselves, ma minette. Though I will admit I was not raised to follow that path."

"That was going to be my next point. I can't imagine your officer's salary would have afforded you the likes of this place?"

He chuckled. "Of course not." Then he finished playing "Scarborough Fair" and turned around fully to face me. "I inherited quite a large fortune, ma minette. My family was very well to do." So that put one of the Drake mysteries to bed. The man in question stood up and lifted his unattended glass of whiskey, taking a sip as he studied me. "Any other questions, ma minette?"

"How is it that we're sitting in the music room? I don't remember this house ever having one," I asked, trying to make idle conversation. The look in Drake's eyes, along with the overbearing silence in the room, was beginning to make me nervous.

"We are in exactly the same room we were in when I requested the pleasure of your company just now," Drake replied before taking another sip of his libation. He was staring at me like I was a turkey on the fourth Thursday in November.

"The guest bedroom?" I asked incredulously. I looked around and shook my head. I could not understand how that could be since the room I was sitting in now was much bigger than my guest bedroom. Probably by at least one hundred square feet or so.

"Oui, the very same, ma minette. It was my music room before someone converted it into another bedroom."

"Hmm," I said as I took in the space again and realized the original room had not only been converted into the guest bedroom, but the guest bathroom as well. That made sense concerning the extra hundred square feet. "It's a bit of a bummer that someone took out the music room," I started, and sighed over the fact. "I like the looks of it."

"Oui," Drake said with a polished smile. "*Vous ne pouvez jamais tenir compte des goûts de l'autre*. You can never account for the tastes of another." He smiled at me quickly before gulping some more of his whiskey. "The reason I called you here, ma minette," he continued, taking a seat in one of the leather club chairs, "is because I am concerned about you."

"Why are you concerned about me?" I asked with a frown. Why did it feel like I was in the middle of an intervention when he was the only one drinking? 'Course, I was the one who couldn't seem to keep her eyes to herself. Ugh! That was frustrating too. I definitely didn't want to give Drake the wrong idea . . .

"I can sense your discomfort regarding the spiritual activity of late," he continued, glancing down at his whiskey, which he swirled amusedly in his glass. "I can feel your anxiety and your fear, ma minette, and your discomfort upsets me."

"Why, because whatever I feel, you feel?" I asked, frowning, and figuring he was irritated that my worrisome nature might be communicable, given our arrangement.

"I will admit that it is less than comfortable to be sharing your body at the moment," he answered nonchalantly, but quickly shook his head. "*Mais non.* But no, my concern stems from a more compassionate and empathetic concern for you, mon amour. I do not enjoy seeing you upset and it was my intention to discuss the matter with you, if only to discover whether there is something I might be able to do to help you?"

Sometimes Drake was so thoughtful and caring, it struck me speechless. After a few seconds, during which I managed to wipe the dumbfounded expression off my face, I also managed to find my voice.

"I'm fine, Drake, and thanks for worrying about me."

"Is there anything I can do?"

I shook my head. "I don't think so, but I appreciate your concern."

"I do not like the fact that the activities of late are upsetting you so, ma minette," he continued, his eyebrows meeting in the middle of his forehead as he scowled.

"Apparently I'm the only one who finds them upsetting. You aren't concerned about any of the weird stuff that's been going on?"

I asked, crossing my arms against my chest as I exhaled. I wondered why no one else seemed to be bothered that New Orleans was becoming a bed of paranormal activity. Well, more so than usual, anyway. Ryan sort of just shrugged it off and now it seemed Drake was following his lead.

Waiting for Drake to respond, I sighed and leaned forward, my elbows on my knees. I didn't notice both of my knees bouncing up and down until I felt the reverberation through my elbows and up my arms. Leaning back into my chair, I took a deep breath and ran the pads of my fingers across the soft leather of Drake's club chairs. The leather felt so real, I had to remind myself, again, that I was simply living in my own mind. Everything around me was no more than a fabrication, created from Drake's memory. It seemed so strange to me that I could smell, touch, and hear things as if they were completely tangible, rather than just mere illusions of my mind.

Drake shook his head finally, after taking his time with a prolonged swallow of whiskey and an even lengthier sigh. "I would not say that I am not concerned about the activities of late, ma minette," he answered before finishing his drink. He paused a little while longer and we just stared at one another.

"Then what would you say?" I nudged.

He stood up and turned around, giving me a view of his taut backside, which did look very fetching in his tailored pants. Groaning inwardly at myself, I watched him reach for the decanter on the desk behind him. He poured himself another generous glassful and took a sip before turning around again to face me. He was wearing the smile of someone who was in the know; as in, he knew I'd been checking out his butt. "I would say that this recent resurgence and awakening of everything spiritual in this town is of primary concern to me as well as to you."

I took a deep breath and my mind raced with the possibilities of why everything ghost-related seemed to be blowing up all around me. Then something occurred to me. "Since you're a member of the spiritual world, Drake, why can't you find out what's going on? You must still have some sort of link to the afterlife, right?"

He looked perplexed. "How would it matter if I did?"

I shrugged, the answer so obvious to me. "Well, those voices that were on Prudence's recording seemed to know something was coming, right? Remember how one of the voices said 'it's coming' or something like that? And then another one mentioned something about hiding?"

"I do recall, yes."

"Well, the spirits on the recording had to have gotten that information from somewhere, right?" I took a deep breath, and, without waiting for him to respond, continued, "So, if we decided to play the what-do-each-of-these-have-in-common game, we'd see that the voices on the recording belonged to the deceased; and since you're deceased . . ."

He chuckled and shook his head. "I am afraid it is not so simple, ma minette. As to my own ties to the paranormal world, I do not know the answer to your question—whether I have maintained them or not. As I am now in a human body, and quite a delectable one at that," he added in a licentious tone, "I believe things will work contrarily to what I used to be accustomed to."

"Okay," I started, and then took a deep breath. "So there's only one way to test that, right?" When he didn't respond, I continued my argument. "Let's test it right now. Let's see if you can still interact with the spiritual world."

Drake flashed me a quick frown that said he didn't necessarily think this was going to be a fruitful exercise, but then he nodded. "*Très bien*. Very well." He eyed me for a second or two as neither of us said anything. "You will need to open your eyes, ma minette, as I cannot access anything with us both in this dream world," he instructed with an amused smile.

"Oh, right!" I answered and then did exactly that. I focused on the television from where I sat on my bed in the guest bedroom, which had once been Drake's music room. "*Okay*," I thought, "*work your magic!*"

I could hear Drake's chuckle as it echoed through my head and died away moments later. "*I am not familiar with the way in which to go about this task, mon chaton*," he started in a hesitant voice. "*This will be a learning experience for us both.*"

"*Okay, that sounds fair.*"

"*Very well, please do not speak or otherwise take my concentration away, ma minette. I am going to attempt to reach out to the spirits, to bypass the limits of your corporeality.*"

I just nodded and thought about closing my eyes in an attempt to help him focus but then worried doing so might return us back to the dream plane where we could more easily interact with each other. And, apparently, Drake hadn't thought that was a good idea. So instead, I tried to allow my eyes to zone out on the wall across from me. And I tried to clear my brain of any thoughts that might derail him on his quest to secure a connection with the afterlife.

As I allowed my eyes to blur while staring at the wall across the room, it didn't feel as if anything was changing inside me. I wasn't sure what to expect but I imagined that if Drake were successful in establishing communication with the beyond, I'd at least feel or see something other than what I currently was.

After another few minutes of receiving nothing at all, my eyes started to tire and I found it increasingly difficult to keep my mind from traveling. I didn't say anything, though, because I was hopeful that Drake might have been making some headway in his attempts.

"C'etait une quête inutile. *That was a useless quest*," he answered at last, his voice in my head sounding drained.

I immediately closed my eyes, thinking it would be easier to interact with him "face-to-face." That, and my eyes were stinging like

SOBs. "So, what happened?" I asked once I recognized his music room and found him standing before me, wearing a frown.

He shrugged. "I attempted to contact the spirits multiple times but was fruitless."

"Damn," I said, and sighed.

"I do not believe it is possible for me to maintain my ties to the supernatural world, ma minette."

"Why? Just because you weren't able to this time? Maybe we should try again?"

He shook his head. "I am afraid I am bound by your body, and, therefore, unable to sustain my ties to the spiritual world. I feel as if I have become corporeal; but, of course, that is just my hypothesis."

"Great," I grumbled.

"I do not know for certain, ma minette, if what I say is true," he started with a handsome smile. "Let us simply call it a hunch. Perhaps your lady friend who assisted with the exorcism would know?"

He was referring to Lovie. Actually, getting in touch with her wasn't such a bad idea. Lovie might know if Drake had somehow maintained his connection with the spiritual world and if he had, she'd know how to tap back into it. Granted, I could have also gotten in touch with Christopher, the warlock, who worked with Lovie. However, when it came to affability, Christopher missed the boat a long time ago. Yes, I definitely felt more comfortable approaching Lovie. "Good idea. I'll try to get in touch with her right away," I said as I leapt up from my chair and closed my eyes, intending to return to my own space and time so I could contact Lovie right away.

"*Attendez-vous!* Wait," Drake called out as I opened my eyes again and turned to face him curiously. "There is one bit of information that I take particular issue over regarding the messages from the deceased that I must first speak to you about."

"Go on," I prodded when he took another sip of his whiskey,

apparently enjoying the fact that I was waiting on pins and needles for his response.

"On the trollop's recording," he started, throwing me for a second before I recalled that "trollop" was his nickname for Prudence. "One of the voices of the deceased said 'the second day.'"

"Right," I said, pausing to ponder where he was going with this. "Oh my God," I whispered aloud. I involuntarily recalled one of the scariest incidents from when the malevolent entity resided in my house, which I now believed was the spirit of the Axeman of New Orleans. He had been a serial killer who attacked his victims by chiseling out panels into the back doors of his victims' homes, climbing inside, and violently doing them in with their own axes, which they most often left by their fireplaces.

"Do you recall the incident, ma minette?" Drake asked, eyeing me purposefully.

I just nodded because it was a moment in my life I could never forget, much to my own chagrin.

"Please try to remember the incident in detail," Drake continued. I closed my eyes and allowed my mind to wander, returning in time to the moment when the entity first made contact with me . . .

I couldn't see through the fog billowing through the guest bedroom but I forced myself forward, forced myself to the bathroom door. Grasping the knob in my palm, I turned it and felt like I was moving in slow motion. I pulled the door open and was blinded by the overhead light while the steam hit me full force in the face.

The air in the room was so incredibly hot, I shielded my face with my arm as I followed the sound of rushing water that was coming from the bathtub. Stumbling forward, I slid the glass door to one side and reached into the bathtub, gripping the hot water knob and turning it off. Standing up again, I turned back around and noticed the steam suddenly evaporating as if on fast-forward.

The memory was so distinct and concrete that it felt as if I were reliving it a second time. I could tell my breathing was getting quicker and that my heart rate was escalating.

"Please do not stop, ma minette, please continue to remember the details. As I was not with you at that moment, I must see what you saw, and experience what you experienced," Drake said in a hushed tone. He hadn't yet taken possession of my body at that point. Instead, he'd been fighting for his own soul against the entity's oppressive power.

I opened my eyes and noticed his were closed, as if he saw the images playing out behind my eyelids as easily as I did. I closed my eyes again and allowed myself to drift backward in time, seizing the imagery of the bathroom and the hot steam pouring from it. Watching myself glance into the bathroom mirror above the sink, I felt my breath catching in my throat. My heartbeat was already racing, pounding through me until I began to feel light-headed.

The steam clung to the mirror, obscuring my reflection. But as the vapor began to dissipate, it left words behind on the mirror, paragraphs of text.

Hell, April 15, 2014

Esteemed Mortal:

They have never caught me and they never will. They have never seen me, for I am invisible, even as the ether that surrounds your earth. I am not a human being but a spirit and a fell demon from the hottest hell. I am what you Orleanians and your foolish police call the Axeman.

When I see fit, I shall come again and claim other victims. I alone know who they shall be. I shall leave no clue except my bloody axe, besmeared with the blood and brains of whom I have sent below to keep me company.

If you wish you may tell the police not to rile me. Of course I am a reasonable spirit. I take no offense at the way they have conducted their investigation in the past. But tell them to beware. Let them not try to discover what I am, for it would be better that they were never born than to incur the wrath of the Axeman.

Now, to be exact, at 12:15 (earthly time) on next Tuesday night, I am going to visit again.

The Axeman

As frightening as the beginning of the letter was, it was nothing compared to that final sentence.

Next Tuesday night, I am going to visit again.

The final sentence was now settling in my stomach like an anvil.

My heart was pumping so quickly, I feared I might pass out. I opened my eyes and saw Drake beside me as he assisted me into the leather club chair again. The visual of the memory was still gripping me, the replay so intense that I wasn't sure if it was still holding me captive. I glanced up into Drake's caring face and shook my head. "I don't understand what just happened," I said in a breathless voice. "It was like reliving the memory again. It felt so real, like I was actually there all over again."

Drake nodded. "I accessed your memories to help you recall the situation, ma minette," he answered evasively. He acted as if his comment wasn't any big deal, as if I wouldn't wonder how that could even be possible. "I needed to understand it, to experience what you saw and felt, so I could try to make sense of it."

"How did you access my memories?" I demanded, but Drake shook his head as if he had neither the time nor the inclination to respond.

"Concentrate, ma minette."

Figuring I could pin him down later about the whole total recall bit, I simply nodded. I remembered seeing the words appear on the mirror, writing themselves as if by an invisible hand, except they had been formed by the steam in the room.

"Next Tuesday night, I am going to visit again," I said, in a flat, empty voice.

"And the words on the recording?" Drake prodded, his police officer roots suddenly visible. I could just imagine him, back in his own day, assuming the role of peace officer. It was really no wonder at all that Drake was so popular with the ladies.

"The second day," I answered hollowly.

"Oui," Drake commented, and said nothing more. He just continued to stare at me, studying me with narrowed eyes.

"Somehow the spirits knew," I said in a daze. I couldn't seem to tear my focus away from the beauty of the piano across from me.

"Perhaps but perhaps not."

"The second day of the week," I continued, not even aware of what Drake was talking about. It was like I was on autopilot, listening to my own stream of consciousness. "The spirits must have been referring to the Axeman's letter." I swallowed hard as the next four words emptied out of my mouth. "To this coming Tuesday."

Drake nodded as he took a deep breath and placed his whiskey glass back on the tabletop. "Oui, ma minette, and the date today is?"

"Saturday, April 19," I answered, starting to awaken from my trance. I shook my head and then my hands to emerge from my stupor. Ignoring the pins and needles that ran throughout my entire body as my feeling was restored, I focused on Drake's handsome face. "That means we have tomorrow and Monday, Drake . . . until . . . until I don't even know what?"

He shrugged. "*Je ne sais pas*, ma minette. I do not know. It could be something, but also nothing at all. Perhaps it is only the sounds of static on a very old recorder."

"How could it be nothing?" I asked, suddenly feeling alarmed as I stood up. I wrapped my arms around myself. Drake was instantly by my side, enfolding me in his embrace as if he feared I might faint. I relished the warmth of his body as it settled around mine, and the tingle of his breathing against my neck. I had to fight to keep my eyes open. The scent of whiskey was still on his breath, and that, mixed with the faintness of the cigar smoke in the room, suddenly overcame me with the urge to kiss him. "What I'm feeling," I started, but immediately felt incredibly embarrassed. I left the words to die unspoken on my tongue.

"Go on," he said in a strained voice.

I swallowed hard and glanced up at him. "Is what I'm feeling coming from you? Or am I feeling my own true feelings?"

"Your own," he answered as his eyes burned into mine.

I nodded, but continued to stare up at him; it was like I couldn't break our eye contact. "Can you feel what I'm feeling?"

His lips turned up at the ends into something that almost resembled a smile. "Oui," he said softly.

Chapter 5

Drake was about to kiss me.

I could see it in his eyes and I could feel his passion when he tightened his hands around my waist, pulling me closer to him. As obviously as he wanted to kiss me, there was a part of me that equally, desperately wanted to kiss him. I was dying—no pun intended—to savor the warmth of his full lips on mine. My eyelashes dusted the tops of my cheeks as I closed my eyes and let his fanning breath tickle my face.

"Ma minette," he started in a deep tone of voice, even though his words came out as mere whispers. My eyelids felt heavy when I opened them and found him staring down at me, studying me intently, as if he planned to etch my features into his memory for a later date. "*J'avais envie de goûter vos lèvres* . . . I have yearned to taste your lips . . . for so very long."

Tipping my chin up with his fingers, he smiled down at me while his eyes smoldered. I suddenly felt intoxicated, as if I were losing myself in the rich hot chocolate of his eyes. But his smirk soon got my attention; it was one of victory, of conquest. I felt my eyelids growing heavier again as my breathing came in shallow spurts. I closed my eyes and listened to Drake's soft chuckle.

Despite the side of me that wanted to know what it felt like to kiss Drake, to taste him and experience him in a way I never had before, there was an undeniable other part of me that rebelled against the idea. That part was in the process of digging my heels into the ground with abject refusal.

It feels right, Peyton, my voice sounded inside my head. *Don't fight it.*

No, I barked back immediately. *It doesn't feel right!*

Why not?

Because of Ryan.

As soon as Ryan's name crossed my mind, I figuratively opened my eyes and felt like I just snapped out of the momentary intoxication. Even though I was still caught in the dreamscape, the influence of whatever sexual elixir I had been under had vanished, leaving in its place shock and guilt. I broke Drake's embrace by dropping my arms from around his shoulders and boldly stepping away from him.

Ryan's name continued to dominate my thoughts, echoing through my mind as I took another few steps away from Drake. I suddenly wanted to catch my breath, and needed to center myself. It was as though a thundercloud hung over my head, raining down the realization that Drake and I should never have gotten ourselves in this situation in the first place. It wasn't right.

It was wrong not only because I cared about Ryan and wanted to explore the possibilities of what might develop between us, but also because Drake and I could never really be together. We could never be a reality. Drake and I could never become anything because only one of us was alive.

The whole situation sounded so completely bizarre and even crazy when I broke it down into its bare components—Drake was a spirit and I was flesh and blood. But in my heart of hearts, I knew it wasn't as simple as just that. Yes, initially, Drake had been no more than a disembodied voice that I heard in my head, but he soon became much more than that. In the brief moments that we met in dreamscapes, he felt just as real as I. I could see, hear, smell, and touch him just as if he were standing right in front of me. During those rare moments, I probably lost touch with what was truly reality and what wasn't.

"*Je m'excuse*. I apologize, ma minette," Drake said, clearing his throat as he ran his hands down the front of his vest and sighed. He seemed embarrassed somehow, frustrated and remorseful. Actually, the more I studied him, the more I realized it wasn't frustration, but rather perturbation. Since it wasn't an emotion I'd ever seen on him before, it threw me for a few seconds.

I nodded, imagining it must've been difficult for him to make sense of what happened between us as well. I offered him a small smile of consolation. For my part, however, I still reeled from the shock of the whole thing. I half wondered if I shouldn't have been consoling myself and not him. Inside, my raw emotions were on a battlefield. Part of me tried to ignore the extreme guilt at coming so very close to kissing Drake when Ryan and I were, more or less, already in a relationship—a new one, but a relationship for sure. Why I even wanted to kiss Drake, I didn't know. I mean, despite how handsome Drake was, and the fact that he was sexier than sin, I couldn't forget that he also wasn't alive!

"I sense your discomfort," he continued, shaking his head as he sighed. "I apologize again, ma minette. I do not wish to be the cause of such chagrin."

"Let's just . . . pretend like it never happened," I answered evasively, refusing to look at him. Actually, I didn't fully know what to make or think of the situation. Needless to say, though, the stupid truth was that I *did* care about Drake—I was very attracted to him, otherwise I never would have lost myself in that moment. Yes, it was true that I enjoyed Drake's company and, who knew? Maybe in another place and time, he and I could have had something . . .

As of now, though, I had to restrain my feelings for Drake and impede their progress because he and I were no more than two ships passing in the night. Even though this pseudo world felt undeniably real—with leather chairs so plush I could sink into them and scents so distinct I could still smell the trace of cigar smoke, which haunted me even now—it wasn't real. It was purely artifice, mere images created by Drake tampering with my thoughts, and allowing his own personal memories of what our home used to look like to filter into mine. They were simply illusions that conspired to trick me into thinking they were real. But when it came down to it, Drake was merely a spirit in possession of my body. Falling for Drake would be like falling for the air that filled my lungs. It would be like falling for nothing!

"Pretending it never happened will not make the feelings between us go away, ma minette. Certainly you realize that?" Drake said, while shaking his head. "*Prétendre est pour les enfants*. Pretending is for children."

"Regardless," I started, "that can't ever happen again." My voice was hoarse. Hoping to avoid the pain in Drake's eyes, I glanced around the music room, taking stock of everything. I saw it the way it looked back in his time, nearly one hundred years ago, and it made me grow angry. I immediately thought to myself that I wanted out of this dreamscape, thereby shattering the visual of the early twentieth century music room in my mind. I had to fight to push away the images of the past, and force myself back into the present, but I gritted my teeth, demanding that history subside.

I found myself lying on my bed, gazing at the television. It took me a few seconds to comprehend the spontaneous exit from my dreamscape and return to the present. Once that realization dawned, I breathed a sigh of relief, but shook my head while remembering what had just happened. Was I starting to lose my mind? Maybe that was a stretch, but at any rate, my visits with Drake were becoming increasingly realistic, which was a thought that disturbed as much as worried me. Was it possible for me to get caught in the surrealism that existed in my head and stay there forever?

Of course, I had no answer to my question, but I had a good idea who might. Without wasting any more time, I jumped up from my bed and started for the chest of drawers in the corner of the guest bedroom. There was a piece of paper lying on top of the dresser with Lovie's phone number written on it.

"*Ma minette,*" Drake started. "*Please do not be angry with me.* S'il vous plaît."

"*I'm not angry with you,*" I replied in my mind. "*I'm angry with myself.*"

"Pourquoi*? Why should you be angry with yourself and not me? It was I who made the advances.*"

"*Because I expected that from you, Drake. You were just acting in accordance with the way you always act.*" I sighed and shook my head, irritated that Drake's advances were actually starting to work on me. What was wrong with me? Usually, we were just like an old married couple: bantering, bickering, and feeling nothing beyond aggravation for one another. Sexual attraction should have never entered the equation.

"*You should not feel guilty for your true feelings, ma minette.*"

But it was too late. I already blamed myself for allowing my feelings for Drake to go way beyond the friendship level. Now, those feelings would be bottled up and dropped off the ship of my mind, where they would disappear at the bottom of my subconscious, never to reemerge into my thoughts again!

"I blame myself for feeling things that I have no business feeling. I should never have allowed myself to get into that . . . kind of situation with you," I said, hoping he would understand where I was coming from. I wanted him to realize the futility of desiring something that could never be.

"*Oui,* je comprends. *I understand.*" His voice in my head sounded hollow, dejected. "*It pains me that your regret runs so deep, ma minette.*"

"*It doesn't run so deep,*" I responded immediately. The frustration and stress of the situation silenced me and I had to take a few seconds to figure out why I was so upset in the first place. "*Drake, you do realize that you and I can never share anything together, right? It's not like we can ever have a real relationship or look forward to a shared future. There is no future for us.*"

"Bien sûr. *Of course, ma minette. I have repeated your very words to myself so many times, I have lost count.*"

"*Then what happened just now?*" I demanded.

In my mind's eye, I imagined him shrugging with his eyes narrowing as he pondered a response. "*I suppose I encouraged myself to kiss you because I have so yearned for that exact moment. I put aside all the reasons why we shouldn't be together and acted on impulse. For that, again, I apologize.*"

"*It's okay,*" I answered immediately, and suddenly felt sorry for him. As difficult as it was for me to have him in my head, it must be even harder for him. At least my body belonged to me. He had nothing to call his own anymore, not even what he once called home.

With no wish to prolong the conversation, and seeing the situation was what it was, I reached for Lovie's phone number and my cell phone, which was sitting beside it. I dialed the number and waited patiently as the phone rang once, twice, and then three times. Just when I worried her voice mail would pick up, she answered.

"Lovie here," she said in her sweet Southern accent.

"Hi, Lovie, it's Peyton," I answered hurriedly. My voice could not conceal my worry.

"Ah honeygirl, where y'at?"

"I'm okay, I guess," I answered, having already been schooled that "where y'at?" was a standard New Orleans way of asking "How are you?" and not a request for my physical location.

"What's wrong, doll?" Lovie continued; the background noise coming through the phone made it sound as if she were in the middle of a parade.

"It's too complex to talk about over the phone, Lovie. I was hoping I could meet with you in person, if that isn't too much to ask?"

"'Course not!" Lovie replied with a little laugh that said my question was a silly one. "Just come on down to my store, honey, an' we'll fix up a cure for whatever's ailin' you."

"Your store?" I repeated, instantly at a loss because I hadn't realized Lovie owned or managed a store.

She laughed. "Guess we never got down to particulars, did we? Come visit my shop on Royal Street in the French Quarter, honey, an' you can tell me all 'bout whatever's ailin' you."

I glanced at the clock on the wall. "Your store is still open at six p.m.?"

"Oh, we stay open until I decide I've had enough!" She laughed. "But with the way business has been lately, the store is just a madhouse, so I've been stayin' open longer than usual. I swear all the dead in N'awlins musta decided to come a-callin' recently! I suppose it's good for my wallet, but not so sure how my health's holdin' up! I swear I haven't slept a wink in the last week or so."

"Well, that, er, meaning the dead, is exactly what I'm coming to talk to you about," I muttered as a sigh escaped my lips. There was a pause on the other line and I assumed Lovie was wondering to which dead I was referring: Drake or the entity of the Axeman she'd previously helped to exorcise. But I didn't want to get into that conversation over the phone. "I don't think you ever told me what the name of your store was?"

"Well, naturally, it's called Ms. Lovie's," she answered with a giggle.

I laughed and suddenly felt like my day was looking up. I wasn't sure why, because I didn't know Lovie all that well, but somehow her presence comforted me. "Okay, Lovie, I'm leaving now."

"Well, you hurry yer sweet hiney on down here, Miss Peyton!" she answered, turning to talk to someone else in a muffled tone.

We said our good-byes and I hung up before taking a deep breath and realizing I needed to check in with Ryan. One of the agreements we'd made in the last few days was that I wouldn't shut him out of my life. He'd been especially miffed when I hadn't told him about the exorcism Lovie and Christopher had performed on my house until afterward. I could just imagine how irritated he'd be when I finally grew the cojones to tell him about Drake. That was a conversation that needed to happen sooner rather than later, because I intended to involve Ryan in everything from here on out. It was a promise I not only made to him, but to myself as well. I lifted my cell phone and dialed his number. He answered on the first ring.

"Is this my incredibly attractive neighbor whom I can't seem to stop thinkin' about?"

I felt myself smiling as soon as I heard his rich Southern baritone. It wasn't lost on me that Drake hadn't said boo since before I called Lovie. I wanted things between us to go back to the way they'd been before our near kiss had thrown everything off course. Hopefully that wasn't just wishful thinking.

"Hi, Ryan," I said with a broad smile. "I, uh, wanted to tell you that I'm headed to Lovie's store, which, coincidentally, I wasn't even aware she owned, to discuss my concerns. Now that the dead seem to be spiraling out of control in this city lately, it has put me into a near panic because I'm afraid of what this might mean where the Axeman is concerned." I took a breath. "Recalling the conversation we had the other day when you told me not to shut you out of my life, I thought I'd extend the offer to you, if you'd like to join me."

There was a pause on the other line before his robust chuckle interrupted the silence. "Well, when you put it that way, how can I refuse?"

I laughed, suddenly feeling remarkably lucky to have this wonderful man in my life. Even if romance never figured into our equation, I would undoubtedly always value him greatly as a friend. A romantic relationship was really just the icing on the cake. Granted, it would be incredibly good icing . . . "I guess you can't."

"It's Peyton," he said to someone else in the room before pausing and apparently listening to the other person's comment. I heard him say something else, but his voice became so muffled, I couldn't make out what he said. "Pey?" he asked.

"Yeah?"

He sighed and laughed. "Trina is over here at the moment, an' as soon as she heard about your little errand to Lovie's, she insisted that she be invited also." Trina was Ryan's younger sister, whom I didn't know too well, but still considered a friend.

"Of course she's invited too," I answered with a laugh. I could hear Trina gabbing on about something in the background.

"You hear that?" Ryan called out to her. "She said you're invited so you better be on your best behavior!" Then he chuckled into the receiver and I could tell by his tone that he was shaking his head. "I'll grab a rain jacket an' pick you up in the truck in, say, five minutes?"

"Roger that," I answered, actually pleased that Trina was accompanying us. I hadn't seen her in a few days and had meant to call her.

Ryan chuckled some more and when he spoke again, his tone was hushed. "I've missed you, Peyton."

I could feel myself blushing as a huge grin broke across my face. "Missed me? We haven't even been apart for twenty-four hours!"

"So what?" he demanded. "What are you, the romance police?"

I giggled, suddenly feeling all of twelve years old, and talking on the phone to my grade-school crush. I cleared my throat, trying to make my voice as deep as I could. "I apologize, Mr. Kelly, but I'm going to have to write you up for your unsolicited romantic sentiments to one Miss Peyton Clark."

Ryan chuckled. "Ah, I apologize, officer. It won't happen again, I do solemnly swear!"

"Very good, Mr. Kelly," I continued, my voice starting to crack.

Ryan laughed again and sighed, clearing his throat. "See you in a few, pretty girl."

"Sounds good, pretty boy."

"Hey, 'pretty' doesn't work both ways, you know?" he answered in mock offense. "Incredibly handsome an' charmin' hunk works better."

"Hmm, I don't know," I responded, pretending to consider it. "I sort of like pretty boy—it seems to fit you."

"Shiiiitttt," he said with a chuckle. "Bye, Pey."

"Bye, Ryan."

"So, I've gotta bone ta pick with you, Peyton Clark!" Trina announced. Ryan had just escorted me from my front door to the passenger seat of his truck, being careful to protect me from the rain with his oversized umbrella.

Once he opened the door for me, Trina popped her blond head around the seat in front of her and eyed me pointedly. Physically, the first thing I noticed about Trina was her striking resemblance to Ryan. Trina was tall, almost as tall as I was, but where my body was more of a curvy type, ample hips and C-cup boobs, Trina was long and lean. Her eyes were the same shade of amber as her brother's, and also possessed the same spark of Kelly fire. With her full lips, oval face, high cheekbones, and golden hair, she often reminded me of a real life Barbie doll.

I laughed as I gripped the handle on the ceiling of the truck and hoisted myself into the front seat, turning around so I could face her. "Well, hello to you too, Trina!"

She smiled prettily before returning to her diatribe. "I can't believe you didn't invite me over when you had the exorcism on your house! An' instead you invited my brother?" She glanced at him in feigned shock and even swatted his shoulder as he seat-belted himself and started the truck.

"Well, I wouldn't say I invited him," I answered with a wink at Ryan.

"It's closer to the truth to say I invited myself," Ryan corrected his sister with a smug smile and a happy wink in my direction.

"At any rate, I felt left out," Trina concluded. She was holding her chin up obstinately as she pouted, sticking out her lower lip like a little child.

I laughed again. I couldn't help it. "Duly noted, Trina. The next time I have to exorcise a horrible entity from my house, you will be the first person I call."

Ryan chuckled loudly as a smile crept through the artificial frown on Trina's face. Seconds later, I could see the glimmer in her eyes as a true smile brightened her face and visible excitement began bubbling up within her. "I'm very excited you invited me along to meet Lovie, Peyton," she said.

"You know who Lovie is?" I asked, surprised.

"'Course, I do! She's got quite the rep as bein' a very gifted priestess, ya know?" Trina asked.

Trina fancied herself a voodoo priestess also; however, the truth did not support her claim. I'd learned that lesson the hard way. "She's very gifted," I answered, taking in the streetlights of the Garden District between the blurry raindrops on Ryan's windshield.

"I am so excited to actually meet her," Trina continued.

"And what about Christopher?" Ryan asked, glancing back at his sister through the rearview mirror. "He's quite a polished warlock."

Trina frowned. "I've heard he isn't exactly friendly."

"Phew, you can say that again!" I agreed with a laugh.

A few minutes later, we turned into the French Quarter and I could already hear the sounds of partygoers on Bourbon Street. "Are we almost there?" I asked Ryan, still rather unfamiliar with the streets of New Orleans.

"Royal Street is a couple more blocks," he answered with a smile, squeezing my thigh just above my knee, and leaving his hand there. I placed my hand on top of his and smiled back at him.

Just then I noticed that Drake still hadn't said a word. He and I would definitely have a conversation once our little errand was over. I certainly didn't want anything to feel strained or uncomfortable between us. The truth was that I did feel as if I'd been too hard on him . . .

"You both are very cute, by the way," Trina commented, while taking turns facing Ryan and me. "I was wonderin' when my silly ol' brother would make a move on you, Pey. I told him more than once that if he didn't move faster an' snatch you up, it was just a matter o' time before some other handsome, sophisticated man did." She sighed, looking at her brother. "You got a lot ta thank me for, big brother."

He chuckled as he nodded and looked over at me. "That I do, Trina, that I do."

Chapter 6

Ms. Lovie's wasn't much of a shop. It looked more like a shack, wedged between an antique store and an art gallery. Even though the place had to be less than three hundred square feet, of which a good half was crammed full of what appeared to be shit—unidentifiable items in mass quantities—the rest of the shop was standing room only. True to her word, Lovie's place was a madhouse.

As I scanned above and around the numerous heads in the room, I noticed the walls were painted bright orange and the ceiling was fuchsia pink. Large, pink paper lanterns covered the bare lightbulbs that hung down from the ceiling, giving the shop a Middle Eastern sort of vibe. The floor comprised gray carpet, covered by numerous small rugs. Each featured a black background with a contrasting bright, paisley print or an even brighter flower in the middle. Black bookshelves filled the walls and sitting atop them were all sorts of vials, candles, beads, and other trinkets that I didn't recognize. Another bookshelf was stacked with books, and another held bags full of colorful substances. Just as I imagined, Lovie's store specialized in the occult, probably retailing in both voodoo and witchcraft artifacts, along with do-it-yourself exorcism kits.

Someone pushed past me and I would have fallen over if Ryan hadn't grabbed my upper arm and kept me upright. The crowd moved and swayed as one, seemingly becoming more agitated as people continued to enter the store, but none exited. The voices, which previously sounded more like a humming background noise, now increased in volume.

"Order! Order!" I recognized Christopher's voice amid the loud cacophony of the room. "Yes, lady, I understand that your Uncle Pete died two years ago an' shouldn't be visitin' you now, but unless you get into line like everyone else, you're going to have ta set an extra table setting for him . . . and I mean long term."

Christopher saw me at exactly the same moment I saw him. With the frown on his face, I could tell he wasn't exactly happy to see me. An accomplished and well-known warlock, Christopher looked pretty young. I guessed he wasn't much older than my thirty-one years. Physically, he was probably about six one with a doughy appearance, like if you poked him in the stomach, your finger would easily sink in. You definitely couldn't get him to giggle though. His hair was completely gray, even white in some parts, and his wide brown eyes were often narrowed into a rather pinched expression. Every time I saw him, he was dressed all in black. That, in itself, wasn't really so odd—but the accessories he chose to complement his black ensemble were, in a word, different . . .

Each time I encountered him, he wore a long, black cape, which, when paired with his pale skin, made him look like Count Dracula. This time, however, he wasn't wearing the infamous cape. His standard black pants, black boots, and long-sleeved black shirt were all in attendance, but he also had on a black top hat. A bow of black tulle wrapped around the front of the hat, cascading down the back of it like a tail. His short black jacket ended at his waist, and an enormous metal belt buckle, shaped like a gothic cross, grabbed my attention. His face appeared even whiter than usual, especially in contrast to his matte black lipstick and black eye liner, which he'd drawn all the way around his eyes. If he was aiming for the crying-with-mascara look, he definitely pulled it off.

"I do hope you saw the long line?" he asked, facing me with a none-too-friendly, tight-lipped expression. Then he crossed his arms against his chest as if his sourpuss expression wasn't enough to ward me away.

"There's a line?" I asked with a smile, glancing around me and shaking my head. "'Cause I'll be damned if I can find it!"

"Well, I can help find it for you!" he replied with one of his trademark snide expressions.

"Oh, Christopher," Lovie said as she struggled through the throng of people and eventually appeared beside him. She pretended to push him away, shaking her head as she smiled up at him warmly. "You'd force yer own motha ta get in line." Holding out her hands to me, she grinned broadly as I accepted them and we both gave each other a hug.

As intimidating as Christopher's overall demeanor and appearance were, Lovie was exactly the opposite. At a head or more shorter than Christopher and slightly overweight, she was still quite beautiful with unblemished chocolate skin, full lips, and wide-set brown eyes. If I had to say, I would guess Lovie was either in her late forties or early fifties. Where Christopher had his own gothic, vampirish style, Lovie also possessed uniqueness. Christopher eschewed all colors, and Lovie welcomed them. Today, she was wearing a green scarf wrapped around her head like a turban. Her blouse was purple and white with another long scarf tied around her middle like a belt, which was punctuated by little jingly bells on each end. As I expected, she had on a floor-length skirt, this one in all the colors of the rainbow.

"Peyton an' Ryan," Lovie said warmly before settling her eyes on Trina. "An', I might be goin' out on a limb here, but you must be one o' Ryan's relations?"

"Yes! I am his sister an' I am so honored to meet you, Ms. Lovie!" Trina gushed. She immediately flung her arms around Lovie, taking the older woman aback for a moment. Then Lovie smiled fondly at Ryan and engulfed his sister in her arms.

When Lovie released Trina, taking a step back and studying her, she addressed Ryan again. "She is every ounce yer kin, Ryan Kelly."

Ryan chuckled. "Yes she is, Lovie." He hugged Lovie, only releasing her to offer Christopher a handshake. The warlock glanced at Ryan's hand with visible distaste on his face before sighing with a shrug. He dropped his arms from his chest and pumped Ryan's hand rather weakly. "Good to see you, Christopher," Ryan said.

"Elated," Christopher answered in a flat tone.

"Peyton?" Lovie interrupted their happy reunion, turning to face me and taking my hands in hers again. "How can I help you?"

Looking around her shop, I found it so chaotic and crammed full of people, it began to make me claustrophobic. I barely made out two people at the front of the room: one was working the cash register, while the other was fetching whatever the people in line were waiting for. Returning my attention to Lovie, I sighed. "I realize this must be the worst time to come visit you, Lovie, but I didn't know what else to do."

From the corner of my eye, I caught Christopher nodding, although Lovie just shook her head. "There's neva a bad time fer you, Peyton," she said with true sincerity. With a look back at the crowd in the store, she exhaled. "We obviously can't talk much in here, though, so let's step outside fer a spell."

"I shall accompany you two," Christopher announced immediately, observing the crowd with utter aversion. "I believe I may be trampled in here if I choose to remain."

Lovie laughed while shaking her head at Christopher's histrionics. As she approached the front door of her store, the bells of the sash around her waist jingled in cadence with her footsteps. Reaching out in front of her, Ryan pushed the door open, holding it for the rest of us as we made our way into the dark, wet, New Orleans night.

"Where to, Lovie?" Ryan asked once we were all assembled together outside, standing underneath the awning as the rain dripped off it menacingly.

Lovie pointed to a black-and-white-striped awning across the street. The sign above the awning read "Café Beignet" in bold, white block letters on a black background. The white accordion doors were fully folded open and a mass of people gathered inside. I was surprised to see the café still open so late since it was usually only open for breakfast and lunch, but there it was. Apparently, the recent resurrection of ghostly activity in New Orleans was proving beneficial for more than one local business.

We hurried across the street and shielded ourselves beneath the restaurant's awning as we all assessed whatever damage the rain might've inflicted upon us. Looking down at my feet, I noticed I was standing on a floor mat that read "Café Beignet" in the same white block letters. On my right was a sign about three feet tall that read: "Beignets, Crawfish Omelet, Sandwiches, Breakfast All Day." Lovie stepped inside the peculiarly small café and motioned to one of the waiters inside who recognized her immediately. She indicated the white, wrought-iron table beside us and the waiter nodded with a big smile.

"Have a seat," Lovie said to our group as Ryan pulled out one of the heart-shaped, white, wrought-iron chairs for her. Lovie thanked him and took a seat while he did the same for Trina. Being across the way, I seated myself, since I was more than sure that Christopher certainly didn't intend to assist me. But I was also a modern woman who didn't need assistance. Sometimes it was just nice, though, when men were mannerly.

As soon as we sat down, the waiter hurried to our table. He'd been standing behind a glass case of pastries at the rear of the restaurant where a long line of people were waiting to place their orders.

"Oh, Howard, we coulda come up ta order jist like everyone else," Lovie argued as the waiter appeared beside her, a stack of menus underneath one of his arms while he held a pen and writing pad in the other.

Shaking his head immediately, he replied, "I'm happy ta take yer order, Ms. Lovie."

Apparently, Lovie was somewhat of a celebrity here—judging by the full royal treatment she received. The waiter handed each of us a menu while making small talk with Lovie. I took in the arched ceiling above, which almost made it feel like we were sitting in a tunnel. Painted on either side of the ceiling were colorful fronds of Birds of Paradise with clouds in the middle. The walls were constructed of brick and featured all sorts of artwork. Hunter-green valances that framed the windows and doors, along with the chandeliers hanging from the ceiling, gave the place a ritzy sort of look. Well, that is, unless you checked out the floor. It looked like someone had tried to piece together broken red and white tiles over old, gray concrete.

Glancing over my menu, I chose a beignet with a cup of regular coffee. The only beignets I'd tried thus far in New Orleans were at the world-famous Café Du Monde, where Ryan insisted the beignets were the best. Admittedly, they hadn't disappointed. I decided to see if this place could give Café Du Monde a run for its money . . .

After seeing that everyone else hadn't quite decided on their orders, my thoughts returned to Drake and his silence. I naturally imagined he'd be thrilled to have another outing, especially one that included the prospect of eating beignets again after nearly one hundred years. But he still hadn't made a peep since leaving the house.

"*Drake?*" I asked. "*Are you there?*"

"*Oui,*" he answered immediately, but I could tell by the tone of his voice, he didn't sound happy.

"*Why have you been so quiet?*"

He paused for a few seconds. *"I have nothing to say, ma minette."*

Yes, something was most definitely wrong. Drake never had *nothing* to say. I sensed Drake's current reason for being upset had everything to do with my reaction when he'd tried to kiss me. Yep, if I wanted things to go back to whatever normalcy we'd previously had, now was time for me to apologize. "*I, uh, I'm sorry about everything that happened earlier,*" I started. "*I didn't mean to upset you, Drake. I'm really sorry if I did.*"

"J'ai déjà oublié," he answered. "*I have already forgotten.*"

Another obvious mistruth. I inwardly sighed and realized I had to apologize more sincerely. "*Drake, I was too harsh in some of the things I said to you, and I apologize if I hurt your feelings. I guess I was just taken aback by everything and I didn't really know how to respond.*" I paused, but he remained silent so I figured I needed to continue. "*I do care about you . . . I care about you a lot, actually, and I want things to go back to how they were between us before . . . the most recent events. I want us to be friends again, Drake. Can we please be friends again?*"

"*Oui, I would prefer us to be friends again too, ma minette,*" he answered, then paused. "*I appreciate your kind words, thank you.*"

"*You're welcome, Drake.*" Figuring I might as well throw him a bone, since this particular bone would certainly lighten his mood, I added . . . "*And, just for the record, I do think you're incredibly . . . handsome.*"

He chuckled. "Bien sûr, tu le fais. *Of course you do, ma minette.*"

I mentally rolled my eyes at him, but felt satisfied that we were back on speaking terms again.

"*Ma minette, on to other subjects,*" he started as he cleared his invisible throat. "*Do you realize that if you ask about the recent spiritual activity in this town and include our latest discussions regarding whether or not I can still maintain ties to the afterlife, you will, in all probability, have to admit that I am residing in your body?*"

I felt my stomach drop. Having been so preoccupied with finding Lovie, I didn't really rehearse the conversation I would have with her in my head. I'd totally forgotten that Ryan would be sitting right there, listening to the whole thing. "*You're right,*" I answered hollowly. "*And Ryan still doesn't know about you. I'm going to have to tell him right now.*" However, I didn't want to tell him in front of everyone else. I was more than sure he wouldn't appreciate that.

"*Oui, I believe that would be a good idea, ma minette.*"

"I'd like a coffee an' the crawfish omelette, please," Ryan said. I pushed away from the table and stood up, not even realizing what I was doing. All eyes landed on me as I approached Howard, the waiter.

"Um, coffee and a beignet please," I quickly ordered before facing Lovie. "I need to excuse myself for a moment."

"Is everythin' okay, Peyton?" Trina asked, studying me intently.

I nodded and addressed Ryan, inhaling deeply. "Everything is fine. I, uh . . ." I cleared my throat. "Ryan, you would mind accompanying me for a second?"

His eyebrows met in the middle of his forehead, quizzically, but he simply nodded and stood up while I started for the front of Café Beignet. I hurried through the small restaurant with Ryan's heavy footsteps behind me. When we reached the sidewalk, I shivered in the cold, rainy night air and wrapped my arms around myself, remaining well beneath the awning so I wouldn't get rained on.

"What's on your mind, Pey?" Ryan asked as he sidled up next to me. He wrapped his arms around me and rubbed my arms to warm them up.

I shook my head and took a deep breath, hoping the information I was about to share with him wouldn't ruin the relationship we both shared. "I, uh . . ." I started, quickly losing my train of thought as I saw a woman and her four kids entering the restaurant. The kids were commenting about eating beignets with unbridled excitement.

"You, uh . . . ?" Ryan repeated with a hearty chuckle.

Looking up at him again, I felt my insides go numb. He had that boyish smile of his and his big amber eyes, and the slight curling of his hair due to the damp air made him look so beautiful. I was suddenly overcome with feelings of adoration and love. But my feelings became parched once I realized that the information I was about to convey might mean the end of us.

I knew there was no going back. "I wanted to tell you this a long time ago," I started as I watched the smile on his face vanish. I steeled my courage and forced myself to continue. "It just seemed like every time I was about to tell you, something came up and . . ."

"What is it, Pey?" Ryan asked as my voice started to trail off. He pulled away from me, but still held onto my shoulders, staring down at me searchingly.

Clearing my throat, my eyes dropped to my feet before I realized it was rude to talk to someone while staring at one's feet. I looked up at him again as my heartbeat started to pound through me and my breathing grew quicker.

"*You can do this, ma minette,*" Drake sounded in my head. "*I have faith in you.*"

"Do you remember when the entity of the Axeman was still occupying my house?" I asked Ryan pointedly, forcing the words. I could not back down now.

"Yes, o' course," Ryan answered, studying me intently.

"Right," I said, thinking it was a stupid question to start out with. There was no way anyone could forget the malevolence of the entity that had haunted my house, especially after everything that had happened when Christopher and Lovie exorcised it.

"Keep goin', Peyton," Ryan said, with a quick glance back into the restaurant. "Don't forget they're waitin' for us."

"Right," I said again with a nod. I took a deep breath. "Before the entity was exorcised, Drake was my protector of sorts."

"Okay," Ryan answered as he let go of my shoulders and crossed his arms against his chest.

"Right," I continued, trying to stay on course. "As the entity started to get stronger, it attached itself to Drake and began basically swallowing him up into itself. He fought and tried to resist it, but in the end, he lost the power to combat it."

"Okay," Ryan said again, studying me as if he were frustratingly intrigued as to where the conversation was headed. His expression showed wary consternation.

"As Drake became weaker, the entity grew stronger and Drake could no longer protect me from it."

"Okay," Ryan replied.

I nodded, but couldn't seem to get the words out of my mouth. This was the part I least looked forward to. "So, uh, anyway . . ." My voice trailed off again as I tried to figure out the best way to tell him I was possessed by Drake's spirit.

"Ne perds pas ton courage! *Do not lose your courage!*" Drake announced.

"Spit it out, Pey," Ryan said at almost the same time.

I wasn't sure how to "spit it out," so I thought the next best thing would be to tell Ryan exactly what happened that night. I closed my eyes for a second to jog my memory. When I reopened them, Ryan was staring down at me. "I could hear water running from the guest bathroom," I said in a soft voice that seemed hollow and frightened. "When I went in to shut it off, it was so cloudy and steamy in the bathroom, I couldn't even see my hand in front of my face." I inhaled as I recalled the particulars, feeling a new sense of fear spiraling within me. "When I turned the water off and started for the bedroom again, I saw words forming on the mirror in the bathroom."

"Words?" Ryan repeated.

"Yes. It was like an invisible hand was writing them in the steam, right there, while I watched. They were the words from the letter the

Axeman sent to the *Times-Picayune* newspaper in 1919." Ryan's eyes went wide, but he didn't comment, so I continued. "Prior to this whole mirror episode, I asked Christopher and Lovie to come over. When they realized how strong the entity had grown and what was happening to Drake, that his soul was dissolving into it, they said there was only one way to save him."

"An' what way was that?" Ryan asked, studying me intently.

I took another deep breath as I decided it was now or never. "In order to save Drake and allow him to continue protecting me, I had to let him possess me."

Ryan didn't say anything for four seconds. He just stared at me, unblinking and unresponsive. When he finally spoke, his voice was low, gritty, and completely devoid of emotion. "So you agreed to become possessed by him?" he asked, his lips tightly pressed together.

"It was the only way I could save him, Ryan!" I protested. "Otherwise, the entity would have grown even stronger and Drake could not continue protecting me from it." I exhaled all the pent-up anxiety that was building up within me for the last few minutes. "As I saw it, it was my only option."

Ryan nodded but then shook his head, rubbing the back of his neck. "This sounds so completely crazy, I almost can't bring myself to believe it."

But there was no way I would accept that. Not for one second. "You saw for yourself what happened in my house when Lovie and Christopher exorcised the entity!" I railed back at him. I remembered how arctic the temperature had become, how the wind had raced through the house and shook it, as if in an earthquake. Ryan had experienced the same thing too.

"Yes, I remember," he answered somewhat reluctantly. It seemed like even though he'd also experienced it, he didn't want to believe it was true. In general, Ryan tended to give credence, albeit begrudgingly, to the idea that ghosts existed. 'Course, living in New Orleans, it was pretty much impossible to deny the existence of spirits, given how plentiful they were. But, when it came down to it, his first impulse was to exhaust all scientific possibilities before accepting the possibility of the occult.

I wrapped my arms more tightly around myself as a cold breeze chilled me. "I had no other choice, Ryan."

He stared at me for a few seconds. "So you're possessed by Drake's spirit then? Is that what you're tryin' to tell me?" I just nodded and watched him shake his head before his gaze settled on something across the street for a few seconds. When his eyes settled on me again, he asked, "So am I talkin' to you or to him right now?"

"To me," I answered immediately. "Drake is just a voice in my head. He can't communicate through me. I basically still control my body. He's just another voice that exists inside my head."

"Can he see what you see an' hear what you hear?"

"Yes," I said, realizing I needed to explain how it all worked. Maybe then Ryan wouldn't think it was such a bad a situation. "Drake can basically see, hear, feel, and taste everything I can."

Ryan nodded as if to say he understood, but his jaw clenched and his lips became even tighter. "Then, when you an' I were ever . . . intimate . . ." His voice faded as he nodded faster, as if he was trying to make sense of it. "That explains why you pull away from me every time I kiss you. An' it explains why you've been actin' so peculiar lately . . . like when we were in my truck the other day."

I nodded with a sigh. "It's not easy hearing someone else's commentary in your head all the time."

Ryan chuckled, but it wasn't a chuckle that in any way revealed humor or amusement. Instead, it sounded like the laugh of someone who found the information very difficult to swallow. He shook his head and ran his hands through his hair. "How long have you been possessed?"

I took a deep breath, still not sure of his reaction. He was pretty good when it came to concealing his emotions. "Since right before the exorcism," I answered. "I wanted to tell you, Ryan—"

"But you didn't," he interrupted, glaring down at me, his anger growing obvious in his handsome face.

"I just couldn't find the right time," I said in a mousey voice.

"You had every opportunity," he spat back at me. "Even after promisin' you wouldn't leave me out anymore! You knew this information even then! You promised you wouldn't shut me out an' yet you never told me."

"I'm sorry." It was the only thing I could think of to say.

He shook his head, clearly upset. "So *now* you decide to tell me! Now, with Lovie, Christopher, an' Trina all waitin' for us to return." His eyes grew wider as he nodded at himself. "An' the only reason you decided to tell me now is because you realized it was gonna come out now anyway. You were forced to tell me; otherwise, you never would have."

"No," I said, shaking my head emphatically. "I absolutely was going to tell you, Ryan!"

"You expect me to believe that?" he railed back at me. "You've had, what? A week or more to tell me an' yet you never did? Save the bullshit, Peyton!"

"Please try to see it from my perspective, Ryan. I wanted to tell you. I really did, but I was afraid of how you'd react." I took a deep breath. "I know it was wrong that I didn't tell you sooner, but I just never could seem to find the right time."

Ryan shook his head defiantly, as if he wasn't buying my excuses. "Peyton, if you an' I are goin' to have a relationship, you can't keep stuff like this from me. A relationship means we're partners." He exhaled with a long sigh. "I can't keep havin' this discussion with you. Either you get it an' agree to it, or you don't."

"I do get it!" I declared. "And I do agree to it! I promise we will never have this discussion again!" I pleaded, reaching out for him. I let my hands drop when it became obvious he didn't want me touching him.

"I can't keep doin' this, Peyton," he said in a soft voice as he frowned down at me. "It was hard enough for me to open myself up after Lizzie died. I never would have, but you came along with your beautiful smile, your pink tools, an' your laugh, an' I couldn't say no."

"Please, Ryan," I started, while tears burned my eyes.

"I thought you were right for me," he said before immediately shaking his head. "I thought you were the one an' now . . ."

"Now what?" I demanded. Fat tears began rolling down my cheeks. "Nothing has changed, Ryan."

"Everything has changed," he answered icily. "I thought I knew you, but now I realize I don't." He sighed again while shaking his head in resignation. "Everything has changed."

Chapter 7

"What does that mean?" I demanded, feeling slightly nauseated. "Everything changing" sounded like a breakup line if ever I heard one.

Shaking his head, Ryan just stared at the wet ground where the rain leaked from the awning overhead, making a large puddle next to us. He was quiet for a few seconds longer before his eyes met mine. They appeared very hollow in their beautiful, amber depths. "Peyton, every time I lower my walls to allow you to get closer to me, I feel like you instantly distance yourself." He took a deep breath and kept shaking his head, as if he didn't have an answer, or didn't know what to make of our situation. "I know you're just gettin' out of a bad marriage, so maybe it's just a problem of you not givin' yourself enough time to get over your ex-husband . . ."

"No," I interrupted as soon as the words came out of his mouth. "My ex-marriage and ex-husband have nothing to do with this. I've been over Jonathon for a very long time." And it was the truth. I'd been over Jonathon for years before I'd finally mustered up the courage to divorce him.

Looking up at Ryan, my eyes implored him to understand, while conveying the feeling that was riding through me. "I want us to be together, Ryan." I took a deep breath and closed my eyes, warning myself not to lose it and start crying. There was really nothing I hated more than losing control. When I felt like I'd regained my composure, I opened my eyes and faced him. "I see your point, and I know exactly how you feel. I would feel the same way. I'm sorry I didn't tell you about Drake sooner; and I can't tell you how much I regret not telling you about him from the very beginning."

"I would have understood, Peyton," he continued. "I wouldn't have liked it, but I would have supported your decision because that's my role as your boyfriend. But I can't help you if you don't tell me what's goin' on."

I nodded. "I know that now. I just . . ." I shook my head, fighting back more tears. "There has been so much going on in my life lately that I kept postponing it. I was just waiting for the right time, but the right time never seemed to come."

Still shaking his head, when he spoke, his voice was softer. "You can't live by that philosophy 'cause the right time never comes." He studied me for a few seconds before he spoke again. "I fully understand there has been a lot goin' on in both of our lives lately, but that is all the more reason to keep me in the loop, Peyton." He took a deep breath and sighed again, cuffing the back of his neck with his hand. "I understand you're an independent woman an' fully capable of takin' care of yourself. You don't need anyone. Your independence is actually one of the attributes I most admire about you. But don't forget, I'm a man an' I need to feel like I'm a man. I need to feel like you need me, an' that I can help you. I need to feel like I can protect you, Peyton, an' most of all, I need to feel that you want me to."

I reached out for him and grasped his hand, folding it between both of mine. "Please, Ryan, please believe me when I tell you that I do absolutely need you. I'm not as independent as you think I am." I shook my head the more I thought about it. "I don't know what I would have done without you. You made New Orleans feel like home to me. Without you, who knows where I would be?"

He nodded, but pulled his hand away from mine, thrusting both of his into his jeans' pockets. "That sounds nice, Peyton, but I can't help but recall that in almost every situation where somethin' big went down, you left me out of it altogether. I would never have found out about your exorcism on the house if I hadn't randomly shown up. An' the only reason I showed up in the first place was because I doubted your whole story about bein' sick. An' now . . . this."

It was my turn to argue. "That isn't true, Ryan. When I found the axe outside my back door, who was the first person I ran to? You. And when I first heard footsteps in my house upstairs, you were the one I called."

"Footsteps that just turned out to be Drake," he remarked with a frown.

"Yes, they were Drake's, but I didn't know that at the time. The point is: I was scared and you were the first person I thought of and the only person I turned to."

He nodded, but it was curt, which meant he would not allow me much of a victory and still had more in his arsenal. "That's true; but both of those instances happened a while ago, before you an' I were in any way romantically involved. It seems things have changed a lot recently." He paused as he apparently considered this angle. "The more I think about it, the more I wonder if maybe you just subconsciously aren't ready for me yet." He began nodding as if his statement made him more convinced of it while the seconds dragged on. "Maybe you just distance yourself without even realizin' it."

I shook my head because that wasn't the case at all. "It might look that way, but it's not, Ryan. I wanted to tell you about Drake, I really did, but I simply procrastinated." I desperately wanted to make him understand where I was coming from, and hoped all my explanations weren't falling on deaf ears. I felt like they were, though.

"I was just afraid of your reaction. I was scared that you would freak out about Drake and wouldn't want to be with me anymore."

He studied me with narrowed eyes. "Can he hear our whole conversation? Is he listenin' to everythin' we're sayin' right now?"

"*Say no, ma minette,*" Drake piped up immediately, reminding me that he was, in fact, listening to the whole conversation.

I swallowed hard. I didn't want to lie to Ryan anymore. "Yes, he can hear our conversation."

Ryan's lips grew tighter. "Then are you talkin' to him durin' our conversation?" He stared at me before he continued. "I need to take a step back from this because hearin' myself right now, it almost seems too absurd to be real. All this talk about ghosts an' demons an' possession." He rubbed his forehead. "Sometimes I feel like I've somehow been sucked right into *The Twilight Zone*."

"Well, you haven't been, Ryan," I said in a sharp-edged tone. "All of this is real and you know that as well as I do. As far as Drake goes, I'm not having a conversation with him right now at all." I suddenly remembered the card I needed to play: my get-out-of-jail-free card. "I can also tune Drake out, Ryan. I can basically shut him out of any conversation or situation that I choose."

Ryan studied me pointedly. "What do you mean?"

"Lovie told me about it when she and Christopher first performed the possession ritual on me. All I have to do is think the words 'I'm shutting you out' or something similar, and Drake can't see, hear, feel, or otherwise experience whatever I'm experiencing." I took a deep breath. "So during the rare times when you and I were intimate in any fashion, I simply shut him out."

Well, that wasn't exactly the whole truth, but there had been plenty of occasions when I didn't want Drake to see whatever Ryan and I were doing, so I'd prevented him from eavesdropping. Yes, it seemed like I usually shut Drake out after the fact, but it was close enough to the truth that I figured I'd better run with it.

"So does Drake intend to possess you forever? Or is there an expiration date on this?" Ryan asked, his eyebrows furrowed in the middle of his brow, revealing his frustration.

"No, he definitely won't possess me forever," I said, both to Ryan and to Drake because I didn't want Drake to get the idea that it could become a permanent thing. "Initially, I figured that after the entity in my house was gone, I would contact Lovie and Christopher to remove Drake from my body and replant his spirit into my house."

"So, what happened then?" Ryan demanded. "The entity is no longer in your house now, right?"

"No, it isn't in my house," I answered immediately. "Well, at least I don't think it is."

Ryan folded his arms across his broad chest, but continued to scowl at me. "Have you noticed anythin' weird goin' on lately?"

"No."

"Why did you hesitate?" he demanded and I imagined he probably thought a whole lot of BS was about to fly his way.

"Well, that's one of the reasons I wanted to see Lovie." I took a deep breath. "I'm afraid that something might happen with this entity . . . with the Axeman."

"Why are you afraid of that?" he barked, obviously still pissed off.

"Because it isn't just a coincidence that the ghosts of New Orleans have suddenly swamped this city! We've heard it now from Prudence, and the waiter at Commander's, and those women who went on the ghost tour, and you saw how many people were in Lovie's store. There's something happening, Ryan. Something is going on!"

He inhaled and exhaled quickly. "So what if there is somethin' to it? What does that have to do with you?"

"That's where Lovie comes in," I answered with a quick glance back at our table to see that our food had arrived. I wasn't sure how long we'd been out there, but after Christopher took his last bite of red beans and rice, and Lovie pointed to her cup for more coffee, I figured it must've been a while. "I don't want to keep them waiting much longer," I continued as I addressed Ryan. "Will you at least come back to the table and listen to the rest of what I have to say? Regardless of what you decide to do about us, please just come back. Besides, your whole dinner is sitting there and waiting to be eaten."

He eyed the table and nodded at me. "That's true."

I took another breath. "Ryan, you've been with me for most of the ghostly encounters lately anyway, so it would mean a lot to me if you'd stay. I'm sure Lovie would appreciate hearing your side of things too."

Ryan nodded, but his lips remained tight and his eyebrows were still bunched up in the middle of his forehead. He held out his hand in front of him, gesturing for me to lead the way. I didn't argue and turned around, heading for our table.

"Je suis surpris," Drake's voice sounded in my head. "*I am surprised, ma minette. That conversation did not go as I expected.*"

"*Yeah, well, that makes two of us,*" I answered.

"*I hope you do not regret telling him about me, mon amour. It had to be done.*"

"*I don't regret telling him,*" I responded. "*I only regret waiting so long to tell him. But I guess it is what it is.*"

I was surprised when Drake didn't say, "I told you so," because I'd lost count of how many times he'd urged me to tell Ryan about him. Yep, all the procrastination rested on my shoulders alone.

"Did we forget to mention how busy we are?" Christopher piped up in an irritated voice as soon as we reached the table. "Argue on your own time."

"Christopher!" Lovie whispered to him while playfully swatting his hand.

"Is everythin' okay?" Trina leaned over and asked me in a hushed tone as soon as I sat down. Even though everything was far from okay, I just nodded because there wasn't anything else I could say. Ryan kept his lips tight, but his eyes were fastened on me.

Suddenly feeling uncomfortable, I faced Lovie and cleared my throat. "I'm sorry that took so long, Lovie," I started.

She shook her head. "Whatever you discussed, I'm sure, was important."

I nodded with an exhale. "Thank you again for agreeing to see us on such short notice," I said to her with a grateful smile. "So much has been going on lately and you're the only person . . ." I glanced over at Christopher and smiled at him too, although somewhat embarrassedly. "You both are the only people I could think of to turn to."

"Take yer time, Peyton," Lovie said as she reached out, placing her hand on mine comfortingly. I didn't dare chance a look at Christopher because I expected he'd be much less receptive.

"I don't want to take up anymore of your time than I already have," I answered in a hushed voice.

But Lovie shook her head. "Babydoll, I knew you were comin' ta see me long before you walked through mah door. I already made time fer you before you even asked fer it."

I felt my eyes widen, but I couldn't say I was *that* surprised. There was something about Lovie and her deep understanding of yin and yang, as well as the natural flow of things. If she claimed she was some sort of goddess or an eternally powerful being, I wouldn't have doubted it for a second. "So we're all pretty aware, it seems, that the spirits in this city have suddenly awakened," I started, eyeing everyone in turn and feeling like I was chairing a business meeting.

"Yes, I haven't seen anythin' like it before," Lovie answered.

"It's a first for me too," Christopher added.

"What do you suppose is causin' all this spiritual energy?" Trina asked Lovie. It wasn't lost on me that Ryan said nothing, but I tried not to fixate on it. Whatever happened between Ryan and me was outside of this conversation. For now, my attention needed to be fully on why the deceased were suddenly establishing their presence all over the city. I had to put my relationship with Ryan on the back burner for now.

Lovie shook her head as she answered Trina. "I dunno fer certain, honey, but from what I've been able ta understand from the spirits themselves, they seem ta believe somethin' is comin', an' it's somethin' pretty big."

I gulped hard as my hands grew numb and I turned to Lovie. "Ryan and I were in Lafayette Cemetery the other day and we came across a ghost tour, which we decided to take. The tour guide said she'd picked up more EVPs in the last two days than in the several years she'd been giving the tours."

"I believe that," Lovie said with a nod, seemingly not at all surprised.

"Well, the information she picked up on her recordings bothered me quite a bit," I continued after a deep breath.

"What did the EVPs say, Peyton?" Lovie asked me, her smile vanishing as she faced me fully.

"They, er, the spirits, talked about something that's coming, and from the sound of it, it wasn't something good."

"What did the voices say exactly?" Christopher asked. "Word for word."

"The first one said, 'It comes,'" Ryan suddenly piped up, although his poker face did not reveal anything more.

I nodded. "Right. The next recording said, 'Save us,' and then we heard a voice saying, 'Make it stop.'" I looked up at Ryan, feeling my heart drop as soon as I saw his undeniably handsome face. "What else did Prudence record?"

"Somethin' about hidin' or needin' to hide," he answered. "I can't remember exactly what now."

"I know Prudence well," Lovie said as she nodded. "I trust that whatever she played fer you wasn't tampered with." The expression on her face was pensive, and more thoughtful.

"What do you make of the recordings?" Christopher asked her.

Lovie cocked her head to the side, pondering the subject. "The spirits know somethin' we don't—"

"There's more," I interrupted, taking a deep breath as my fear tried to work its way up into my stomach. "The EVP that frightened me the most said, 'The second day.'"

"The second day," Lovie repeated before becoming momentarily silent.

"Do you remember the Axeman's letter that appeared on my bathroom mirror in the steam?" I asked.

She nodded as, apparently, the puzzle pieces started to fit into place. "The letter said the Axeman would return Tuesday . . . the second day o' the work week."

"Yes," I responded.

"The letter from the Axeman?" Trina repeated, her voice revealing her utter confusion.

I nodded at her, realizing I needed to back up and explain the origins of the letter, both for her and for Ryan. "A letter was sent to the *Times-Picayune* newspaper back in 1919 purportedly from the Axeman himself. In it, he said he would strike again on a Tuesday and then went on to say he wasn't a human, but a demon and so on." I took a deep breath. "The important part is that sections of the very same letter appeared on the mirror in my guest bathroom, written in the steam. The only difference was that the date was written as last Tuesday, April 15, 2014, instead of 1919."

"Oh my God," Trina whispered, covering her open mouth with her hand. "That is insane, Peyton. I can't believe you're still livin' there!"

"Well, we already exorcised the demon," I answered, doubting my own words as soon as they left my mouth.

"The letter stated that this demonic entity plans ta return on Tuesday," Lovie continued.

"Any Tuesday?" Ryan asked, leaning forward and suddenly appearing much more interested in the conversation.

"No, in the letter, it said 'next Tuesday' which would mean this coming Tuesday," I answered.

"As in three days from now, Tuesday?" Trina asked, the pitch of her voice escalating with panic.

"Yes," Lovie and I answered at the same time.

"This is so much worse than I feared," Lovie exclaimed as she swallowed another sip of her coffee before placing the mug back on the table. She didn't release it though. Instead, she tipped it toward her so she could see into it. She studied the mug intently without saying anything. When she rolled the cup in her hand and stared at it even more fixedly, I knew something was up.

"Lovie?" Christopher started. "What are you receiving?"

She shook her head. "I'm tryin' ta reach out ta Samuel, but I detect interference."

"Samuel?" I asked, shaking my head to show I wasn't following. Christopher faced me while Lovie continued to zone out on the coffee mug.

"Samuel is Lovie's familiar," Christopher explained before staring at Lovie again.

"Like a witch's familiar?" I asked.

Christopher nodded. "Exactly the same. Samuel is a spirit who guides Lovie on her explorations into the other world. He can take the shape of any person or any thing." He motioned to Lovie's mug, which she clutched in her hands. "He has an affinity for the taste of coffee, which is why Lovie usually chooses to contact him after a coffee run." Then he addressed Lovie again. "Have you made contact with him yet?"

She shook her head. "There's too much static on the line between us," she answered. When she finally exhaled, placing the mug back on the table, she glanced up at me and her eyes seemed full of worry. "It's been this way fer the last three days. I've been unable ta reach Samuel an' this is the first time it's happened to me in my whole life." Apparently, witches and familiars were lifelong buddies. Interesting.

"That sounds really bad," Trina said as I nodded my concurrence. My entire stomach began to cave in on itself. I was beginning to believe firsts of anything were never good.

Now it was time to turn to the other questions I had regarding Drake . . . "The other reason I contacted you both was to ask if you might know what all the rules are regarding spiritual possession." Lovie frowned as if to say my comment was too general. I didn't bother to look at Christopher or judge his reaction. "What I mean is," I continued while my legs bopped up and down nervously. I had to place my hands on them to keep them from bouncing. "Does Drake have any ties to the afterlife that I might be able to share? I mean, now that his spirit is tethered inside my body, does that mean he lost his other ties to the spiritual world, which he once had?"

Ryan shifted uncomfortably in his chair, but didn't say anything. I refused to look at him because I was afraid of what I might see in his eyes. It was more than obvious that he was having a difficult time processing all of this, but I was well beyond that stage. I was ready for answers, so I did my best to find out what awaited us; and if it *was* something bad, how best to avoid it.

"Whenever the spiritual and the tangible worlds intersect, each benefits from the other," Lovie said. She might as well have been speaking Swahili because I had no clue what she was talking about. Or maybe I was just dumb.

"Um," I started, chewing on my lip as I inhaled long and slow before exhaling just as deeply. "I'm not really sure what that means," I finally admitted, as my eyebrows furrowed in the center of my forehead.

Lovie laughed at me, sounding like the bells jingling from the sash tied around her waist. "The answer ta your question regardin' whether Drake still possesses ties ta the spiritual world even though he now resides inside your body is yes, honey, he does."

Chapter 8

Okay, that's good," I said, nodding as I inwardly sighed over the realization that Drake would be able to maintain his ties to the spiritual world even though he was now sharing my body. Christopher turned to face me with his left eyebrow arched dramatically and his lips forming a straight white line. I often wondered if he even knew how to smile.

"But your physicality is a barrier to his spirituality," Christopher said, enunciating every consonant, and making me think he might be a barrier to my rationality.

"What does that even mean?" Ryan demanded, frowning at both of them. He shook his head vigorously and appeared, for all intents and purposes, frustrated. "Layman's terms here, folks." With an irritated glance at Trina and me, he turned to address Lovie and Christopher again. "Remember, we aren't on the same cosmic level as y'all are."

"It's difficult to forget," Christopher grunted, eyeing me before he frowned. I chose to be the bigger person and pretended not to notice his snide comment.

"Pour l'amour de Dieu," Drake piped up in an irritated voice. "*For the love of God, ma minette, you must find out how we both are able to access the spiritual world. I am not certain I can stomach much more of this drivel!*"

"*I'm working on it, Drake! Calm down!*" I railed back at him.

"*Humph,*" he groaned. "*Allow me to remind you, mon amour, that time is of the utmost importance, owing to how little we possess of it.*"

He was right. We basically had two days to figure out what in the hell was coming and, more importantly, how we could stop it. We didn't have time for idle and confusing conversations while Christopher mocked us to feel better about himself. "We don't have time for this!" I piped up, slamming my hands on the tabletop as I stood up. Bending over my outstretched arms, I took turns glaring at everyone. All eyes focused on me as I took a deep breath and forced myself to stop staring everyone down. "We have two days! Two days!" I exclaimed. "Let me remind you that Tuesday could mean a lot of shit hitting the fan!"

Ryan narrowed his eyes at me. "Or it might mean no shit hittin' the fan at all."

My nostrils flared as my heartbeat increased and my breathing grew rapid. I faced him fully and when I spoke, I kept the tone of my voice stonily calm. "I think, in this case, it's best to play the devil's advocate and bet that the odds won't be in our favor."

"Peyton's right," Lovie agreed with a nod. She gently placed her soft hand on my lower arm and pushed lightly against me, hinting that I needed to take my seat again and calm down. I obediently complied and, with an encouraging smile at me, she returned her attention to the others. "Somethin' is certainly upsettin' the natural balance between this world an' the next in N'awlins." She took a deep breath. "I believe we ignore it at our own peril."

"Then what's to be done?" Ryan asked as he leaned back into his chair and crossed his arms against his chest. He looked at her and Christopher with a frown. Although I still didn't know what would happen between the two of us, the thought of losing him sliced like a blade right through my heart.

"Vous ne devez pas mettre l'accent sur des choses que vous ne pouvez pas changer. *You must not focus on things you cannot change,*"

Drake said. "*Or at least the things you cannot change at this moment, ma minette.*"

"*Obviously, you can feel how depressed I am about the whole Ryan situation,*" I responded, feeling a little guilty that he'd witnessed my dejection firsthand. I needed to shield him better.

"*Oui, mon amour. Everything you feel, I can feel.*"

"*Sorry,*" I answered mentally before attempting to change the direction of my thoughts. I was pretty sure Drake didn't appreciate my nausea.

"Donnez-vous du temps," he continued. "*Give yourself time. Le barbare will come around, I am certain.*"

Although I couldn't help smiling at the mention of "le barbare," it was bittersweet, and laced with gloom. Lovie seemed to study me for a few moments, her gaze penetrating mine as I forced myself to stop thinking about the relationship, or lack thereof, between Ryan and me. It was almost as if she knew my thoughts weren't on the subject at hand. "Peyton, you must open yourself ta be able ta share in Drake's gifts," she started. Before I could ask her what that meant, she added, "Currently, you aren't sharin' Drake's knowledge o' the otherworld 'cause you closed that part o' yourself off ta the possibility."

"I don't understand," I said. "Drake can and does talk to me about any and everything, so why can't he just tell me what he knows about the spiritual world? I seem to be able to access all his other knowledge."

Lovie shook her head. "It isn't the same thin'," she said and then took a deep breath which she exhaled for a count of three. "Think o' it like this . . . jist as Drake experiences the modern world through you, you have the ability ta experience the spiritual world through him, but you gotta open yerself to the possibility. It's different than simply explainin' his world ta you."

"Okay," I said, nodding and finally understanding what she meant. "So, can I open that part of myself?"

She nodded, but it wasn't very convincing. "Yes, but it'll take a bit of work on yer part."

"Work?" I repeated, frowning and shaking my head. We didn't have time for work on my part. I needed to be able to interact with the otherworld, like, yesterday.

"Nothing comes easily," Christopher interjected in a scolding tone. "In order to indulge in the gifts of the universe, you must first prove yourself worthy."

"Okay, how do I do that?" I asked impatiently. I wished everyone understood that I was in over my head and had no idea what I was doing or how to do it. Last I checked, they didn't teach "Ghost Encounters 101" in college.

"Wait just a second," Ryan interrupted, holding up his hands as if to say we were going about the whole thing way too fast. "Just what exactly is the outcome we're hopin' for here?" he asked, frowning at each of us in turn, before facing Lovie specifically. "What do you mean when you say Peyton could benefit from Drake's knowledge of the otherworld? An' by 'otherworld,' I'm assumin' you mean where the ghosts hang out?"

"Yes, the otherworld is the spiritual world that we cannot see with our eyes, but it exists all the same," Lovie answered, flashing a quick and encouraging smile, as if she appreciated him asking the question. "To answer yer first question, as Drake is a spirit, he has the ability ta interact with the spiritual world in ways you an' I cannot, since we are corporeal bein's. We are limited an' bound by our own bodies, an' our own mortality."

"When you say interact," I started, studying her quizzically, "do you mean Drake could find out what's been going on around here lately? And, more importantly, if there *is* something bad heading down the pike, could he find out how to stop it?"

Lovie glanced from Ryan back to me and smiled reassuringly. "Yes, he could, simply by interactin' with the spirits an' asking them.

Remember: he would've been privy ta this information before he ever took up sanctuary in yer body, so, naturally, he should also be privy to it now, Peyton." She took a breath and continued. "I imagine Drake's ties ta the spiritual world might help us immensely, because those of us who are still bound by our bodies have lost contact with the spirits."

"Samuel?" I asked, just to make sure I was following along. Lovie nodded.

"So, to make sure I understand," Ryan continued, "if Peyton can bring her walls down an' tap into this connection with the spiritual world through Drake, then could she find out just what in the hell has gotten into this friggin' city lately?"

"Not so elegantly worded, but yes," Christopher answered, his expression pinched, like he just swallowed a mouthful of vinegar.

"Okay, great," I continued, trying to ignore my overwhelming irritation at Christopher. "So how do we go about helping me to drop my walls?"

Lovie glanced at me again as she started drumming her fingers against the tabletop. I could tell by the blank look on her face that she was pondering the question. Finally, she stopped fidgeting and glanced over at Christopher, but doubt appeared in her eyes. "We can't do this alone, Christopher. We need Guarda."

Christopher nodded and sighed, shaking his head, only to sigh again. Then he dropped his shoulders and grumbled something unintelligible to himself before sighing audibly once more. He reminded me of someone in drama class, trying to convey despondency or maybe impatience. Whatever it was, it was over the top, like all things Christopher did. He faced Lovie and, yes, sighed again. "Much though it pains me to admit it, I believe you're correct, Lovie; we cannot rely on ourselves alone in this situation."

Lovie raised her brows and nodded, saying nothing for a few seconds. Then she cocked her head to the side and rubbed her eyes as if she was suddenly exhausted. "I would usually attempt it ourselves first, but in the interest o' savin' time . . ."

Christopher shook his head. "We cannot consider taking this upon ourselves, Lovie! It is foolhardy to even imagine we could."

"What is it that needs to be done?" I asked, frowning as I alternated my concerned gaze between the two of them.

Lovie faced me again and cleared her throat. "Removin' a psychic wall isn't an easy feat, Peyton. It requires advanced knowledge o' magic that neither Christopher nor mahself possess at this stage." I was surprised. I actually thought Lovie was an unstoppable psychic force.

"But Guarda does possess the abilities," Christopher finished.

"Who is Guarda?" Trina asked, sounding awed and perplexed at the same time. She'd been so quiet throughout the conversation, I'd nearly forgotten she was sitting next to me.

"Guarda is a voodoo priestess who's also schooled in witchcraft," Lovie answered. "Magic runs through her veins; it is in her blood." She paused for a second and then sighed. "She possesses more power than I have ever seen in any one person."

Christopher nodded as he faced me. "Guarda is a relative of Marie Laveau's."

"Oh my goodness!" Trina commented as her eyes went wide. "She must be incredibly powerful if she's related to Marie Laveau!"

"Yes, Guarda is very powerful," Lovie said, and sighed as if she was more than concerned. She glanced at Christopher and raised her brows.

"Her power is what makes her dangerous," Christopher interjected. Then he faced me and shook his head. "But I see no alternative."

"Well, if anyone can help me, someone sharing the Queen of Voodoo's blood is probably the best bet," I said, and exhaled as I shook my head and wondered what new adventures awaited me. I couldn't help the shiver that ran up my spine.

Not only was I concerned about meeting Guarda after hearing Lovie and Christopher's less-than-glowing description of her, but it also didn't help that she lived in Slidell, Louisiana, otherwise known as BFE.

It took us the better part of forty-five minutes to get to Davis Landing Road, taking the Military Road exit off the 10 freeway. Slidell, on first impression, looked as if it was a sizable city, situated on the northeast shore of Lake Pontchartrain, but the particular area in which we were looked more like Hillbilly Central.

Davis Landing Road was a single-lane street that wove through a forest of dense foliage, punctuated periodically by a few rusty trailers that looked like they'd seen much better days. Random furniture, lean-tos, and enough junk heaps to look like a metal-recycling lot were the only other objects that caught my attention.

"Mess with me an' you mess with the whole trailer park," Trina whispered, and shook her head. She was sitting in the middle seat of the back row of Ryan's truck, planted snugly between Lovie and Christopher. She glanced over at me and smiled as I laughed. "Funny, huh?" she asked. "I read that on a sign yesterday."

"Sounds like the sign was talking about this place," I responded with a smile as we hit a pothole and Ryan's truck bounced violently in seeming indignation. Yes, I was beyond amazed when Ryan had offered to drive the five of us to meet Guarda. We still had yet to discuss where our relationship stood, but I took it as a good sign that he cared enough to accompany us on this little trip. Of course, as soon as Ryan offered to drive, everyone scurried for the backseat, which left me sitting shotgun, next to him, albeit uncomfortably. He remained quiet for the entire trip, which I guessed didn't bode well for us; but, again, I had to remind myself to focus exclusively on the task at hand. Our relationship, or what was left of it, would have to wait.

We followed a bend in the road, and just on the other side, through a copse of bushes and trees, I made out the banks of a river.

"Old Pearl River," Lovie said as rain started to splatter Ryan's windshield. He responded by turning on the window wipers at full speed. "Do you see that driveway up ahead?" Lovie asked as she leaned forward. She pointed to a dirt road, weaving between an old, green trailer and a slightly newer, white trailer with brown trim. Water-filled potholes perforated the dirt road and a chicken-wire fence ran down one side, while tree skeletons lined the other. The place was many things, but welcoming wasn't one of them.

Ryan simply nodded as he slowed the truck down and took a right onto the road. The truck bounced irregularly as he navigated around the potholes. Up ahead, I spotted a shanty that looked as if it had been painted sky blue a long time ago. Now, the paint was peeling in some areas and so dirty in others, it was dark brown. A blue tarp covered what looked like a stack of firewood on the side of the house.

"You can park alongside the tarp," Lovie said, and Ryan obeyed her. When he killed the engine, none of us said anything for a few seconds before Lovie broke the silence. "It's probably best if we don't make this a field trip." Then she tapped me on the shoulder. "Let's you an' I go in, Peyton. Guarda doesn't do too well with strangers."

I didn't say anything, but nodded as I glanced over at Ryan and smiled. "Thanks for driving," I said, but he didn't respond. Unwilling to stress myself about it, I opened the passenger door and jumped down, breathing in the wet air as I wondered what awaited me in Guarda's lean-to.

"Do you want me to accompany you, Lovie?" Christopher asked, leaning forward in his seat. He was still buckled in.

"No, Christopher, I think that would be a bad idea," Lovie answered with a little laugh. Apparently, I wasn't the only one Christopher rubbed the wrong way. Somehow, that information cheered me slightly.

The light rain began to grow heavier as Lovie and I hurried for the cover of a makeshift porch in front of Guarda's blue shanty. Once we reached the shelter of the porch, the rain continued to pelt down, seeping through large cracks and gaps in the rotten wood overhead. A cold wind whipped around us, causing some nearby bottles, which were hanging from a dead tree beside Guarda's house, to clank together noisily.

"Those are spirit bottles," Lovie explained when she caught me looking at the bottles, probably with a vacant expression on my face.

"Spirit bottles?" I repeated.

Lovie nodded and we watched the bottles clank against one another in the wind before she responded. "As part o' N'awlins voodoo hoodoo, spirit bottles are meant ta capture good an' evil spirits an' ta protect the home. Some believe she who imprisons the spirit in the bottle can force the spirit ta do her biddin'." A chill crept up my back. "Some say if you listen real close, you can hear the spirits talkin' an' sometimes even singin' in the bottle."

"*I believe you should avoid the bottles all together, ma minette,*" Drake suddenly piped up. "*I must admit, I do not feel comfortable here in the least.*"

I concurred. "*We have no choice, Drake. Apparently, Guarda is the only one who can help us,*" I responded.

For some reason, my instincts were on high alert and I had an undeniable feeling that it was in our best interest to head straight back to Ryan's truck. "What is voodoo hoodoo?" I asked, trying to change the subject. I wasn't even really sure I understood what voodoo was entirely, let alone hoodoo.

"That requires a very long answer, but fer the sake o' time, I will tell you that it is our Creole voodoo, unique ta N'awlins. Unlike other voodoo an' hoodoo elsewhere in this wide world, ours blends spiritualism, African roots, Native American traditions, Catholicism, an' Pentecostalism."

"Oh," I answered, making a mental note to follow up on it later. I had to admit that Trina's dabbling in voodoo had piqued my curiosity.

Lovie pulled open the rusted metal screen door and knocked stridently on the wooden door beneath it. It seemed like a mere two seconds went by before the door flew open and a woman who appeared to be in her late seventies or early eighties faced us. She wore a blue bandanna wrapped around her head. It was pulled down tightly around her ears so I couldn't see any of her hair underneath it. Her style of dress was very similar to Lovie's: a loose blouse and a long skirt that dusted the ground when she walked. As far as presentation went, though, they were worlds apart. Where Lovie's outfits were always colorful and clean, the hem of Guarda's skirt was ripped and smeared with mud, apparently from dragging along the ground in the rain.

Guarda's face was narrow and lean, making her rather obvious cheekbones a prominent feature. Her skin was dark and ashy with age, and somewhat slack in its looseness. Her face was covered in lines and raised age spots, particularly beneath her eyes. But her eyes were in a word . . . captivating. At one time, I believe they would have been considered beautiful—high, open eyelids that appeared very round—but now, advanced cataracts had made them cloudy and opaque. I didn't know why, but an unnerving thought suddenly crossed my mind that they could be the eyes of death itself.

"*I do not know if the worry I sense is yours or mine, ma minette,*" Drake said. "*But I do not have a good feeling about this woman in the least.*"

I couldn't answer him, however, because the very presence of Guarda made my skin crawl. I decided not to reply and just watched as Guarda stepped back and silently granted us entrance into her home. Lovie didn't say anything either. She simply nodded before stepping into the dark house. I looked down at Guarda, who stood as tall as my chin, and she bowed to me as well, allowing me to enter.

Stepping into her house, I was immediately struck by the odor. It wasn't a bad smell necessarily, but it reminded me of earth mixed with something spicy, like incense, maybe. The air was stale and surprisingly warm, considering it was raining and the air outside was decidedly cold. It took a while for my eyes to adjust to the darkness inside, but when they did, I instantly wished they hadn't. What little light there was came from various candles that were placed around the room. They illuminated rows of human skulls mounted to the wall directly across from me. Some were missing their jaws.

"*Ma minette, we need to leave this place immediately,*" Drake continued, his tone of voice more than concerned. "*This place gives me a terrible feeling. I do not want you in here for another second!*"

"*I trust Lovie,*" I answered, although I could only hope my trust wasn't blind and, worse, stupid. "*If this is the only way for us to move forward, then we have to stay, Drake. We have to find out if there is a way to stop whatever is coming.*"

"*There is just something about Guarda,*" he continued.

"*I know. She's creepy.*"

"*Oui, ma minette,* très *creepy.*"

I continued scanning the perimeter of the room, noticing all the windows were covered, either in cardboard or dark fabric. To my right stood what I imagined was an altar—a small table covered with white material. On the top of the table sat a human skull with a mound of fruit off to one side, while various bottles filled with God-only-knew-what occupied the other side. A gold cross stood out in the middle of the altar, catching the candlelight on either side and reflecting it garishly.

On the opposite wall was another table covered in red fabric. Sitting atop was a huge cow's skull, candles, and four jars stuffed with naked baby dolls. As frightening as the human skulls mounted on the wall were, I found the dolls stuffed inside the jars infinitely more disturbing. When I looked at them, I had the uncanny feeling that they were looking back at me.

I forced my attention to the center of the room where I noticed there wasn't any furniture at all, just a badly stained carpet. I couldn't discern anything beyond the living room because the rest of the house was so dark.

"Guarda," Lovie said at last in a voice that seemed to echo the emptiness of the room. "Thank you fer seein' us."

Guarda didn't say anything as she closed the front door and hobbled into the living room. Her walk was peculiar—she was slightly bent over, presumably from old age, but the way she limped looked as if she'd broken an ankle sometime in the past, or maybe her knees were bad.

"We've come—" Lovie started.

"I know why you've come," Guarda interrupted. Her voice was deep and gritty, but she spoke in such a whisper, she was difficult to understand.

"Of course," Lovie said, smiling apologetically. "Then you believe you can remove her block?"

Guarda hobbled up to me and narrowed her cloudy eyes as she studied me. Given how milky her eyes appeared, I half wondered if she could even see me. Reaching down, she grabbed my hand, and I felt myself gasp as soon as she made contact with me. It was as if every nerve in my body suddenly sprang to life.

"Yesss, I can," she announced, her tongue visible through the gaps of her missing teeth as she spoke. She reminded me of a snake, using its tongue to detect the scent of prey.

Hobbling past Lovie and me, she disappeared into what I assumed was the kitchen, but it was too dark to tell. I could hear the sounds of rustling and glass hitting glass. It reminded me of the spirit bottles colliding in the wind . . .

"Mah wormwood oughtta fix her up real good," Guarda announced when she returned and handed Lovie a bottle of clear green liquid, followed with a smaller vial of what looked like water. "She gotta drink the neutralizer first," she said and motioned to the vial with the water-like substance in it. "Wait a hour an' then she drink mah wormwood an' then ya return within the hour. You can come wit' her, but I don't want none o' them others. Ya know how I feels 'bout strangers."

I didn't know how she felt about strangers but I did know how I felt about her. Suffice it to say that I was more than happy I wouldn't have to hang around Guarda's while drinking the neutralizer or the wormwood. There was just something about her, some intangible inkling that warned me to keep away.

Chapter 9

"So what if she doesn't want us comin' back with you!" Ryan exclaimed after we returned to his truck and Lovie told everyone what had happened at Guarda's. "I don't give a damn!"

"Well—" Lovie started, her lips pursed together tightly with stiff composure.

"Sorry to interrupt you, Lovie, but I just don't feel right about the two of you goin' back in that shack on your own," Ryan continued. "I had to hold myself back from insistin' you take me with you when you first went in."

"I must agree that I don't feel good about you both going in alone either, Lovie," Christopher concurred from the backseat as we pulled into the parking lot of a Winn-Dixie grocery store a few miles away from Guarda's hovel.

"You know how Guarda is, Christopher," Lovie argued, shaking her head. "If I want Guarda's help, I gotta 'bide by her rules." With a sigh, she rubbed her forehead as if she was frustrated with the whole situation. Considering our interaction with Guarda earlier, and her less-than-friendly approach to Lovie, I guessed Lovie didn't like the idea of going back alone any better than Ryan or Christopher did.

I glanced down at the remaining glass vial in my hand, which Guarda called wormwood. I'd already downed the "neutralizer," which had tasted strangely of ginger, about an hour ago. Now all that was left was the wormwood. The vial of wormwood seemed to glow green in the dark midday, amid the shadows of the rain still splattering Ryan's windshield. "What is this stuff anyway, Lovie?" I asked as I held it up to what little light the sky rendered. "Isn't wormwood a different name for absinthe?"

Lovie nodded. "Yes, wormwood an' absinthe are the same."

"La fée verte," Drake added. "*The green fairy.*"

"Isn't that illegal here in the US?" Trina asked.

"*Oui. It has been illegal since 1912,*" Drake answered as Ryan talked over him.

"It used to be," Ryan said. "But it's been legal for a while now."

"Well, what the US refers to as absinthe is legal, anyway," Christopher corrected him with a nod. "But the absinthe you find here isn't the same as the absinthe in Europe or what Peyton's holding in her hand," he explained, nodding his head in the direction of my vial. "The thujone, which gives absinthe that buzz, is missing in the legal varieties available, so it really isn't the same species at all."

"The thujone is also responsible fer enhancin' psychic visions an' creatin' spiritual clarity," Lovie added. "Absinthe without it is basically useless . . . well, as far as contactin' spirits is concerned anyway."

"So that's why we came to Guarda?" I asked, glancing down at the vial in my hands again. "For this?"

Lovie nodded. "Guarda pretty much prescribes her wormwood recipe for any ailment. When paired with the power o' her voodoo magic, she can heal the sick, see the future, ensure that yer man ain't spendin' his time with yer best friend . . . the list goes on."

I took a deep breath and hesitantly glanced back at the smallish vial, which was maybe comparable to the size of my thumb. "So we don't know what's in it exactly?" I asked in a cautious tone, which revealed my true feelings when it came to the idea of drinking the stuff.

"We know the essentials," Christopher started. "Absinthe is basically wormwood, combined with various herbs like hyssop, lemon balm, fennel, peppermint, or angelica, along with sixty-eight percent alcohol."

"What makes it that greenish-blue color?" Trina asked, eyeing the vial with interest.

"The chlorophyll content," Lovie responded.

"So what's so special about Guarda's version?" I asked, glancing back at Lovie and Christopher as I narrowed my eyes. I was still wondering why we needed to involve Guarda at all. "Sounds like you both know how to make it?"

Lovie shook her head. "We don't know the magic she adds to it. We don't know her magical recipe."

"Making absinthe is a long and difficult process," Christopher added in a didactic tone. "Between collecting the ingredients, macerating them with a pestle and mortar, steeping them, and then straining the nearly final product, it takes a few days." He took a deep breath before resuming his sermon again. "Making absinthe is an intimate process between the creator and the absinthe itself. You have a close relationship with the herbs and the power of your intent breeds the absinthe, and flavors it with your own magical imprint."

Lovie reached down between her feet and gripped the handles of a large, colorful fabric bag with a paisley pattern, which she plopped on her lap. Looking through it, she pulled out a glass and handed it to Trina without any explanation. Trina just shrugged and accepted it while Lovie continued digging through the enormous bag that occupied her entire lap. The next thing she pulled out was a ziplock baggy full of what looked like mint, then a small vial of something syrupy, and, finally, a can of club soda.

"What's all that stuff?" I asked in wonder.

"It's the N'awlins lagniappe recipe fer drinkin' absinthe," Lovie responded as she folded the bag, but left it sitting in her lap. Taking the glass from Trina, she settled it on top of the sack while she opened the baggy and took out a handful of mint leaves. She pushed the leaves into the glass and unscrewed the cap of the bottle filled with syrupy stuff.

"What's that?" Trina asked.

"Sugar syrup," Lovie replied, emptying about an ounce of it into the glass. Reaching into her bag again, she produced a slotted metal spoon. She placed the spoon over the top of the glass, being careful to balance it. Then she reached back into her satchel and retrieved a single sugar cube, which she placed on the spoon. "Peyton, hand me the absinthe, please," Lovie said.

I nodded and handed her the absinthe, which she took, pulling the cork from the top of the vial. She carefully poured the green liquid—no more than an ounce or so—on top of the sugar cube. The sugar cube soaked up the dazzling green liquid before it began to dissolve, falling through the slots in the spoon. When the absinthe mixed with the sugary liquid in the glass, it went from green to a milky white. After all of the absinthe was in the glass, Lovie unscrewed the top of the club soda bottle and added it, filling the glass right up to the rim. She handed the glass to me once it was full, and as soon as I accepted it, she held up her hand to motion me to stop.

"Before you take a sip o' it," she started as she reached into her bag of tricks and took out a red flannel bag the size of my palm, "you must keep this close ta you. It's easiest jist ta slip it into yer pocket." She handed the small bag to me and I studied it curiously. Attached to the drawstring holding the sack shut was a blue bead. The inside of the bead was white. There was a lighter, aqua-blue spot inside the white circle, and a black center in the middle of the aqua spot. The overall effect made it look like an eyeball.

"What is it?" I asked, rotating the red flannel bag around in my hand. The back looked exactly the same as the front.

"It's a gris-gris fer protection," Lovie responded.

Immediately, the gris-gris—pronounced *gree-gree*—at the tourist trap, Marie Laveau's House of Voodoo, came to mind, which was sold to me when I first tried to eject the malevolent entity from my house. It hadn't worked. I eyed the thing with little interest and looked back at Lovie. "Do these things really work?"

Lovie nodded emphatically and seemed irritated that I asked the question in the first place. "If the gris-gris is created by someone who is strong enough in her magic, then yes, it does work."

"What's in it an' what's it supposed to do?" Ryan asked, eyeing the thing suspiciously.

Lovie faced him with a perturbed expression, and one of her eyebrows arched up dramatically. Apparently, she didn't appreciate having her methods questioned. "This gris-gris is filled with snake skin, frog bones, cigarette ashes, an' horsehair; an' it's all tied together with an evil eye bead," she started. "As fer what it does? Why, it protects." Apparently, satisfied with her response, she turned to me. "Now, Peyton, usin' both hands, hold the gris-gris in the palms o' yer hands an' close yer fingers ova it." I did as she instructed. "Then bring it ta yer mouth an' gently blow into it. Yer breath is what activates the gris-gris."

Taking a deep breath, I released it into the bag. I didn't feel different, and as far as I could tell, the gris-gris didn't seem any more active than it had been a second ago. "Okay," I said.

"Good, honey. Now the gris-gris knows ya need its protection. I want ya ta wear this gris-gris at all times, from here on out, whenever we're in Guarda's company, or whenever ya take her magic into yerself, ya hear?"

I nodded and placed the gris-gris into my pocket for safekeeping as I contemplated Lovie's words. As far as taking Guarda's "magic into myself," I figured Lovie meant I had to down the magical absinthe concoction Guarda had brewed up in her House of Horrors. Then something occurred to me. "Why didn't we take this precaution before we walked into Guarda's house? Or before I drank the neutralizer?"

"Guarda didn't tamper with the neutralizer," Lovie answered. "Remember how the cap was sealed in plastic?" I nodded as she continued. "Nothin' there ta worry 'bout. As to why we didn't take any precautions 'fore enterin' her house?" She shrugged. "Well, you hadn't ingested any o' her magical potions yet so there was no need." Then she focused on the vial of wormwood. "Now you gotta drink that downright after we create yer spiritual barrier."

"Create my spiritual barrier?" I repeated, clearly dumbfounded. "I thought we were trying to uncreate it?"

Lovie shook her head. "We're makin' a barrier 'tween you an' evil influences. We are protectin' yer spirit from forces that would do you harm."

"Will I still be able to hear Drake though? Or will this barrier block him as well?"

Lovie shook her head. "It won't block Drake. You'll still be able ta pick up what he tells ya," she answered, reaching into the satchel on her lap and producing yet another vessel of what looked like olive oil. She opened the bottle as she faced me. "It might be better if we did this outside the truck."

I nodded and handed my untouched absinthe cocktail to Ryan before opening my door and jumping down onto the asphalt of the parking lot. Lovie followed suit, taking hold of each of my arms and rotating my body so that I was facing her. Then she popped open the cork of the bottle she just fished out of her bag and dipped her index finger into it. She brought her finger, which smelled strangely of almonds, to my face, drawing a straight line from the center of my forehead to the tip of my nose. She dipped her finger in the oil again and drew lines across each of my cheeks. She finished by drawing three lines from my jaw to the bottom of my neck.

"What is this oil?" I asked, finding the smell of it strangely appealing. It was sweet, but subtle.

"It's angelica oil—rosemary, bay leaves, an' mandrake root, all combined into a base o' almond oil. Workin' together, they'll protect you 'gainst anyone or anythin' wants ta do ya harm."

"Aren't you supposed to say a prayer or a chant or something?" I asked when it became clear that she wasn't going to.

Lovie shook her head and laughed. "Not all magic is magic you can see, Peyton. Remember how Christopher mentioned the power of intent an' how it breeds magic?" I nodded. "Well, there's yer answer."

I nodded again as the image of Lovie making the oil and imbuing it with thoughts about protection arose inside my head. That image, however, was ruined at the memory of the deathly stillness I saw in Guarda's opaque eyes. I instantly felt my stomach recoiling on itself. "Why are you and Christopher so worried about Guarda?" I asked, studying Lovie carefully. In our short association, I hadn't really seen her get apprehensive or fearful about anything, not even when she'd expelled the entity that was squatting in my house and all hell broke loose.

Lovie glanced up at me as she screwed the lid back onto the vial of spiritual barrier oil. "Guarda delves inta good an' bad magic. She's powerful an' she's selfish. Those two make a frightenin' pair." After a long, deep breath, she smiled. "You're protected as much as I can protect ya. Now you're gonna have ta drink that absinthe down an' let's hope Guarda doesn't have anythin' up her sleeves."

"*Ma minette,*" Drake piped up. "*Are you fully resigned to drinking that bizarre concoction? I cannot say I approve of this entire mission. Perhaps it is wiser just to see what awaits us Tuesday rather than jumping over such hurdles?* Après tout, *after all, perhaps nothing awaits us and we are simply being foolish in taking these precautions?"*

"*You already know how I feel about the subject,*" I responded.

"*Oui,* je sais, *I know, ma minette. But that is not to say that I approve of your feelings. This Guarda woman gives me an eerie feeling and I do not think it bodes well that Lovie appears quite distressed about her as well.*"

"*The situation is what it is, Drake,*" I responded, trying to avoid getting into an argument. I wasn't in the mood to debate the pros and cons. In my mind, Guarda was the only avenue for me to communicate with the dead. With a deep breath, I nodded to Lovie to let her know I was ready to get the show on the road. I turned toward the truck and opened the door, glancing up at Ryan and smiling. But my smile wasn't genuine—it was a reflection of my rattled nerves. "I guess I'm ready to drink that stuff," I said.

Looking down at the glass, he didn't hand it to me right away. Instead, he looked back at Christopher and then at Lovie. "Are you sure it's safe?" he asked.

Christopher nodded immediately. "The last thing Guarda wants is the po-lice on her tail. Legally, it's safe. It's our spiritual safety that worries me."

"She'll be fine," Lovie insisted. "She's protected with the gris-gris an' the oil." She eyed Ryan and nodded as he handed the glass to me. Then she faced me and smiled. "You good, babydoll, you good."

Figuring that was my cue, I brought the glass to my lips and swallowed the bitter liquid as soon as it hit my tongue. The aftertaste was something less bitter and slightly herbal. It wasn't as overpowering as I expected.

When I finished the contents of the glass, I handed it to Lovie, who was studying me. She examined me as if she half expected me to drop dead right there. "You good?" she asked with narrowed eyes.

"I think so," I answered.

"*I do not notice any change in your body as of yet, ma minette,*" Drake announced. "*Though I must admit, I quite enjoyed the taste of that spirit.*"

I smiled inwardly at Drake's boyish charm. "*Maybe it takes a while to start working.*"

"Peut-être," he responded. "*Perhaps.*"

"We gotta go back to Guarda's now," Lovie announced as she motioned for me to get back into the passenger seat. She walked around to the other side of the truck and opened the rear door, piling in as I did the same in the front.

"You okay?" Ryan asked as soon as I sat down. I turned toward him and found him studying me quizzically.

"Yeah, I feel fine so far," I answered with a shrug. He started up the truck and we exited the parking lot without further conversation.

"I don't want you both goin' back in there alone," Ryan began, breaking the silence once we turned onto Davis Landing Road.

"We have no other choice," Lovie argued. "Guarda specifically said no one else was ta come with us." Then she sighed. "Why don't ya just park here on the street where she can't see the truck from her house? Peyton an' I can walk the rest o' the way. I got my cell phone with me, so if somethin' comes up, I'll give you a shout."

Ryan took a deep breath as if to argue, but must've realized he was out of order, and simply nodded. I offered him what I hoped was a reassuring smile, but his expression didn't change. He pulled over to the side of the road, right before it curved around a bend, and where Guarda's shack was visible from the street. He put the truck in "park" and turned off the engine.

"Good luck, Pey," Trina said in a soft voice.

I turned around and smiled at her while Lovie opened her door and dropped down to the asphalt below. "We gotta hurry now,

Peyton," she said. I simply nodded and opened my door, taking a deep breath as I jumped down onto the road and closed the door behind me. A cold wind whipped through the trees and splashed rain onto my face, but I hurried to catch up with Lovie, who had already started down the long, muddy driveway leading to Guarda's. I caught up to her just as she reached Guarda's front door.

Stepping onto the porch outside Guarda's door, the wood below our feet whined in protest. Or maybe it was my stomach. It suddenly sprang to life and started groaning as if I were hungry. My attention was momentarily diverted at the sound of the spirit bottles as they clanked against each other while the wind rattled them unapologetically.

"Yer stomach growlin' is normal," Lovie said as she eyed me, probably well aware that I was anything but relaxed about the whole situation. "There's quite a bit o' alcohol in the absinthe an' sometimes, yer body don't know how ta deal with it." She brought her hand to the door, intending to knock, but the door opened to reveal Guarda standing there, staring up at us with a frown.

"She drink it?" she demanded, addressing Lovie.

"Yes," Lovie answered quickly.

"Then come in. We ain't got us much time remainin'," Guarda ordered as she held the door open wider. Lovie stepped inside and I followed suit, finding, again, that my eyes needed more time to adjust to the darkness of Guarda's small house. I instantly felt heat around my ankles, ambling up my legs and seizing the middle of my body. The heat continued to travel up my chest and seemed to linger around my neck. I wasn't sure if Guarda's house was incredibly hot, or if I was having a reaction to the absinthe. I had a feeling it was probably the latter.

"Sit there," Guarda said to Lovie, pointing to an old, white, plastic outdoor chair she'd moved into the living room, beside the wall of skulls. Lovie didn't say anything, but merely obeyed as she was instructed. Then Guarda turned to me, studying me with those milky eyes that made my skin crawl. "Ya gonna lay down in the center o' the room," she said curtly.

Looking at the living room floor, I saw she'd set out a red piece of fabric that was maybe six feet long by four feet wide. Holding down the corners were lit candles sitting on white plates. Each candle was a different color—white, blue, silver, and black—and all were dressed in oils and herbs. "Guess you were expecting us?" I asked with a hesitant laugh.

"'Course," Guarda answered somewhat evasively. I figured I shouldn't attempt to make any more small talk. Instead, I took my seat on the red fabric and hoped it wasn't as soiled and dirty as the carpet appeared to be. "Take off yer shoes an' socks," Guarda said gruffly. I just nodded and did as she instructed, pushing my socks into my shoes and piling them neatly on my right, beside the red cloth. "Now ya gotta lay yerself down," Guarda continued.

I lay down on my back and faced the ceiling. That bizarre heat began working its way up my legs again, only this time, centering on the parts of my body that touched the fabric below me.

"*Are you well, ma minette?*" Drake asked. "*I feel hot.*"

"*I know. I'm not sure what it is but, yeah, so far I'm okay.*"

I didn't realize Guarda had left the room until she returned with a handful of what appeared to be even more candles. These candles, however, were shaped differently. I wasn't sure, but it seemed one of them was shaped like a snake. I found it hard to pay much attention to Guarda because I was growing hotter by the second and my vision became blurry.

The heat inched up from my backside and traveled in tiny rivulets of warm electricity toward my face, breasts, stomach, and the tops of my legs. My body seemed incredibly heavy, dense, and weighted. Then my feet suddenly felt as if they were miles away from my head. I found myself completely shrouded in darkness, which threw me for a second until I realized I had simply shut my eyes. When I opened them, I couldn't focus on anything—the candlelights surrounding me became blurry, casting strange shadows around the room that diffused into the background. It felt as if everything around me was moving, and I couldn't concentrate on any one thing because nothing remained stationary.

"Baron Samedi." Hearing Guarda's voice, I tried to focus, but I couldn't see her. I shifted my head to the side, but it felt so heavy I could barely move. Hardly able to make out the silhouette of Guarda kneeling beside me near my stomach, I recognized a white candle in her hand that was shaped like a skull. With her eyes closed, she said, "I call on you, Loa Baron Samedi. I come ta serve you."

Having never heard the term "Loa" before, somehow I knew that it was a spirit Guarda was contacting. But not just any spirit. I could feel the weight of this particular spirit, and his significance. I didn't know how I possessed that knowledge, but I knew he was a being, an entity, that was endowed with tremendous power.

"Loa o' the dead," Guarda continued, her voice wavering in and out, as if it were being picked up and carried away by the wind. "Spirit o' death, hear me."

The heat began to boil inside me and even though it tortured me, like it was burning right through me, I couldn't make a sound. It was as if any control I'd previously possessed over my body was now lost. I opened my mouth and tried to yell, but no sound came out. Then I tried to think of Drake, tried to contact him, but I couldn't. My entire body was paralyzed while my mind knew and felt everything going on around me. However, I couldn't think in sentences or words.

Suddenly terrified, I tried to move my head to make eye contact with Lovie and tell her I'd had enough and we needed to leave, but my body wouldn't budge. I just lay there, staring at the ceiling, rigidly immobile. I closed my eyes again, and was suddenly struck with the image of Lovie lying slumped over in her chair, her body unresponsive and flaccid. In my mind's eye, I watched her drop off the chair and fall onto the ground in one fluid motion. Even though I couldn't actually see her to verify it, I had the uncanny knowledge that Lovie wasn't with us any longer. She was under Guarda's spell, and at the mercy of Guarda's powers. Suddenly Lovie and Christopher's fears about Guarda started to make sense to me. I was overcome with the absolute certainty that whatever spell Guarda was weaving, the purpose behind it wasn't simply to aid me in unblocking my psychic walls. No, there was definitely more to it than that.

"Baron Samedi, hear me, I'm yer servant," Guarda's voice continued to ring through my mind. "I need you, oh great Loa. I plead fer yer help an' in return, I offa you this vessel, this woman."

I didn't understand what her words meant but I was suddenly very frightened by them because it appeared that I was being offered to some spirit of death.

"*Drake!*" I whispered. "*Drake, can you hear me? Are you still there?*" But Drake didn't respond.

"*I hear you.*" It was a man's voice, which resonated clearly. It was deep and I could understand it, which meant he was speaking English. But somehow, I had the feeling that my brain was translating his words, and giving his words meaning.

"See him," Guarda said and it suddenly seemed as if she removed the block restricting my movement. I felt my body sitting up of its own accord where before, I'd been frozen. I leaned up onto my elbows and perceived a man kneeling before me, studying me curiously. I was immediately conscious that he was no ordinary man. There was a presence about him, an aura, that hinted of his dynamic power.

"I offa you this woman, Baron Samedi," Guarda announced again. "In return fer yer help. I offa you her willin' body ta do wif as ya please."

"*Hello, baby!*" the man said to me with a wide and toothy grin.

Chapter 10

Baron Samedi, the Loa of the dead, was, in two words: primitively sophisticated. He was dressed in a black top hat and a matching tuxedo with a gigantic, live snake (maybe a boa constrictor?) wrapped around his shoulders. He wore dark, perfectly circular glasses that rested on the tip of his bony nose. Cotton plugs stuck out of his nostrils. Somehow, and I couldn't tell you how, I possessed the knowledge that he was dressed like a corpse in Haitian burial style. His face was completely white, abnormally so, and awfully gaunt. It resembled a skull even though there was flesh on top of the bones. He held a lit cigar between the bony fingers of his right hand. When he brought the cigar to his lips, the smoke wafted out from behind his sunglasses and ears.

"Who are you?" I asked, amazed to find my own voice. I didn't know why, but I suddenly felt as if I was in complete control of myself again, as though the powers of the absinthe had released their hold on me.

The spirit laughed a dark, disturbing sound. But even more intimidating was that he never opened his mouth. I could only hear his laughter in my head. He continued smoking his cigar and staring at me, or so I had to imagine, since I couldn't see beyond his dark glasses. The snake around his shoulders swayed this way and that, seeming to mimic the wafting of Baron Samedi's cigar smoke.

"She ignorant, great Loa," Guarda piped up, crawling toward the spirit as if she were an abused dog, trying to appeal to her master's rare moment of kindness. "She dunno her place."

"*Quiet,*" his voice sounded in my head as he faced her with an angry expression. Guarda immediately pulled away and appeared shocked or stunned into silence. She stayed on all fours, staring up at him curiously. When he turned his attention back to me, the protruding lines of his jaw appeared to slacken a bit. "*You don't know me, mortal?*" he asked, sounding surprised.

I had a feeling that not knowing who he was wouldn't win me any favors, but lying about it was probably even worse. "Um, I know you're a spirit," I started. That was about the full extent of what I knew about him, though. As to his reputation, I could only hope he was a good Loa . . .

His chuckle sounded through my head again. "*It depends on what yer definition o' good is,*" he said, his voice reverberating through my mind as his toothy grin vanished and he bent down onto his hands. I couldn't stifle the shock that traveled through me as I realized he could read my mind. But that shock wasn't given much time to brew because moments later, he was crawling toward me until barely three inches of air separated our faces. The snake continued to waver this way and that, but never touched me. Thank God.

"*I'm the all-knowin' Loa o' death, baby.*" Who knew Baron Samedi had a distinctly Southern accent? It seemed to have tinges or remnants of his Haitian beginnings, but the accent wasn't exactly obvious. Again, there was something inside me that told me his English was merely for my benefit—just so we'd understand one another.

"Do ya approve o' my offerin', Loa?" Guarda asked, her voice taking on a lilt that hinted at her excitement. But Baron Samedi ignored her. Instead, he ran his hands down my waist, pausing at my hip bones. He palmed the lump in my pocket—the gris-gris meant to protect me.

I could hear his chuckle in my head as he shook his. "*You want protection, baby?*" he asked. "*This ain't enough. You need me.*"

"You're offering me protection?" I asked, frowning because he didn't seem the protective type.

"*I might be known fo' debauchery, obscenity, an' being a wild lover, but I'm also the protector o' all children,*" he answered stonily. "*And it up ta me whetha you live o' die.*"

I swallowed hard. "Are you going to kill me?"

He chuckled again as he ran his bony finger down the side of my face. "*Do you wanna die, baby?*"

"No," I answered immediately.

"*Your wish is mah command.*" I figured that meant he wasn't going to kill me . . . or so I hoped.

"But about your protection . . ." I started, suddenly worried that Lovie's gris-gris wasn't all she thought it might be. 'Course I couldn't say I was surprised—I didn't think anything could compete with the power of Baron Samedi.

"*If you desire mah protection, baby, you must ask fo' it an' you gotta offa me somethin' in return.*" He smiled more broadly as I realized he regarded that offering as something sexual in nature. "I *am the Loa o' the dead, which means if you want mah assistance, you must come where I dwell.*"

"The graveyard?" I asked, repeating the first word that occurred to me.

Baron Samedi nodded.

"How do I find you there?" I asked, growing nervous. "I mean, what do I do once I'm there?"

I could feel him grinning at me. "*I can't give you all the answers, baby.*"

Somehow, and maybe it was because I'd lost my grip on sanity, I wasn't afraid of him. Figuring he told me all he intended to on the protection subject, I turned to my other concern. "Are you going to remove my block?"

He chuckled and leaned closer to me until I couldn't help inhaling the smoke wafting out from behind his glasses. It tasted rather heady, but sweet when it hit the back of my tongue. "*Have you heard the one 'bout the guy who died from a Viagra overdose?*" Baron Samedi asked me.

Was he really going to tell me a joke? My knotted eyebrows reflected my puzzlement. "*No,*" I answered, without speaking either. I was thinking my responses. Hmm, very strange.

"*They couldn't close his casket!*" Baron Samedi replied, his deep laugh echoing through my head as his lips slightly turned up at the ends.

"*That's a good one,*" I answered with an uneasy smile, finding his crass sense of humor slightly endearing.

"*You tell me one,*" the Loa of death demanded. It almost felt like we were just two kids exchanging dirty jokes on the school playground.

"*Um,*" I started while wracking my brain, trying to remember a crude joke that might impress him. He seemed to favor the obscene ones. "*Okay, got one,*" I thought with a smile. "*How does a woman scare a gynecologist?*"

"*Tell me,*" he answered, not missing a beat.

"*By becoming a ventriloquist!*" I answered, silently hoping he wouldn't kill me for telling him such a stupid joke. He pulled back and I could hear the roar of his laughter in my head. When the moment passed, he leaned back down and the snake disappeared from around his neck, vanishing into thin air. My eyes went wide. "*I am Baron Samedi, mortal,*" he started, his tone now more serious. He reached his bony hand up to his face and removed his glasses. I gasped in shock when his glowing, white eyes met mine. He didn't have pupils and the irises of his eyes were as white as freshly fallen snow. "*I am head of the Guédé family and my wife is Manman Brigit.*" He paused and then smiled more broadly. "*She knows of my vast sexual appetite,*" he added, almost as an aside. Then he dropped his attention from my eyes to my breasts and lower still. When I glanced at my body, I found I was suddenly naked. I bucked in response, but the Loa's hand on my upper thigh calmed me. "*Be still. Allow me,*" he whispered as he continued to gaze at me unabashedly. His smile showed obvious appreciation when his eyes centered on the mound between my thighs. I felt my thigh grow hot beneath his hand and watched him close his glowing white eyes as he inhaled, and a smile pasted itself across his broad mouth.

"*What?*" I said, my voice sounding quivery because I didn't understand what was going on.

"*Quiet,*" the Loa responded. "*I am acceptin' mah offerin',*" he added in a softer tone, seemingly feeling sorry for reprimanding me. He opened his eyes and they seemed to glow more brightly. "*I am experiencin' yer body as best I can.*"

"*Oh,*" I responded, still not understanding what that meant but at the same time, I couldn't say I felt defiled at all.

"*I stand at the crossroads o' this world an' the next,*" he continued, apparently after having gotten his fill of experiencing my nudity. He brought his glowing eyes back to mine and I found myself zoning out as I gazed at the white orbs that dominated his face. "*I decide who passes ta Guinee an' who stays on this plane.*"

"*Oh,*" I said again, shaking my head, trying to force myself out of my trance-like stupor.

"*You have death in ya,*" he announced in an inquisitive tone of voice. He leaned closer to me and stared so hard it felt as if he were peering right through me and into my soul. Maybe he was. It seemed like he was trying to detect what sort of death resided inside me. I figured he must be channeling Drake's essence.

"*Yes,*" I answered. "*I'm possessed by a spirit, but I also have a spiritual block and can't communicate with the spiritual world because of it.*"

"Now that you have accepted mah payment, oh great Loa, we call on you ta unblock her," Guarda suddenly interrupted, crawling toward us, with one of her hands extended out, as if she wanted to touch him.

He turned toward her sharply and his eyes grew brighter, blazing with an angry intensity. "*Silence!*" his voice roared through my head. Guarda dropped back down to a slump again and nodded, cowering as she crawled away.

When Baron Samedi faced me again, the anger blanched from his expression. He leaned back down until we were inches apart and took a long drag of his cigar before exhaling it into my face. I suddenly had the desire to inhale the smoke and breathe it in as deeply as I could. I closed my eyes and sucked it in for three counts as the headiness of the smoke filled me. I felt his bony fingers grasping my upper thighs as he pushed my legs apart and settled himself between them. Somehow, though, I had no worries that he might try to take advantage of the situation and penetrate me.

I suddenly felt very dizzy. Upon opening my eyes, I found it wasn't Baron Samedi at all who hovered above me, but Drake. He knelt between my legs, gazing down at me, and tightly grasping each of my thighs. "*Drake?*" I asked with a laugh as I felt something euphoric erupting inside me. I pushed my pelvis against his waist and rocked back and forth, riding the waves of elation that rippled inside me. I opened my eyes again and found Drake staring down at me. He was so incredibly handsome with his dark hair and up-to-no-good smile. But there was something that didn't fit; something was definitely off. His eyes were glowing white. I reached up and cupped the back of his head with both of my palms, forcing him down on top of me. "*Why aren't you talking to me?*" I demanded.

"Que voulez-vous que je dise, *ma minette?*" he responded and I understood the French to mean: "*What would you like me to say?*"

I ran my fingers through his hair, continuing to grind myself against him. Heat began building between my thighs. "*I don't want you to say anything,*" I responded. "*I want you to kiss me.*"

He chuckled and his smile was undeniably wicked. He gripped the back of my neck none too gently and forced my face upright. Gazing at me, his eyes glowing that unholy white, he pressed his lips on mine, demanding my reciprocation with heated urgency. I wrapped my arms around him and allowed my tongue to mate with his as I undulated against him. When he pulled away, I found it wasn't Drake at all, but Ryan I was kissing. He chuckled as stray locks of his honey-gold hair dropped down into his face before he pushed them aside. Just as with Drake, Ryan's eyes glowed fiercely white.

It only perplexed me for a moment before I wanted to feel Ryan on top of me; no, I wanted to feel him inside me. I gripped his neck again and pulled his face down to mine, forcing my tongue into his mouth. He returned my eagerness and we both lapped at each other almost ferociously. When he pulled away, he looked down at me, shaking his head as his smile widened. "*Yer block is officially removed, impetuous creature.*"

Before I could question how Ryan could remove my spiritual block, he simply disappeared right in front of me. I blinked and sat up straight, searching for any sign of him, but there was nothing. I found only the wispy clouds of cigar smoke enveloping me before dissipating into the ether. I blinked again and found Guarda standing above me, but she was gazing at something in the distance, something right behind me. I glanced back and noticed nothing was there.

"It weren't enough?" she asked, shaking her head before she began to nod. "Yes, I will do yer biddin', Loa. I will find ya a suitable vessel." She nodded. "She yours, Loa, she yours."

"Is he still here?" I asked, wondering if she was still talking to Baron Samedi, and why it was that I couldn't see him.

Guarda turned to face me immediately, as if she was surprised I was still in the room. She wore a bizarre expression that I half thought could have been astonishment in her old, faded eyes. She held an unlit candle that smelled like some sort of oil, which dripped off the end of the candle and landed on the carpet. "Where did he go?" I asked.

Her eyes narrowed. "His work here was done so he done left."

I closed my eyes as a wave of dizziness overtook me. When I opened them, I focused on the wick of the candle in Guarda's hand, only to find it was suddenly burning, and the red wax was pooling at the top. I could just make out very crude scratch marks in the side of the candle. The more I studied the markings, the more they took shape until I recognized them as letters, a P and a C.

"P, C," I repeated out loud, suddenly feeling woozy. All of the clarity I'd previously experienced with Baron Samedi was gone, leaving me with the feeling of inebriation. "P, C," I said again, shaking my head as I tried to understand why the letters seemed so familiar. "Peyton Clark!" I burst out as soon as it dawned on me that the carvings in the side of the candle were my own initials.

Guarda took no notice of my jubilance. Instead, she chanted something I couldn't understand as she placed the burning candle on the floor right between my feet. Suddenly remembering that I'd been buck naked only moments before, I glanced down at myself only to find I was clothed again. I instinctively felt for the gris-gris in my pocket and started to breathe a sigh of relief once I felt its familiar outline. That relief was transient, though, after I remembered Baron Samedi's comments that the thing was basically useless. I could only hope he meant that it was only useless against his power . . .

As a flood of dizziness overtook me, I closed my eyes again and tried to decide which way was up and which was down. When I reopened my eyes, I found Guarda kneeling before me. There was a bunch of objects on the floor in front of her, but my vision was growing so blurry, I found I couldn't focus on any of them, and their identities remained a mystery.

Instead, I fought to keep my eyes open and tried to focus on Guarda, who was now holding three pieces of ribbon in her hands: black, red, and yellow. They were tied together at one end and I watched her study me as she started to tie knots into the ribbons, repeating "Peyton Clark" with each knot she tied. She continued tying knots and chanting my name until she had about nine knots. Then she reached for what looked like a little gingerbread man at the base of her knees. When she lifted the thing up, I realized it was a crudely constructed doll made from what looked like burlap. It was maybe the size of my hand, and naked except for two buttons of different sizes and colors, which were sewn onto the doll's face to resemble eyes. Guarda was tying the knotted ribbons around the doll's neck. Then she reached back down between her knees and produced a needle.

"Gimme yer hand," she said coarsely. I glanced down at my right hand, but it seemed as if it were miles away from me. I waved it a few times, wondering why my arms had grown so long. Guarda reached out and gripped my hand, wrapping her gnarled, tree trunk fingers around my index finger. Then she held the needle up to the pad of my finger and pierced the end of it. At the unexpected jabbing pain, I cried out and tried to pull my hand away, but her grip was too strong. She squeezed my finger until blood pooled on the top of it. Then she grabbed the button-eyed doll and smeared my blood all over its face.

She pushed my finger away and reached back down to her knees where she grasped what looked like a small piece of rough bark, or maybe it was an old, petrified nut. She attached the thing to the doll by tying it with the three ribbons. Then she retrieved a large, black pen from the floor, and, holding the doll in place, started drawing on its stomach. When she was finished, she placed the doll beside the lit candle, between my feet. I glanced down at the doll, curious to see what Guarda had drawn on it. It looked like two snakes facing one another and sticking their tongues out. Between them were three stars.

When I looked back up at Guarda, I found her milky eyes focused on mine. "Damballah Wedo, I give you the blood o' her who I wish ta command. I beg ya ta grant me victory ova her will," she continued as she held the doll before reaching for a vial of oil at her knees. She poured the oil over the doll and I suddenly felt as if she were pouring the oil over me, and my entire body. My skin felt slimy and wet. I ran my hands down my arms, feeling for slickness, but found none. I closed my eyes against another bout of extreme dizziness. I could faintly hear Guarda chanting and when I attempted to open my eyes again, I couldn't because they were clasped tightly shut.

"I command ya, I compel ya," she chanted in a whispered voice. "I command ya, I compel ya, Peyton Clark. Ya will do as I bid."

I felt a cold wind blast my face and seconds later, I could smell the acrid scent of smoke, and the candle's wick being blown out. I fought to open my eyes, but it was no use, my body seemed as if it no longer answered to me.

"When ya open yer eyes, you'll forgit all o' this," Guarda continued. "I command ya, I compel ya. Open yer eyes now an' forgit!"

A bolt of what felt like electricity surged through me. I heard myself scream out as my eyes fluttered open. I found I was lying on the floor, looking up at the ceiling. I took a few deep breaths and tried to orient myself, but my mind was completely blank. I didn't know where I was or what I was doing on the floor.

"Peyton?" It was Lovie's voice. I blinked a few more times and looked at her face where it appeared above me.

"Lovie?" I asked, my voice coming out rough and hoarse, like I'd pretty much lost it.

She gazed down at me while rubbing the side of my face, and nodded. I took comfort in her sweet smile. "Are you okay?" she asked.

I wasn't sure I was okay. I had no memory of what had just happened and that realization stuck in my gut. "Is the block gone?" I asked, feeling like I'd just emerged from a deep, long sleep and not really sure whether I was still dreaming.

"It gone," Guarda answered, holding her jaw tightly. I looked at her and felt something unpleasant bubbling up inside me. I couldn't put my finger on the emotion, though, and decided I was just incredibly exhausted. Lovie extended her hand, which I accepted, allowing her to help me into a sitting position. Once there, I rolled onto my hands and knees and took a few deep breaths as the room circled erratically around me. I shook my head, attempting to clear the cloudiness that remained in my mind. Leaning back onto my knees, I waited until I felt up to it, then started to stand. I was a bit wobbly on my feet, but Lovie was instantly beside me, wrapping her arms around me as she supported my body weight and assisted me to the door.

"Why do I feel so woozy?" I asked.

"You've neva experienced magic before," Lovie answered. "Sometimes it can put yer body through the wringer."

"*Drake,*" I thought, suddenly wondering why he was so quiet. "*Are you okay?*"

"*Oui, ma minette,*" he answered, his voice sounding unsteady and faint. "*I am afraid I do not quite feel myself. I share your lethargy.*"

But lethargy wasn't exactly the right word for the way I felt. This was more like delirium. I tried to see my feet, but almost needed to remind myself to lift my foot up and then put it down again in order to walk to the door. I was vaguely aware of Lovie discussing what sounded like payment with Guarda.

"*Ma minette, are you well?*" Drake asked. "*I am concerned for you.*" I got the distinct impression that he was shaking his head, seemingly confused. "*I do not possess any memory of what just occurred.*"

"*Neither do I,*" I responded. "*It's like there's a big void in my head.*"

"*Oui, I feel the same. I do not understand this, mon chaton.*" I could suddenly feel his anger. "*I do not trust this old woman! I believe she has done something to us, ma minette!*"

I couldn't say I disagreed but I also didn't have the wherewithal to think about it any further. As it was, I felt like I was about to pass out.

Upon reaching the front door, I paused momentarily and took a deep breath, my mind full of buzzing insects, all fluttering around in my skull and causing pressure between my eyes. I closed my eyes and thought about the haven of Ryan's truck. Then an image of Ryan arose in my head and I instantly felt relief and warmth around and inside of me. All I wanted to do was see Ryan. Then I would be safe. Ryan would take care of me. I opened my eyes and with Lovie's help, worked my way onto the porch and the muddy ground below. I heard the sound of Guarda closing the door behind us, but I kept my attention strictly facing forward, blinking away the rain as it landed in my face.

"We need yer help," I heard Lovie say, presumably into her cell phone. "She can barely walk."

"*Take one step at a time, mon chaton,*" Drake whispered through my head. "*Breathe in and breathe out. One step at a time.*"

I focused on his words, trying not to allow myself to succumb to the darkness that was beginning to weigh down my eyelids. Only seconds later, I watched Ryan's white truck rolling into the driveway. Lovie stopped walking and held me as I stood gasping for air because I felt like I couldn't get enough oxygen. It crossed my mind that Guarda wouldn't be too happy about strangers in her yard, but I quickly dismissed the thought as one I really didn't care about.

Ryan put the truck in "park" and opened his door, jumping down to the muddy ground below. I brought my eyes to his and noticed his were wide with worry. He ran up to Lovie and me and wrapped his arms around me, lifting me bridal-style as Lovie stepped aside.

"What's wrong with her?" he asked as I wrapped my arms around his neck and happily let my head rest against his chest. I closed my eyes and relished the feeling of safety his body offered. His scent filled my nostrils and I held onto him even more tightly.

"I'm so glad you're here," I whispered.

"Nothin's wrong with her, Ryan. She's jist been put through a magical wringer. She's okay. She's just gonna need ta sleep it off," Lovie assured him.

"How are you feelin', Pey?" he asked as he pressed me more firmly against him and I thanked my lucky stars that he was there.

"I'm tired," I answered without opening my eyes. I couldn't remember the last time I'd felt so safe, protected, and content. There was nothing quite like being in Ryan's arms.

Moments later, he set me down on my feet and I reluctantly opened my eyes, watching Trina as she jumped down from the backseat of the truck and opened the passenger door for me. "How is she?" she asked, regarding me nervously.

"I'm okay," I muttered, although I wasn't convinced that was true. I just didn't feel like myself at all. Ryan lifted me up again and settled me into the passenger seat, carefully buckling me in. Then he gave me a little smile and closed the door. I still didn't know where we stood relationship-wise, but I didn't fret about it.

I could hear the sounds of shuffling as Lovie and Trina climbed into the backseat.

"Well?" Christopher asked.

"Everythin' went as expected," Lovie responded.

“Then my block is removed?” I asked, my voice sounding as though my throat were raw.

“Your block is removed,” Lovie answered. “But Guarda said it took a lot o’ work ta remove it an’ lots of magic, which is why ya feel the way ya do. Ya need ta listen ta me when I tell ya ta get lots o’ rest tonight, ya hear?”

I just nodded, thinking sleep was about the only thing I could handle in my current state.

Chapter 11

I blinked a few times and blinked again, but still had no clue where I was, or how I'd gotten there. The sterility of the white ceiling glared back at me. I rolled my head to the side before I recognized my chest of drawers and my lamp on top of it. Looking down, I found I was in my pajamas, in my bed and in my bedroom. The sound coming from the television comforted me with its monotone—but comforting or not, it still didn't explain how I'd gotten home. The last thing I remembered, I was leaving Guarda's house . . .

"You slept like the dead," Ryan's voice accosted my confused ears. I glanced up to find him in the doorway, holding two brown paper bags of what looked like takeout. He was smiling his devilishly charming, boyish smile, the one that never failed to make my insides melt like butter. He held the bags up, drawing my attention to them. "I picked us up some lunch."

"It's lunchtime?" I asked in a rough voice, sitting up and rubbing the back of my neck, wondering why I felt so exhausted after so much sleep: all night, all morning, and, now, into the afternoon.

Ryan chuckled. "It's one in the afternoon, Sleepin' Beauty."

"Oh God," I groaned, not at all happy over the passing of so much time. "What day is it?" I grumbled, imagining this was probably what the recovery from a lobotomy would feel like.

He chuckled again. "Sunday."

I felt panic riding up into my stomach. "Sunday!" I repeated as I shook my head, almost annoyed that he let me sleep for so long. Then I spotted the bags of food and further shook my head. "I don't have time to eat! Tuesday is nearly here!"

"Calm down, Pey," Ryan started. "I already talked to Lovie an' she's comin' over shortly. In the meantime, you need to eat somethin' so you have some energy." His expression told me he wouldn't be swayed.

"Lovie's coming over?" I repeated, my tone suspicious as I studied him from narrowed eyes.

"Yes," he repeated with finality, even nodding. "Once she gets here, we'll figure out our next steps. For now, though, I just want you to focus on eatin' so you'll be able to get through the rest of the day. I got a feelin' it's gonna be a long an' busy one."

I took a deep breath, relieved that Ryan had already asked Lovie to come over. Maybe we weren't in as bad shape as I'd previously supposed. I smiled at Ryan when he placed the two bags of takeout on my bedside table and leaned against the doorjamb, crossing his arms against his broad chest and regarding me playfully. "You are one tryin' woman, Peyton Clark."

I wasn't sure if that was a compliment, so decided to ignore it. I didn't know how to respond to Ryan in general because I still didn't know where we stood relationship-wise. But that was a conversation we'd have to ease into. "Have you been here since last night?" I asked. I was a little surprised because as far as I could tell, he and I very well could have been broken up after the whole Drake conversation.

"Yep, you passed out in the truck an' after everyone went their separate ways, I took you home, carried you into your room, put you in your jammies, an' then to bed. After that, I basically kept myself occupied by watchin' your television all mornin'. Which, I have to tell you, wasn't a pleasurable experience in the least. Just how small *is* your screen?" He pointed to the offending object in question before frowning.

I laughed, taking a deep breath and standing up before I approached him. "Thanks for staying with me, Ryan," I said. I decided not to overanalyze it and, instead, threw my arms around him and hugged him. He returned the hug, but neither of us said anything. When he released me, I hesitantly stepped back and tried to read him. So far, it seemed like we were good; he was acting like nothing had happened between us. "Given our situation, I'm surprised you did stay with me," I started, figuring someone had to broach the subject sooner rather than later. "It was really thoughtful."

"Surprised?" he repeated, almost appearing offended. "Why would you be surprised to know I care about you? I'll never stop carin' about you." He didn't give me the chance to reply. "An' what did you mean when you say 'our situation?'"

"Um, I don't know," I said with a shrug as I took a deep breath. I was irritated at myself for bringing the subject up. The more I thought about it, the more I realized how much I wanted to avoid delving into a long, drawn-out explanation; not now, when so much was riding on whatever might happen on Tuesday. My stomach started to growl deeply in hunger as I opened one of the bags to see what was inside of it.

"Sweet an' sour chicken; your favorite," Ryan piped up.

"Yum," I said, opening the other bag. "Mmm, you even got egg rolls!" I added with a huge smile, eyeing him momentarily before indulging my relentless need to know what was inside the foiled box at the bottom of the bag. "What did you get for yourself?"

"Well, I was tempted to go for the kung pao chicken, but you always complain that it's too spicy. Since we both know your incorrigible tendency to mooch my food, I decided to get almond chicken instead."

"Wow, Ryan, you're so good to me," I said, grabbing a fortune cookie, and tearing off the plastic wrapper. "Thanks for getting all of this."

"You're welcome."

I broke open the fortune cookie and shoved half of it in my mouth before unfolding the small, white fortune. "Conquer your fears or they will conquer you," I read with my mouth full before remembering my manners. "Ha, that's fitting." Then I stuffed the other half of the cookie into my mouth while Ryan shook his head and smiled with unmasked amusement.

"So, do you want to eat in here or in your kitchen?" he asked.

"In here," I answered, forgetting I had a mouthful of cookie again. "I'm starving, plus, the kitchen isn't even finished." Then I gave him a look, even going so far as to arch one eyebrow, inferring that it was his fault.

He frowned at me, but I noticed a smirk on his face, which made it pretty clear that he knew I was just playing with him. "Well, it's not like you've been askin' the crew back here to get it finished, have you?"

I laughed and shook my head. "No, I guess you're right." Then I took a deep breath. "If the world doesn't blow up on Tuesday, let's plan to resume construction on Wednesday, if that works for you?"

He smiled and nodded. "I'll see what I can do." Then he looked into the larger of the two paper bags. "Well, good thing they gave us plates an' plastic silverware, so we *can* eat in here," he said as he started unloading and arranging the contents of the Chinese food on my narrow bedside table. He handed the box of sweet and sour chicken to me and I took it greedily, sitting down on the end of my bed. I grabbed a fork from the pile he'd set down, and, after folding my legs Indian-style, I dug in. After a few bites, I realized I hadn't heard a peep from Drake since waking up.

"*Drake? Woo-hoo! Are you there?*" I asked him. "*Still sleeping?*"

"Non," came his immediate reply. "*I have been awake these last few hours, wondering when you might grace me with your presence. Your mind can be a very lonely place when you aren't awake, ma minette.*"

"*So why didn't you say anything?*" I asked while shoveling an enormous bite of chicken and pineapple on my plastic fork before chomping down on it. "*I've been up for twenty minutes or so now . . .*"

"*Oui,* je suis au courant," he answered. "*Yes, I am aware. I simply wanted to allow you some personal time with le barbare.*"

"*Well, thanks,*" I answered, unable to keep from smiling at hearing his nickname for Ryan. But even though Drake seemed to be trying for humor, I picked up an undercurrent in his tone, which sounded strangely detached. "*Is everything okay, Drake?*"

"*Oui, I suppose,*" he responded but I could tell everything wasn't okay.

"*What's the problem?*" I pushed.

"*It is not easy for me, ma minette,*" he answered. "*Experiencing your interactions with this man firsthand and recognizing the way you feel for him . . . It is not an easy situation for me, that's all. But I suppose the situation is what it is and I, therefore, must force myself to grow accustomed to it. I am attempting as much, mon chaton, though I find it exceedingly difficult.*"

"*I'm sorry.*" I didn't know what else to say because he was right, the situation was what it was and I couldn't help my feelings for Ryan.

"*Would you mind tuning me out, ma minette? I find I need some peace of mind.*"

"*Of course,*" I answered immediately and then thought the words that would disallow him to overhear or oversee the interactions going on between Ryan and me.

"Are you talkin' to Drake?" Ryan asked as I stuffed my face with another massive forkful of Chinese food before I saw he was studying me pointedly.

I felt myself blush as I realized he just caught me red-handed. "Sorry, I was just making sure Drake was okay," I answered. "I did disallow him to hear any of this conversation, though. So it's just you and me at the moment."

Ryan nodded, but I couldn't read his expression. He just seemed guarded somehow, and wearing his poker face. Biting into his almond chicken, he seemed to deliberately take his time chewing it. After he swallowed it, he took a sip of sweet tea before facing me. "Every time you talk to him, you get really quiet. At first, I just thought you might be losin' your mind or somethin', but now, I know it's called multitaskin'. Now I know what to look for."

I laughed and shook my head as I sighed. "That's what I figured you thought—maybe Peyton Clark was going batshit crazy." I took a deep breath and jabbed another piece of chicken, but suddenly didn't feel hungry anymore, so I just played with it.

"You're not batshit crazy, Peyton," Ryan responded. "Do you make batshit crazy decisions?" he asked while cocking his head to the side and pretending to consider the question. "Yes. Do you drive me crazy with some of the decisions you make? Absolutely."

"But you still love me?" I asked before I could censor myself. Feeling suddenly vulnerable, I shrugged my shoulders right up to my ears.

He exhaled a long breath, placing his forkful of almond chicken back on the plate, while I felt my heart sink into my belly. "God help me, but I still do."

In an instant, the sinking feeling was replaced by elation. "Then you aren't dumping me because of the whole Drake situation?" I asked hopefully. Plastering a huge grin on my face, I tried to soften him up a bit. "Because, you know, I thought about it, and I don't think today is a good day to get dumped."

Ryan chuckled as he shook his head. "I never know what to expect when it comes to your mouth, Peyton Clark." I didn't respond because, once again, my mouth was full of Chinese food. Ryan's chuckle faded, but the smile stayed on his lips. "As for the Drake situation . . ." He looked down at his half-eaten plate of food. Then, turning to face me again, he said, "Was that what you were talkin' about when you referred to 'our situation' earlier?"

"Our situation?" I repeated, trying to stall for a little time. "Oh yeah, that's what I was talking about," I said, only pretending to remember it.

Ryan cleared his throat. "As to the whole Drake situation, I won't lie to you, Pey, I was an' still am upset that you didn't tell me about the possession," he said while rubbing the back of his neck. "I thought we agreed that we were going to be a team."

"We *are* a team, Ryan," I interrupted. "And I meant it when I promised you I wouldn't keep anything from you again."

He looked at me and nodded. "I've been debatin' with myself about whether or not I want to continue havin' a relationship with you," he started, as I felt my stomach drop. "I've since realized my feelings for you will never be anythin' other than romantic. I realized this at Guarda's. I didn't want that crazy old woman touchin' you. I didn't an' I still don't trust her."

"I feel the same way," I admitted, cocking my head to the side as I further considered it. "What bothers me is that no matter how hard I try, I can't remember what happened when Lovie and I went inside her house." I took a deep breath. "It's like that whole part of my memory is missing."

Ryan frowned and his eyebrows met in the middle of his forehead. "I asked Lovie as much an' she couldn't seem to remember anythin' either." He inhaled deeply and sighed. I could tell he was stressed out. "She seems to think y'all are fine though based on the protection spells she performed before you went into Guarda's."

"Well, I hope she's right."

He nodded, somewhat absentmindedly. "Anyway, as to the relationship between you an' me," he started again before he sighed. "Lord help me, but I can't seem to keep away from you, Peyton Clark."

"Is that so?" I asked, smiling, as I walked up to him, adding a little sashay. Even though I appeared cool and confident, inside I was shouting "Hallelujah!" I was so glad I hadn't lost him.

"Yeah, that's so," he answered as his voice grew deep. He took the few steps that separated us and picked up my Chinese food, placing it on the table beside my bed. He tilted my chin up, forcing me to look into his eyes. "Although if you ever keep somethin' big from me again, I might have to resort to cruel an' unusual punishment."

"Like what?" I asked, taking his bait.

He chuckled. "I might be forced to . . . seduce the truth out of you."

"That doesn't sound especially cruel or unusual," I started. "In fact, I would go so far as to say seduction by Ryan Kelly couldn't even be categorized as punishment."

My giddiness started up from deep inside me and I realized Ryan was about to kiss me. He dropped his head and used one hand to lift my chin up, until his soft lips found mine. When he kissed me, his lips and mouth felt warm, while his tongue seemed eager as it danced with mine. I wrapped my arms around him and stepped onto my tiptoes.

"I won't ever keep something from you again, Ryan, I promise," I whispered, pulling away from him and cupping his cheek, wanting him to realize I was completely serious.

He smiled and his dimples framed his sumptuous lips. "If you do, there'll be hell to pay!" he answered, still grinning. "Now on to more important conversations: Are you sure Drake isn't able to overhear or oversee any of this?"

I nodded. "Yes, I'm sure. Why?"

His eyes narrowed as his hand stroked the nape of my neck and he wetted his lower lip with his tongue. I could tell his breathing was coming faster. "Because I intend to make love to you, Peyton, an' three's definitely a crowd."

My stomach plummeted all the way down to my toes. "But Lovie—" I began to argue, immediately putting the damper on my elation as the image of Lovie knocking on my front door at the worst possible moment suddenly crossed my mind.

"Isn't comin' over until I text her," Ryan interrupted me. "So we won't have any interruptions."

"Famous last words," I answered with a laugh, remembering the last time we'd tried to get busy. All the mirrors in Ryan's house had suddenly started cracking, thanks to the malevolent entity that had followed me there.

"As far as I'm concerned, nothin' can stop me from lovin' you," Ryan said, and his tone of voice seemed deeper, more determined.

I swallowed hard and hoped he would keep his promise. But then, all of a sudden, doubt crept into my head. "Um, Ryan, I haven't been with a man in a very long time," I started, worrying my lower lip.

"Shhh," he said, holding his index finger up to my mouth. "I don't want you to doubt yourself at all. Not with me, Peyton. You an' I are too close for that." He was silent for a few seconds as he just gazed at me. "You're beautiful . . . even when you chew with your mouth open, I think you're stunning." He chuckled and shook his head.

I smiled up at him just as I realized that we really didn't have time for sex. Not with Tuesday looming ahead of us like a nightmare. But then again, I figured if Tuesday really would bring the apocalypse, what better time to have sex than now? I mean, what a damned shame it'd be to face the end of my life without ever knowing Ryan intimately . . . "Too much talking!" I declared.

He chuckled. "Agreed."

Stepping away from me, he rested his weight against the side of the bed. His eyes never left mine. He crossed his arms over his chest and looked me up and down. "Take your clothes off for me, Pey," he said in a deep, gruff voice.

I felt my nerves shoot through the roof, but I knew better than to stall or argue with him. Instead, I kicked my nervousness in the ass and started unbuttoning my long-sleeved pajama top. "So if you were the one who put me in my jammies, that means you already saw me in my birthday suit," I announced.

Ryan shook his head. "I left your bra an' panties on, smart ass," he said with a smile. "An' while I admit it was impossible not to notice your rather shapely backside, especially when you insist on wearin' a G-string, I behaved myself, just like the Southern gentleman I was raised to be."

I didn't say anything as the pajama top dropped onto the floor and Ryan's eyes zoned in on my light-pink lace bra. His wolfish leer thrilled me to the core and I responded by sliding the less-than-sexy, gray flannel pajama bottoms down my legs. Stepping out of them, I stood up straight, allowing Ryan's eyes to travel from my bust to my barely-there pink G-string.

"You make me think very naughty thoughts," Ryan confessed as he stood up and approached me. He didn't wait for any invitation, but gripped the back of my neck and pulled me toward him, thrusting his tongue into my mouth as soon as our lips met. His other hand found one of my breasts, which he started fondling, teasing my hardened nipple through the lace. Releasing my neck, his hand traveled down to my back where he battled with the clasp of my bra for maybe half a second before it released under his deft fingers. The bra straps slipped over my shoulders before Ryan slid it off me altogether.

"Gorgeous breasts," he whispered as he bent down onto his knees, taking my left breast into his mouth. He wrapped his hands around my waist and held me in place while he sucked and nipped at my nipple. I ran my hands through his hair and my head rolled back as I closed my eyes and enjoyed the sensuous feel of his body next to mine.

His fingers lightly skimmed my skin as he traced the line of my lower back to my bottom and the swell of my derriere, his fingers lingering on my upper thighs. He probed inward until he found the hem of my panties and then moved upward, obviously trying to tease me. When I couldn't stand it anymore, he intuitively pushed his finger beneath the hem of my panties and started rubbing the firm nub between my legs in slow, fluid motions. I kept growing slicker as the tingling of my arousal spread throughout my pelvis.

Ryan pulled his finger out and yanked my panties down my thighs, his gaze settling on my lady bits. When he ran his finger down my crease, I moaned loudly and gripped his hair.

"You are beautiful," he whispered. He brought his finger down my crease again, this time separating my lips so he had more access to me. I cried out, and my hips began swaying of their own accord.

Before I could catch my breath, he gripped my waist. Lifting me up and over his head, he pushed me against the wall for support. My bare feet found purchase on top of his shoulders as he splayed my legs wide and gripped either side of my bottom cheeks to keep me suspended against the wall. He glanced up at me with a devilish smile. "I need ta taste you," he said as if I'd demanded an explanation. Then his tongue was inside me as he moaned and buried his face deeper in me. He licked me and then sucked, driving me mad with ecstasy. Seconds later, I experienced such a blissful release that I screamed out as my legs began to shake uncontrollably. My heartbeat thundered through my body. Just as I started to descend the crest of passion, I felt his large finger tracing my lips before rubbing me from top to bottom. I moaned out when he pushed his finger deep inside me. I bucked against him, but he held me firmly in place. When he pulled his finger out, he added another one before pushing them inside me as I arched against the wall.

"I need it," I whimpered, shaking my head, knowing I couldn't take much more of this teasing. I wanted to feel his body inside mine.

"Are you ready for me?" he asked in a voice thick with desire.

"Yes," I managed as he lowered me down from the wall, his biceps bulging under my weight. He carried me to the bed and deposited me on it gently, never taking his eyes from mine as he pulled his shirt over his head. I was instantly drooling at the amazing view of his tanned and deeply muscled chest. I swallowed hard when he unbuttoned his jeans and pulled his zipper down. His erection proudly burst forth when he removed his boxer shorts and allowed me to savor his perfect nudity.

"You are breathtaking," I whispered, my voice filled with awe.

Leaning down on top of me, he pushed two fingers inside me as I bucked underneath him. He slid them out and pushed them back in again while he situated himself between my legs. "I need to feel all of you, Peyton, bad," he whispered.

I just nodded and let him center the head of his penis at my opening. We didn't break eye contact as he slid into me ever so gently. I had to stretch to accommodate him, and I threw my head back, moaning and arching my back to receive him. He pushed into me deeper while gripping my hips, and lifting my pelvis up so he could enter me even deeper.

"Oh God," he groaned. "You feel amazin'."

Speechless, I pushed against him as hard as I could, sliding him as deeply inside me as possible. He pushed me back down against the bed as he sat up, apparently just to get a better view. With his hands kneading my breasts, he began pushing in and out of me. I stared up at his eyes and neither of us broke each other's gaze.

I didn't dare blink because I was afraid I'd miss the look of pure delight in his eyes. He reached down and began touching my sensitive nub as he pushed deep inside me, watching me intently. "I want you to come for me again," he whispered.

I smiled, already incredibly close. As the urgency within me began to spiral until I couldn't handle it anymore, I screamed out at the same time that Ryan started to speed up, thrusting deep inside me with renewed vigor.

"Do it for me, Ryan," I crooned into his ear, wrapping my legs around his waist. He smiled down at me before driving into me as deeply as he could. He closed his eyes and moaned, lowering his body on top of mine as I wrapped my arms around him and inhaled the spicy yet clean scent that was so uniquely his.

"Wow," he said, smiling at me as he kissed my lips and then pulled away, gazing down at me as he traced my hairline.

"Wow," I repeated with a little laugh and then ran my hands through his soft hair.

Neither of us said anything more for a few seconds as we continued to look at one another, but then Ryan smiled lasciviously. "I'm thinkin' that after that performance, we might need an encore."

Chapter 12

Lovie arrived within the hour. When the doorbell rang and Ryan answered it, Lovie had her usual beaming smile while Christopher wore his customary frown. I was surprised to see Christopher with her because he didn't exactly act like he enjoyed spending time with us. Go figure. Lovie was dressed, as always, in her colorful turban, blouse, and floor-length skirt, while Christopher looked like an escapee from the *Sleepy Hollow* set. I looked at Ryan, who was dressed in jeans and a white T-shirt, and we smiled in mutual wonder at Christopher's fashion choices.

When Ryan closed the door, I couldn't stop my eyes from traveling the length of him, pausing for a few seconds on his tight butt and broad chest. Now that I had experienced a sample of his bedroom sports, I couldn't turn that part of me off. Nor did I want to! I shouldn't have been surprised though—sex with Ryan absolutely and unquestionably blew my mind. I couldn't remember the last time I'd enjoyed it so much. It certainly never happened with my ex-husband, Jonathon, whose nickname should have been, "Wham-bam-thank-you-ma'am." Ryan did anything but wham or bam.

I finished the last sip of my Starbucks coffee, which Ryan had brought to me about twenty minutes earlier. I plopped the cardboard cup into a nearby trash bin that was sitting in the hallway, owing to the yet unfinished construction going on at my house. "Hi, guys," I greeted Lovie and Christopher, after Ryan said his hellos.

Lovie hugged me, kissing both of my cheeks in turn, like we were in Paris. Then she pulled away from me, but held my hands in hers as she smiled and asked, "How are you feelin', Peyton?"

"Lots better than last night," I answered with a sigh. "I slept half the day today."

"That's real good," she said with a nod. "Your body needed it. An' I'd insist ya take more time ta recuperate if we weren't in such a rush."

I agreed with a nod. "Yeah, we can't afford any more delays."

Lovie bobbed her head as she dropped my hands and turned to face Ryan and me. "There's one last step we must take in order ta open ya up ta communicatin' with the dead," she started.

"I thought my block was already removed?" I asked, shaking my head in curiosity. I glanced down at my bare feet and realized I really should have been wearing shoes, considering all the bent nails and other debris that lurked in the corners of the house. I almost appeared sloppy in white sweatpants and a fitted, heather-gray thermal shirt. I didn't exactly look the part of good hostess.

"The block is removed, but you haven't enabled that part of yourself yet, in order to take advantage of it," Christopher explained with an arched eyebrow and a lot of exaggeration. "You still haven't tapped into the flow of spiritual unity that now drifts through you."

I was at a complete loss as to what he was talking about—the flow of spiritual unity? I did, however, figure that whatever I needed to tap into was probably very important. "What do I need to do?" I asked, crossing my arms over my chest and sighing. It seemed to me that nothing came easy in the spiritual world.

"This part won't be too difficult," Lovie answered with an encouraging smile. "You simply hafta open yerself up ta the connection ya share with Drake through meditation."

Drake! I felt my stomach drop as I realized I completely forgot to remove the ban I'd placed on him while Ryan and I had been intimately engaged!

"*Drake, I permit you to experience what I experience,*" I said to myself, scrunching my eyes shut tightly, which often allowed me to reach out to him faster than usual.

"*Humph!*" came his irritated reply, giving me the distinct feeling his muscular arms were crossed over his chest while he glared at me. "*You could have prepared me in advance before leaving me in the dark for half of the day!* La souffrance!"

"*Sorry,*" I muttered as I opened my eyes. I looked at Lovie and then at Christopher, who was now standing beside her.

"*Why are they back?*" Drake demanded, his tone sounding suddenly concerned. Apparently, he disliked all of this mumbo jumbo stuff as much as I did.

"*Lovie just informed me that there are some more steps required before I can tap into your spiritual ability. So they're both here to assist me with those steps,*" I responded.

"Mon Dieu! *Is this task never ending!?*"

"*Yeah, you're telling me!*"

"Peyton?" Lovie asked, facing me with an amused smile while awaiting my response.

"Uh, yeah? What?" I replied, since I had no clue what she'd just said.

She laughed, shaking her head, but I sensed no irritation in her composed appearance. It seemed to me that, generally speaking, it was very difficult to ruffle Lovie's feathers. I mean, if her feathers weren't regularly ruffled by Christopher, I could only assume they simply never got ruffled. "I imagine you were talkin' with Drake just now?" she asked.

I nodded guiltily. "Yes, sorry."

She laughed again with bell-like cadence before replacing it with a much more serious expression. "We need ta find a place in yer house that's very quiet an' where you'll be comfortable."

"The only place that's finished in the house is one of the guest bedrooms, the one I'm currently sleeping in," I answered. "And, yes, I'm very comfortable there."

"That'll do jist fine," Lovie responded. Then she turned to Christopher and Ryan. "You two keep yerselves preoccupied while I see 'bout connectin' Peyton ta the spirit world." Then she faced Christopher. "You good?"

Christopher frowned down at her. "I shall manage," he replied testily.

I made the mistake of looking at Ryan, who responded with an expression that told me how much he was looking forward to hanging out with Christopher for who knew how long. I smiled apologetically and shrugged at the same time. Then, realizing Lovie was waiting for me to lead the way, I started for my bedroom.

"How long will this take?" I asked, opening my door and immediately blushing as soon as I saw the unmade bed linens. I smoothed the duvet back down on the bed, and fluffed the pillows from where they lay drooping against the headboard. I could only hope my lovemaking with Ryan wasn't too telltale.

"How long it takes depends entirely on how good ya are at meditatin'," Lovie answered. She had a knowing smile on her face after watching my hasty ministrations over the bed linens.

"Well, I've never done it before," I started. "Er, that is, meditated."

She nodded with another secretive smile and motioned for me to take a seat on the bed. When I did, she placed her brightly colored, paisley-print bag on the bed beside me and began rummaging through it, humming a tune I didn't recognize. She pulled out a vial that was about the height and width of my middle finger, then folded her fabric purse over onto itself while pulling the cork from the bottle.

"What's that stuff?" I asked.

"Creole water," Lovie answered as she dipped her little finger into the brownish-looking stuff. "It's a traditional spiritual water that's used ta contact N'awlins spirits specifically."

"We're only contacting New Orleans spirits?" I asked, instantly realizing what a silly question it was because we were in New Orleans. Naturally, the spirits we would encounter would be local.

She nodded. "For the time bein'. You need answers an' Christopher an' I have a good idea on where you'll find them."

"Where?" I asked immediately.

She glanced over the vial of Creole water and smiled at me. "We'll git ta that part in a bit, Miss Peyton. Fer now, I need yer focus."

"Okay," I answered as she approached me. Using her pinky finger, she drew a line wet with Creole water down the center of my face, then down both of my cheeks. "What's in that stuff?" I asked, trying to trace the slightly floral, citrus smell.

"Orrisroot, French brandy, oil o' orange blossom, oil o' geranium, an' coumarin," she answered, closing her eyes. "Now close yer eyes an' remain quiet fer a spell."

I obeyed her instructions and listened to the soft sounds of her chanting and humming. The smell of the Creole water filled my nostrils and I could honestly say I liked the aroma. It was earthy and floral and sweet, all at the same time.

"Are ya sittin' comfortably?" Lovie asked.

"Yes," I answered.

"Good. Now I want ya ta focus on yer breathin'. Find yer navel an' focus on that spot in yer mind. Notice how yer abdomen rises an' falls as you breathe in an' out. Imagine a coin sittin' on the spot jist above yer navel, risin' an' fallin' with yer breath." She was quiet for a few seconds as I focused on my navel and my breathing. I could feel my head clearing, and the sounds of my breath coming in and going out were soothing; it was almost like listening to waves.

"Now I want you ta imagine a place in yer mind where spirits rule. There're only thoughts in this place, no bodies, no tangible things, jist thoughts, jist bein'. Time doesn't exist there, jist air. Now deepen yer breathin' an' really let yer abdomen expand an' contract with each breath you take."

I did as she instructed, but it made me feel light-headed. Then I focused on the magical, spiritual realm and my dizziness immediately faded.

"Now imagine there's a door standin' right in front o' you. The door is closed an' it's separatin' you from this ethereal, weightless place where you want ta go," Lovie continued. "Do ya have it in yer mind? Do you see the door, Peyton?"

"Yes," I answered in a soft voice.

"Good. I want you ta imagine unlockin' that door with a key. When you put the key into the door an' turn yer hand, pull the door toward you." I could see the door unlocking clearly in my mind. "When you look beyond the door, ya see nothin' but the stars, just the galaxy. That is the spiritual world, Peyton. Now I want you ta open that door as far wide as it'll open." She was quiet for a second or two. "Is the door wide open?"

"Yes, it is," I answered.

"Now imagine that door fallin' apart, little by little, the wood begins ta splinter an' the door starts fallin' off the hinges. When it hits the floor, it melts away inta nothin', an' all that's in front o' you, an' all that's below you, behind you, an' above you, is space."

I imagined exactly what she described and felt my breath catch as the sensation of complete weightlessness overtook me. I was flying, no, floating, in a void where time and gravity meant nothing to me.

"Now focus on yer breathin' again, Peyton," Lovie continued. "Focus on the up an' down o' yer abdomen as you come back ta this plane. Focus on the coin as it rises an' falls with yer breathin'. Are you with me, babygirl?"

"Yes," I answered.

"Now open yer eyes," she finished.

When I opened my eyes, Lovie was standing before me. Beside her stood what I first mistook for a medium-sized dog. Upon further inspection, though, it definitely was no dog. It sat on its haunches, but was probably about two feet tall. It looked similar to a human except for its enormous, round eyes, which made it look like a tarsier. Its limbs were surprisingly human-like, though much longer and thinner than the average person's. It possessed five fingers on each hand and five toes on each foot. Its fingers didn't look like a human's though. They were more like long, thin spindles with balls on the ends of them. Its skin was an orangey brown and it had such large ears, I imagined it must also have very good hearing.

"Putain! *Bloody hell!*" Drake roared out. "Quelle est cette créature? *What is that creature? Stay away from it, ma minette!*"

"Um," I started as I backed away, not exactly sure what the thing was, or whether I should be afraid of it. "There's something really weird standing next to you, Lovie," I said in a warning tone.

Lovie just laughed away my concern and waved a dismissive hand in my direction. "That's jist Samuel, my familiar," she answered. She glanced at either side of her, but never looked directly at it, making it evident that she couldn't actually see the thing.

I studied the bizarre creature again and found it staring unblinkingly back at me. I took a deep breath and sighed. "So, I guess this means the block is completely gone now, right? I mean, since I can see your familiar?"

Lovie nodded. "It would appear that way." Then she closed her eyes and extended her hands, looking like a blind person searching for a light switch. "I can't feel Samuel," she announced after a few seconds of groping for him. "Can you ask 'im why he hasn't been connectin' with me?"

I glanced down at the little creature, and although it didn't move to open its mouth to speak, I got the distinct impression that it was being silenced against its will in some way. "Um, I think it's—"

"Samuel," Lovie corrected me.

"I think Samuel's trying to tell me that there's some sort of block on him. He's not able to talk to me, but I get the distinct feeling from him that he's being silenced involuntarily. He's been trying to tell you, but the magic between the two of you has also been affected," I finished and frowned. "At least, I think that's what he's trying to say."

Lovie nodded. "Thank you," she said, chewing her lower lip. "I have a feelin' this block has everythin' ta do with whatever's goin' down in this city." Then she took a big breath as she faced me again. "Now that ya have this gift, Peyton, ta see an' interact with the spiritual world, ya also need ta understand how ta turn a blind eye."

"Why would I want to do that?" I asked, watching as Lovie started for the door. Samuel momentarily vanished, only to reappear on her shoulder. It didn't seem as though his weight affected her in any way so I figured he probably didn't weigh much, if anything at all.

"You'll be able ta see things you never could before," Lovie continued as I followed her out of my bedroom and down the hall. "There will also be times when you might want ta shut the spiritual world out."

"And how would I do that?" I asked, suddenly anxious about the topic.

"The same way you shut Drake out," she answered. " You simply think the words."

"Okay," I nodded as we emerged into the foyer and found Ryan and Christopher exactly where we'd left them. Neither one said a word.

"How did it go?" Ryan asked after a short pause, studying me with caring eyes.

"Good," I answered. "I can now see Lovie's familiar!" With a fleeting glance at Christopher, I noticed there weren't any strange creatures looming around him. Apparently, his lack of popularity extended into the astral plane as well.

Lovie turned to face me. "The next step is fer you ta gather up as much information as possible regardin' what's goin' on in the city," she started. "You need ta talk ta the spirits, Peyton, an' find out what they hafta say. We need ta know what Tuesday will bring."

"Okay," I said as I nodded. "And where do I go to do that?"

Lovie seemed to have expected that question next. "Christopher an' I were discussin' it, an' we decided yer best chances ta uncover info-mation would be at either the LaLaurie Mansion or . . ."

"The Sultan's Palace," Christopher finished for her.

"Of course," Ryan interrupted, rolling his eyes. "The two most infamous haunted houses in N'awlins."

Not knowing what to make of his comment, I decided to ignore it. Lovie and Christopher followed suit and neither replied.

"Okay," I started. "Why those two places?"

Lovie cleared her throat and her expression was pensive, as though she was deeply pondering something. Then she sighed. "Usually, the places that possess the most spiritual energy are where the spirits have reasons ta remain."

"*Oui, that is so,*" Drake said, and I had the distinct impression that he was nodding.

"Meanin'?" Ryan asked, alternating his gaze between Lovie and Christopher.

"In general, there are four types of haunts," Christopher announced. "The first we refer to as residual energy. These types of specters simply repeat actions, sounds, words, and emotions that occurred back when they were alive. Many relive the scenes of their deaths."

"*I refer to these types of spirits as inutile, useless,*" Drake announced. I didn't respond.

"The second type of haunting is one in which the spirit is trapped or stuck on our plane."

"*Is that what type of spirit you are, Drake?*" I asked.

"Non," he answered immediately. "*I was given the option to move on, ma minette, but I have chosen to remain here.*"

I didn't have the opportunity to ask him why because Christopher was busily continuing his explanation. "Spirits who are stuck on this plane oftentimes died suddenly and, usually, violently. The third type of haunt is one where the spirit willingly remains on this plane, either to protect someone or because it's attached to something or someone."

"*That's you!*" I announced to Drake.

"*Oui, mon chaton,*" he responded with a chuckle. "*That is me.*"

"*Did you stay here to protect someone?*" I continued.

"*Oui, ma minette, I remained to protect you.*"

"*But, that's impossible because we only met recently and you've been dead for a while.*"

"*Perhaps it would appear that way, ma minette, but spirits are privy to information that humans are not. I knew I would be needed here and, therefore, I stayed.*"

"*But—*"

"*That is all you need to know, ma minette,*" Drake announced resolutely. "*I cannot explain the whys and the hows to you. Some things you must just accept at face value.*"

Call me nosy but I wasn't very good at accepting things at face value. Before I had the opportunity to argue with Drake, Christopher cut me off again.

"The fourth type of spirit can travel between this plane and the spiritual plane. These spirits can be both good and evil. The good ones usually offer advice, or protection, and often send us messages. We refer to these haunts as spirit guides."

"And the evil ones?" I asked, shelving the questions I had for Drake for the moment.

"The evil ones travel to this plane to harm us. We refer to these spirits as demons," Christopher responded without flinching.

"And that's what you think the entity in my house was?" I asked.

Christopher and Lovie nodded together, but it was Christopher who answered. "Yes, indeed." Then he cleared his throat. "As I was saying," he started with a discouraging glance directed my way. "The spirits who we are most interested in contacting are those who travel both planes and can, therefore, give us the information we seek."

"An' we have had the best luck in contactin' these sorts o' spirits at the LaLaurie Mansion an' the Sultan's Palace," Lovie interjected as Samuel rubbed his back against her legs, like a cat eager for attention. "Both places witnessed horrible crimes an', understandably, many o' the spirits are still stuck, reenactin' their final moments."

"Bien sûr," Drake piped up. "*Of course. Only the two most infamous houses in New Orleans.*" I didn't have the chance to comment because Christopher immediately started talking.

"But we've also come across some very lucid spirits and those are the ones you will wish to speak with," Christopher said.

"So where to first?" I asked.

Lovie frowned while Christopher shook his head. "It's not quite that simple."

"Of course not," I answered with a sigh.

"We need to prepare you for what to expect in both locations, Peyton," Christopher continued. "You should not be surprised to find yourself in another space and time. The spirits can cast a dreamscape before your eyes, a dreamscape of their choosing, and it might be a vision of the goings on that ended their lives. And, if you should find yourself in such a situation, we need to prepare you beforehand, because it won't be pretty."

"*Oui, this is very true, ma minette. This will not be an easy adventure for you to take upon yourself,*" Drake announced.

"Is this where I get another history lesson?" I asked, deciding to pay attention to Christopher at the moment.

"Yes," Lovie answered. "Y'all handle the Sultan's Palace, Christopher. I'm much more familiar with the history o' the LaLaurie Mansion."

Christopher nodded. "The story of The Sultan's Palace takes place in the late eighteen hundreds on Dauphine Street in the French Quarter. The home was built in 1836 by Jean Baptiste Le Prete, a wealthy plantation owner. He purchased the house as a winter home for his family. Now, you must keep in mind that back in Louisiana Plantation society, it was not unusual for wealthy families to keep more than one home, usually one in town and one in the country."

"Right," I answered when Christopher looked at me as if he expected me to comment, before continuing with his story.

Apparently satisfied for the moment, he went on. "Le Prete decided to rent his home in the city during the summer months that he and his family spent at the plantation. Now, this is where the story gets interesting. As far as I understand, based on books I've read on the subject, Le Prete rented his home to a Turkish man who claimed to be descended from deposed royalty.

"*The Turk was none other than the Sultan of Turkey,*" Drake corrected.

"He claimed to be the brother of the Sultan of Turkey," Christopher continued as I got the distinct impression that Drake was shaking his head and crossing his arms against his chest in disagreement. "Apparently, he absconded with the Sultan's treasures, as well as his harem, and found sanctuary in New Orleans."

"I've also heard tell that the Sultan's entourage included eunuchs an' guards armed with scimitars," Lovie added.

"*I had not heard that,*" Drake piped up. "*Funny how the truth becomes distorted over time. You would do better to listen to my knowledge of the incident, ma minette.*"

"*Well, continue to correct them where they go astray,*" I answered with an internal smile.

Christopher nodded. "Yes, I also heard those accounts, Lovie. At any rate, Le Prete did rent his home to the Turkish Sultan's brother, which did not please the neighbors. They complained of noisy parties, strange-sounding music, laughter, the stench of opium, and even scandalous orgies."

"*I must admit, the scandalous orgies were of most interest to me,*" Drake said.

"*Of course they were,*" I muttered in response.

"Then, one day, the joviality ceased," Christopher finished.

"What happened?" I asked, feeling like I was perched on the edge of my seat, even though I was standing.

"*Everyone was murdered!*" Drake interrupted.

"There are divergent accounts on that point," Christopher continued. "But it seems the most popular story is that a neighbor happened to be passing by and noticed blood dripping down the front steps; blood which was coming from beneath the door. The neighbor instantly alerted the police and an investigation was conducted," Christopher said.

"Now, this is where things get a little ugly," Lovie warned.

"Inside the house, police discovered a very gruesome scene," Christopher continued. "Body parts were strewn all over the rooms. Blood covered the walls and had congealed on the hardwood floor. But the corpses were all unrecognizable because every one was missing his or her head."

"*Oui, that is so,*" Drake concurred. "*And though I have never personally interacted with the Sultan or any of his harem, I do understand that it was quite a shame that the ladies were murdered, as they were rumored to be quite voluptuous and stunning.*"

"*Well, maybe if you're lucky, I'll play your wingman at the Sultan's and you can set yourself up with some hot ghost action,*" I grumbled.

Drake chuckled. "Très drôle. *Very funny, ma minette. But you know you are the only woman for me.*"

"*Right,*" I responded before turning back to Christopher and reminding myself I needed to pay attention to the conversation that wasn't going on in my head. "How many bodies did they find?"

"*I believe the count was twenty-five,*" Drake responded.

"Accounts differ, but most agree there were eleven bodies," Christopher answered.

"*Hmm, perhaps it was eleven,*" Drake finished.

"No, more than eleven," Christopher said. "Some seem to think the true Sultan of Turkey located his brother and murdered everyone who had helped him in retribution; others think that pirates marauded the place; while still others believe the crew of the ship that brought the Sultan's brother overseas took notice of the riches and came back later to rob and murder everyone."

"*It was the men from the Sultan's ship,*" Drake announced.

"As ya probably can imagine, Christopher an' I have had lots o' luck gettin' in contact with spirits in the house," Lovie started. "The house is a hotbed fer spiritual activity so you should have no trouble findin' someone ta talk to. An' even though the Sultan's Palace is now apartments, we've been lucky enough ta be invited in a few times by some o' the residents when we were hostin' our own séances. They told us their own stories o' ghosts as well. I'm sure we could easily git another chance ta go back."

"Okay," I started, sighing as I resigned myself to the unenviable task awaiting me.

"The other location where I've sensed a lot o' activity is the LaLaurie Mansion," Lovie started.

"What happened there?" I asked.

"The story dates back ta 1831 when the home, which sits on Royal Street, was sold ta Delphine LaLaurie. Madame LaLaurie, as she came ta be known, was a member o' the French Creole upper class."

"*She was an evil, evil woman,*" Drake announced.

"Madame LaLaurie was wealthy an' connected," Lovie continued. "Three years after the LaLauries moved in, a fire swept through the house an' when the fire department was called in, they discovered the bodies o' slaves in a nearby outbuilding. One that hadn't been burned. The slaves were chained ta the walls an' some were dead an' rottin'. Others were near death from pure torture an' starvation. Some were in cages, an' body parts were everywhere, litterin' the room. Stories claimed they found holes in some o' the slaves' heads, broken limbs, maggots in their wounds, the list went on. There was even some talk 'bout experimentin' where some o' the slaves had been subjects o' sex changes."

"*Oui,*" Drake concurred sullenly.

"Oh my God," I said, shaking my head, finding it inconceivable that anyone could do such hideous things to another living being.

"Another account had LaLaurie chasing a young slave girl around the house and the poor child fell from the third story right to her death. Supposedly, her body was buried in the courtyard sometime during the night." Christopher added, "I believe I have been in contact with the apparition of that slave child."

"What happened to Madame LaLaurie?" I asked, not missing Christopher's frown. He definitely didn't appreciate any interruptions.

Lovie shook her head. "She 'scaped."

"What?" I asked, suddenly angry.

"Once N'awlins po-lice discovered the horrible scene, the citizens demanded Delphine be brought ta justice, but as the story goes, she 'scaped by carriage. Some say she returned ta France, but many believe she jist retired ta Lake Pontchartrain."

"*Drake?*" I asked, wondering if he knew what became of her.

"Je ne sais pas. *I do not know, ma minette. I have always attempted to keep my distance from this case in general as I am not convinced that Delphine LaLaurie was truly a human and not possessed by some malicious demon. In instances such as this one, it is best to leave well enough alone.*"

"There is a tombstone in St. Louis Cemetery Number One that bears Delphine's name," Christopher interrupted. "And it lists her year of death as 1842. It's commonly believed that her children arranged to have her body returned to N'awlins."

Lovie nodded. "Christopher an' I've been ta the mansion on more than one occasion an' we found it very spiritually active. Ya know, Nicholas Cage used ta own the house, an' he permitted us ta visit whenever we desired, but unfortunately, he lost the house in foreclosure in 2009. I introduced myself ta the new owner 'bout a year or so ago, an' he asked me over twice, I believe."

"I was in touch with him recently," Christopher added, "and I do not believe we would have any difficulty in obtaining a personal invitation."

Lovie nodded as she faced me. "So now you jist hafta decide where you'd like ta visit first: LaLaurie or Sultan's . . . ?"

Chapter 13

Even though I hadn't thought much about whether or not I was prepared to venture beyond the confines of my house, now that my spiritual block was removed, I definitely wasn't prepared. Yes, Lovie and Christopher did their damndest to try to prepare me for the fact that there was no longer any interference between the spiritual world and me, but it still wasn't enough. 'Course, to be fair to them, I didn't believe any amount of preparation would truly have made any difference. Until you see your first ghost, you can't quite understand what the situation is like.

As we drove through the French Quarter, on our way to 1140 Royal Street, otherwise known as the LaLaurie Mansion, my eyes went as wide as my gaping mouth. My heartbeat pounded throughout my body, leaving me slightly light-headed.

"Les voyez-vous?" Drake sounded from inside my head. "*Do you see them, ma minette?*"

"*Yes.*"

Spirits. They were everywhere: on the street, floating through buildings, and disappearing into walls. New Orleans seemed to be the residence of more dead people than living. In fact, the real people I saw, strolling up and down Royal Street, remained completely unaware of the spirits that sauntered right through them. The living people just continued to talk about this and that, completely oblivious of a whole other world invisible to their eyes. Sometimes the spirits would float through the tourists and other times, the tourists would walk right through the dead.

"I can't believe how many there are," I said in awe, not able to tear my attention away from the view beyond my windows. But the spirits weren't just located outside Ryan's truck. We drove right through a small mob of them. Some of them reappeared inside the truck, while others just disappeared into the ground, like puffs of transparent smoke.

"*Oui, ma minette,*" Drake responded. "*I, myself, am quite surprised. Lacking the ability to leave the confines of our home, I never had the opportunity to behold so many spirits.*"

"Until you witness the spiritual world for yourself, it is utterly indescribable," Christopher commented. "I share the amazement of which you speak."

"Hmm," I answered, paying little attention to him. I could not restrain my awe and wonder at seeing the sheer number of specters in New Orleans. Some appeared fully detailed, as if a very talented artist had outlined them with a white pencil. Others merely appeared as balls of glowing light, floating and weaving between and through the more defined spirits.

"*Why do some look like people, while others just appear as balls of light?*" I asked Drake.

"*It requires more energy for us to appear in the physical form,*" he responded. "*Those who appear as light are quite simply on their way elsewhere. Those are the types of spirits who can travel between this plane and the spiritual plane, as the warlock explained earlier.*"

"Yes," Christopher continued, confusing me for a second when his timing made it sound like he was commenting on my conversation with Drake. "If you do recall, I played host to quite a few spirits in my time."

I nodded, but his words failed to interest me. Instead, I stared at the ghost of a woman, who was clad in what appeared to be nineteenth-century garb. She stood at the front doors of a stately building on the corner of Royal and St. Philip Streets. The building looked European, featuring the wrought-iron detailing that so iconically signified New Orleans. The figure of the woman was only visible from her waist up. Below her waist, she was no more than a thick fog. Studying her, I could barely make out her tightly curled hair, which was hardly visible beneath her dark-colored bonnet, adorned with an enormous ostrich feather. She wore an empire-waist dress trimmed in velvet. Even though she was somewhat transparent, she wasn't white, as I always imagined a ghost would be. I could see hints of color in her face and clothing—and her bonnet was clearly dark red, her dress gray, with the velvet piping in the same shade of burgundy as her bonnet. She wore a blank expression.

"What do you see, Pey?" Ryan asked, turning to face me.

Glancing over at him, I noticed the spirits of a black woman and a young boy, whom I assumed was her son. They were floating alongside the truck and dressed in tattered and stained clothes. The boy's pants were much too short for his long legs. Their feet were bare and they both wore floppy hats that were purely meant to shade their faces, and were certainly not a fashion statement. The woman's eyes met mine and she seemed to look right through me. There was a misery in her eyes, a certain despair and hopelessness that instantly made my stomach plummet. "Slaves, I bet," I whispered, turning around to face Lovie. "So . . . just as I can see them, can they see me too?"

"Yes," Christopher responded immediately. "Your walls are gone now. If you can see them, they can see you. Think of yourself as linked to the spiritual world. You are no longer bound by your corporeal body."

"Okay," I said as I gulped and faced forward. We drove right through four male ghosts who were working on the road. When I saw their red hair and freckles, as well as their overall haggard appearances, I imagined they must have been Irishmen who fled their own country during the great potato famine. I'd often heard stories about the impact the Irish had on New Orleans history. It appeared that I was reliving a time in history long past—which, unfortunately for these poor, restless souls, they were doomed to re-experience, forever.

"We're here," Ryan announced as he pulled up in front of a beautiful three-story house.

"Béni soit Dieu dans ses anges et dans ses saints," Drake said. "*Blessed be God, in his angels and in his saints.*" I got the distinct impression that Drake was crossing himself, as well as me. "*The LaLaurie Mansion was known for its horrors and spiritual phenomenon even in my day,*" he added.

"*Have you ever been inside?*" I asked.

"Non," he responded immediately. "*I never had the desire.*"

I didn't respond because I had nothing more to say. I looked up at the intimidating property and shuddered. The house was painted the color of dark thunderclouds, fringed with a black wraparound wrought-iron balcony on the first story, which became the porch for the second story. The ten floor-to-ceiling windows on the first floor were oval-shaped on top and square on the bottom. The detailing of the balcony and its intricate black ironwork also covered all the windows. The windows on the second story were square, trimmed by black plantation shutters, while the windows on the third floor featured white ironwork.

"Wow, it's huge," I started.

"As in ten-thousand-square-feet huge," Christopher interjected.

Ryan parked the truck and killed the engine with a glance back at Lovie. "Um, I hope y'all realize I'm goin' in with Peyton?"

Lovie nodded without showing much concern as Samuel appeared around her shoulders and stretched his limbs before dropping his head down on her shoulder and closing his eyes again. "I don't believe the owner will care. He's not 'round here ta care, anyways. He's back in Texas."

"So it's a moot point," Christopher said as he opened his car door and stepped out onto the sidewalk. Eyeing the house, he made the sign of the cross for protection. "Let's hope you get the answers you need here, so we won't have to pay a visit to the Sultan."

"Amen to that," I muttered, still feeling slightly faint at the prospect of entering the LaLaurie Mansion. From the outside, it appeared quite innocent—as if none of the rumored horrors had ever occurred behind its walls. But, appearances could be deceiving.

Searching for spirits, I couldn't see any on the balcony, nor from the windows. I stepped down from Ryan's truck and closed the door behind me. It felt like my feet were anchored in tar with every step I took toward the dreadful place.

"So, who's meetin' us? If the owner isn't here?" Ryan asked Lovie as he appeared beside me, and wrapped a protective arm around me.

She just shrugged. "Dunno. Guess we're 'bout ta find out."

Starting for the front door, but thinking better of it, Lovie turned around and extended her hand to me. When I took it, she closed her fingers around my hand and squeezed it, smiling at me encouragingly. "Jist you remember that I'm here with ya the whole time, Peyton. If it gets ta be too much fer ya, we can always take us a breather. Okay?" It wasn't lost on me that Samuel suddenly sat up, glanced at the intimidating structure, and in a flash, was gone.

"Samuel just disappeared," I said.

Lovie nodded and didn't seem concerned. "He doesn't like ta accompany me on these types o' outins."

"*Remember, mon chaton, we do not have to venture inside. You can always forfeit,*" Drake started.

"*No,*" I responded stonily. "*We're going in.*"

I nodded to Lovie, and my nerves rose to high alert. As we walked across the sidewalk, a deceased group of nuns paraded right through us, no doubt headed for the Old Ursaline Convent on Chartres Street, which was maybe a block away. It felt like we were walking through an exceptionally cold wind, and the hairs stood up on the back of my neck.

"We just walked through a bunch of nuns," I said in a shaky voice. It seemed so surreal, like I was in a dream, and my mind couldn't really accept what I saw as really happening.

Lovie smiled and said, "That's good luck."

When we approached the front entryway, I noticed the black wrought-iron gate, which stood about five feet in front of the door and was opened maybe a foot wide. Gripping one of the spokes on the gate, I pulled it all the way open, figuring it was deliberately left unlocked in anticipation of our visit. We walked into the vestibule and Lovie knocked on the door while I admired the beauty of the arched ceiling, which was adorned with squares of floral reliefs. Even the white, carved front door was a work of art, featuring columns on either side of it. The floor was a checkerboard pattern of white and gray squares.

The door opened to reveal a plump African American woman who greeted us warmly with a big smile. "We been expectin' ya, Ms. Lovie," she said. "I'm the caretaker o' LaLaurie. My name's Hannah."

Lovie smiled as the woman held the door open for us and we went inside. I hesitated only momentarily but Lovie squeezed my hand and I took a deep breath. I could only hope and pray I wouldn't see something that would traumatize me for the rest of my life. As the thought crossed my mind, I observed a couple of balls of light emerging from the staircase. One disappeared into the wall beside the stairs while the other floated into the next room.

"Well, come on in," Hannah said as she closed the door behind us. Then she faced Lovie and ran her hands down the front of her apron, almost nervously. "I had me many a strange experience in this here house, Ms. Lovie." Then she started to fidget with the ties of her apron. "I was wonderin' if it might be okay fer me ta tag along witch y'all?"

Lovie turned to face me. "As long as it's all right with Peyton."

I nodded, giving Hannah a smile, but was unable to speak. I'd been trying to ignore the sudden heaviness I felt in my stomach. I wasn't sure if I was channeling something in the house, or if my unexpected stomach upset was purely the aftermath of my hyperactive nerves.

Hannah beamed at me and began nodding her head vigorously. "Ah, thank ye, Miss Peyton, thank ye."

"Perhaps you can escort us to the rooms where you experienced the most occurrences," Christopher said, seemingly irritated with the eagerness of the woman.

"'Course I can, Mr. Christopher," Hannah answered as she led us through the foyer. Its interior doors were painted white and carved with floral patterns. They were breathtaking. The floors were so dark, they almost looked black and contrasted nicely with the off-white walls. Balls of light continued to appear and reappear at random, some blinking and dissolving into the ether, while others chose to follow us, always keeping within a safe distance of a few feet.

Hannah led us up the stairs to the second level as the dread in my stomach continued to expand. I tried to concentrate on the details of the house to briefly ignore my growing fear. Upon entering the kitchen, I told myself to examine the woodwork, which was painted black against the light-peach color of the walls and the marble island. There was a round table in the kitchen, and Louis XVI-style chairs, also painted black to match the woodwork. The chairs were upholstered in a cream fabric, with a repeating black paisley pattern, interlaced with skulls. As I traced the outline of the skulls with my eyes, three small, bluish lights emerged from the tabletop, spinning around one another as they floated up to the ceiling before they disappeared.

"There were rumors back when Madame LaLaurie owned this place, that she chained the cook ta the oven," Hannah said as she looked at us, nodding her head as if to say she believed the rumors were true. "Some folks say the fire that broke out in 1834 was set by the cook." She sighed while shaking her head. "I ain't nevah had no experiences in here though."

The kitchen opened into the dining room where the walls were painted a light gray with white wainscoting. The silvery silk drapes kissed the dark hardwood floors delicately, but the frieze of angels along the tops of the walls were what arrested my attention. The angels were white, set above a background of gray, which matched the rest of the room.

"Those angels be original," Hannah offered with a proud smile as we all glanced up at the three-dimensional angels and nodded. Seeing the appearance of something holy in this forsaken place planted a shimmer of hope, which I hoped would soon blossom within me.

The dining room was dominated by an eight-person table painted black, and the seats of the dining chairs were upholstered in faux python skin. We continued through the dining room until we emerged into the hall. I spotted a parlor across the way, which was painted the color of heavy cream. Two armchairs upholstered in another shade of the rich cream color faced a bright-red velvet sofa.

We stepped onto the spiral staircase that led to the third floor. As soon as I took the first step, my breath hitched. I paused and inhaled deeply, trying to fight the sudden feeling of dizziness growing inside me.

"Pey?" Ryan asked, and I felt his hand on my back.

"*Ma minette, the spiritual energy here is very strong,*" Drake said. "*You must not let it overwhelm you.*"

"I'm okay," I said immediately, though my voice sounded rather strained. "I'm just feeling a little bit dizzy, that's all."

"We can take our time," Lovie answered.

Taking another deep breath, I noticed Hannah was staring at me curiously. "It's jist the spirits," she said in a low voice. "I feel it sometimes too. It's like they're chokin' me wif their sorrow an' anger." She tightly gripped the banister and took the stairs one at a time, huffing and puffing all the way. I couldn't tell if it was the spirits that caused her such difficulty, or just her lack of exercise.

"Try ta take another step," Lovie said to me as she held my arm, allowing me to lean on her. I took another step, and another, without feeling any better, but, fortunately, no worse. When we reached the third floor, the constrictive feeling I had in my throat disappeared altogether.

"It's gone," I said, rubbing my throat, hoping the discomfort was permanently over.

"Where have you noticed the most ghostly activity?" Christopher asked Hannah, after studying me for a moment or two. He seemed to be trying to decide if I was fit to continue. Apparently, I was.

"Mostly in the Heaven Room," Hannah answered. "Lotsa folks say the torturin' o' the slaves happened in a shed at the back o' the house, but I dunno 'bout any shed. I had mo' scary stuff happen ta me in the Heaven Room than anywheres else."

I spotted a bedroom that was painted in various hues of blue. An enormous four-poster bed dominated the room, covered in black bed linens that only made the room appear darker. The floor-to-ceiling purple taffeta drapes were drawn closed on the windows, imbuing the room with an even eerier ambiance.

"I done left them drapes open," Hannah said, almost to herself, as she shook her head. "Seems whenever I do, though, them drapes jist close theyselves up 'gain."

Two armchairs flanked a large fireplace, which appeared to be constructed of some sort of bluish-green marble. Each of the armchairs was upholstered in bright-blue fabric. "Is this the Heaven Room?" I asked Hannah. My furrowed eyebrows showed my obvious doubt and confusion.

"*It would be more apropos to name it the 'bottom of the sea room,'*" Drake piped up from inside me as I nodded in agreement.

"Oh no," Hannah responded as she continued leading us down the hall. She stopped outside of a small room, which was done up in hues of white and cream. A glass chandelier hung from the ceiling, its ornateness enhanced by the floor-to-ceiling drapes, which were a warm shade of beige. The floor was covered by a soft, white flokati rug. It wasn't lost on me that Hannah didn't or wouldn't enter the room. She chose instead to cling to the railing.

"This be the Heaven Room," she answered, her voice soft.

I nodded, suddenly feeling the urge to enter the room. I knew the drive couldn't be coming from me, so I figured the sprits were somehow calling out to me. I couldn't see any balls of light or anything spectral, just the furniture in the room. Nevertheless, I still felt the undeniable impulse, as though the spirits were pushing me to enter the room.

"Do ya see anythin'?" Lovie asked me pointedly.

I shook my head. "No, but I have an overwhelming need to enter the room," I answered, knowing the fear had to be evident in my voice.

"The spirits want ta tell ya somethin'," Hannah said as she nodded several times. "Sometimes I git that feelin' too, whenevah I'm walkin' past this room. I gotta fight not ta go inside."

I didn't want to find out why she resisted entering the room. I just wanted to get on with my business so I could get the hell out of the LaLaurie Mansion. I vowed to myself, right then and there, that if I was lucky enough to survive this incident, I would never come back. I took a step toward the door when I felt Ryan's hand on my arm. I turned around and looked up into his caring face.

"You don't have to do this, Pey," he said and nodded. "I can tell you're scared to go in there."

"But I do have to," I answered solemnly, trying to smile at him. I removed his hand from around my arm and took a deep breath. With three agonizing steps, I was in the doorway to the Heaven Room. All of a sudden, my breath caught in my throat again and the sensation of complete doom overcame me. I got the distinct warning from my gut that I should stop right now and not go on. But I knew I had to.

With another big breath, I closed my eyes and took a final step, knowing that I would be inside the Heaven Room as soon as my foot touched down. A feeling of numbness started in my toes, working its way up my legs, seizing the center of my body, before maneuvering into my arms and taking over my head. When I opened my eyes, I wasn't in the Heaven Room at all. I wasn't sure exactly where I was. Worst of all, however, I was completely alone. Lovie, Christopher, Hannah, and Ryan were nowhere to be seen.

I heard what sounded like moaning. Turning around to confront whatever was making the noise, I almost couldn't believe my eyes. I gasped as my heartbeat escalated tenfold.

"Mon Dieu!" Drake's startled voice sounded in my head.

There, chained to the wall in front of me, were twelve slaves. They were anchored to the wall by their necks. I wasn't entirely sure, but it looked like four of them were dead—they weren't moving, at any rate. They just hung there, limp and lifeless. The others looked up at me, but seemed to see beyond me, as if I wasn't even there. One girl was missing her arms; the man next to her was missing an eye and had limbs hanging limply by his side that seemed to have been stretched from his body.

"Oh my God," I heard myself whisper. I sensed the tips of my fingers as I brought them up to cover my mouth. I closed my eyes, hoping the horrific scene before me would flee once I opened them again. I wasn't so lucky. Instead, I noticed a mound of amputated limbs in the corner of the room. I never stopped to consider why I couldn't smell anything as putrid as what I saw. The images before my eyes were so terrifying that I couldn't ponder much more than the sight of them.

One woman wore an iron collar with spikes all the way around it, to prohibit her from dropping her head. Beside her was a very old woman who had a deep and festering gash on her forehead. She was mumbling incoherently. Every one of the slaves, whether alive or dead, was incredibly emaciated. Their ribs were clearly visible under their skin and their cheeks were hollow and gaunt. The man with the missing eye also had welts that covered his face and body, the scars from having been flayed by a whip.

Unable to resist, I reached out and tried to pull out the chain that fettered the man to the wall, hoping I could somehow free him. When I touched the chain, however, my fingers went right through it. I opened my palm, but it just passed through the chains again. I realized with some shock what was happening. I was visualizing a dreamscape, like what Christopher mentioned would happen, a video of a time long gone that now only existed in my mind's eye. I swallowed hard as I tried to comprehend what that meant.

Saddest of all, it meant there was nothing I could do to help these defenseless, wretched victims.

I dropped down to my knees, facing the woman wearing the collar. When she didn't focus on me, I waved my hand in front of her eyes. She didn't even blink.

"*She cannot see you, ma minette*," Drake's voice sounded in my mind. "*These people exist on another plane of being. They are not actually here. They are not real.*"

Looking at the woman again, I realized Drake was right. She was simply zoning out on something behind me, something she saw in the distance. I remembered Christopher explaining dreamscapes and the four types of ghosts and figured this must be a case of residual paranormal energy. These spirits were simply reliving the most horrid time in their lives, which was probably also the cause of their eventual deaths.

But residual energy couldn't help me. I had to find a spirit I could converse with, who might explain what was happening in the spirit world. I stood up and looked at the old woman who continued to mutter helplessly. I figured she was also a lost cause. The man with the missing eye was staring vacantly into the distance.

"Are any of you coherent?" I asked, my voice overcoming my panic. I had to get information, and find out what was in store for us on Tuesday. The only way to get that information was to ask these spirits.

Scanning the room, I tried to see if maybe there was someone else there, someone who could help me get the information I so desperately sought. Unfortunately, there was no one else in the small room.

"He comin' the second day."

I heard the voice from the far side of the room, on my right. It was the voice of a woman, but it sounded deep and gravelly, perhaps even pained. I hurried to the corner of the room and dropped down to my knees, spotting a woman looking up at me. She was chained to the wall by her neck, similar to the other slaves, only her hands were also fettered to the floor, held in place by two large wrist cuffs that were bolted to it.

"Mon Dieu," Drake whispered through my mind.

Her right ear was hanging by a shred and her lips were sewn together, the skin bruised and swollen where what looked like rough twine was used for stitches. Of course, I second-guessed myself, wondering how it was possible to hear her voice when she obviously couldn't speak. But when I heard the sound of her breathing in my mind, I realized I was listening to her thoughts.

"Who comes on the second day?" I asked, leaning toward her. I wished there was something I could do to relieve her pain and fear. But that was an impossibility because this was nothing other than a mere whisper from a time long past. I was helpless and there was nothing for me to do but listen to her thoughts.

"He come," she responded, her empty eyes seeming to look right through me.

"*Find out who 'he' is, ma minette,*" Drake prodded.

"Who is he?" I asked, my voice panicked.

"He a demon," she replied, her voice eerily calm, even detached somehow. "He evil."

"Is he coming Tuesday?" I asked. "Is the Axeman coming Tuesday?"

She tried to nod but couldn't because the iron collar she wore jabbed her in the jaw, forcing her head to face the floor again. "He comin' ta kill." Her eyes dropped down to the floor before she immediately glanced up at me again. "He comin' fer you first." I felt my stomach drop as I swallowed hard.

"*You must find out how to stop the Axeman, ma minette.*" Drake's worry echoed through his voice.

The woman's eyes narrowed as she studied me. "You the one got away. He comin' ta finish his bidness." She was quiet for a few seconds. "He comin' ta finish you an' then he goin' after the city."

Suddenly realizing this woman might know the answers to many questions I'd wondered about the Axeman, I decided to try my luck. "The Axeman is a demon," I started. "Does that mean he was released from hell?"

"Yes," she answered immediately. "He do the bidness of his master down far below."

"What is his reason for being here?" I continued, shaking my head to convey that I was at a complete loss as to the Axeman's motives. "Why did he kill all those people almost a hundred years ago and then go silent for so long? And why is he coming back now?"

The woman regarded me blankly for a moment, and I realized maybe I'd asked too many questions. "Evil exist ta balance out good," she said simply, her voice raw and soft. "Whereva ya find good, evil is always lurkin' jist behind." She was silent for a moment or two. "When a demon excape from the heat down below, his sole purpose is ta destroy," she continued. "A demon's goal is ta cause fear an' that fear feeds him."

"So the reason he killed before was to cause fear in New Orleans?" I asked.

She nodded. "He did what he programmed ta do. He a destroyer o' life."

"Then why did he suddenly stop killing and wait almost a hundred years to start up again?" I prodded.

"'Cause the magic of N'awlins is strong," she answered. "An' the magic bound him, kept him from continuin' ta destroy. But like all things, that magic weakened ova the years an' the demon kept growin' stronger wif every day that gone by. He sat back an' waited fer the magic ta fade an' his own self ta grow stronger, mo' powerful."

"And then once he was stronger than the magic binding him, he made his move," I finished for her. She merely nodded and then we both fell silent for a few seconds.

"He comin' back ta continue his killin' streak an' he comin' fer you," she finished, her voice echoing through my mind.

I couldn't speak, couldn't even think. I just stared at her as I got the distinct impression that she wanted me to touch her.

"*No,*" Drake announced as I reached out and settled my hand on top of hers, feeling the cold weight of the cuff that held her in place. As soon as I touched her, I felt a bolt of energy pulse through me. I heard my own gasp as images began filling my head. It was like watching a film reel on fast-forward, with rapid pictures of people I didn't know flashing in front of my eyes. The imagery I saw wasn't pleasant, not by a long shot. There were mounds of bodies littering the streets of New Orleans. One of the offensive visions was of people being bludgeoned by axes. Another showed blood flowing everywhere. I could hear the sounds of people screaming and all hell breaking loose in New Orleans. But most frightening of all, they weren't images of a long-ago era. Each image in my mind reflected modern-day New Orleans.

"Many gonna be murdered," the woman's voice continued in my mind.

"How do we stop him?" I asked, shaking my head as the images continued to plague me. She didn't answer right away. Instead, a visual of the front of my house suddenly interrupted the flow of images in my mind.

"*Release her, ma minette!*" Drake demanded. "*We have seen enough!*"

"*No,*" I answered and continued to focus on the images revealing themselves before my eyes. It was like a camera started zooming into my house as I watched in frozen terror. Once inside my house, I recognized my guest bedroom, only there was blood everywhere and a stray axe left on the end of the bed. The bed linens were stained red and strewn around the room, but it was the body on the bed that made my skin crawl.

"Non, *ma minette! I have seen enough!*" Drake yelled at me.

Even though I didn't want to continue watching, I couldn't stop the pictures from unfurling in my mind's eye. The camera lens of my mind continued to hone in on the lump lying on my bed until I recognized my pink sweatpants and what was once my white, long-sleeved thermal T-shirt, now scarlet red. I could see my blond hair matted with blood.

"*Peyton . . .*" Drake said, and his voice sounded haunted, pained.

"He been let out," the woman continued, her tone of voice now sounding futile. "He been released inta the air. Ain't no stoppin' him now."

"Released into the air?" I repeated, shaking my head and trying to understand what she meant, at the same time attempting to force the images of my own death from my head.

"*Clear your mind, ma minette!*" Drake ground out. "*I cannot stomach these images of you still and lifeless. You must clear your head!*"

I focused on emptying the pictures from my mind and heard Drake's sigh once we were both faced with the blankness of my thoughts.

Drake sighed. "*Now we must understand what she means by the demon being released,*" he said.

"I don't understand," I started, focusing on the hapless woman in front of me as I shook my head. "What does it mean that the Axeman, this demon, was released into the air?" I took a deep breath. "How was he released? Who released him?"

The woman did nothing but incline her head slightly as she seemingly stared right through me. Her hollow brown eyes echoed the answer to my question. I felt my stomach drop as realization dawned through me, causing a bitter taste to crawl up my throat. "We let him out," I whispered as I shook my head, wishing such hadn't been the case.

The woman said nothing but the condemnation in her eyes verified my answer. All of a sudden I was overcome with memories of the time when Christopher and Lovie performed the exorcism on my house. When they had evicted the malevolent spirit of the Axeman, all the windows had blown out.

I felt my heart stop for a moment and recalled Christopher's first words after the entity had shattered the windows: "*We forced the entity from the house. It is only natural that it blew all the windows to escape.*"

"Oh no," I heard myself whisper as I continued to shake my head. "We forced it out. *We* allowed it to escape."

The woman nodded slightly. "It been thrivin', growin' stronger, gettin' mo' powerful." She was silent for a few seconds. "It been pullin' energy from the spirits o' N'awlins. It eatin' us up ta make isself bigger. Ain't a thing we can do, neither. Jist lettin' it swallow us up whole."

I figured the fact that the entity was "eating up" the spirits in New Orleans, feeding on them, was the reason why they were all in a flux lately and the reason why Samuel hadn't been able to make contact with Lovie. The spirits were losing their power.

I looked closely at the slave woman and felt my eyes widen. "There has to be some way to stop it."

She shook her head as far as her restraint collar would allow her. "It too strong ta stop now. N'awlins gonna be a river o' blood."

I shook my head, refusing to accept her prediction. "No, there has to be some way to stop it. Just tell me what I need to do. Tell me how to stop it."

I heard the sound of the woman's laugh echoing through my mind. "Only way ta stop him was ta stop him 'fo' he got so powerful. You shoulda stopped him when he first made hisself known."

"We tried to stop him!" I argued, remembering the exorcism.

But the woman shook her head emphatically. "No. You shoulda stopped him the *first* time he made hisself known!"

I shook my head, not following her. "But the first time he attacked anyone was in 1918," I said as my voice began to trail. The slave woman just nodded, as if I'd hit the answer right on the head. "You mean stop him by going into the past?" I asked, thoroughly confused.

"Yesss," she hissed, her voice now sounding more pained. "The madam comin'," she explained as her tone of voice became precarious. "She gonna punish me fer talkin'."

"Wait, please," I said, raising my other hand to her wrist. "Please tell me how to stop the Axeman."

She brought her face to mine with piercing eyes. "Ya gots ta go back ta the beginnin', back a century, an' git rid o' him. You gotta rid yourself o' that demon. Then he nevah gonna come back."

I nodded as I stood up and backed away from her. She was beginning to grow transparent. I glanced at all the other slaves and realized they, too, were fading. Little by little, the glow of cream-colored paint consumed their outlines. I blinked and found myself facing a white ceiling. Turning to my left, I realized I was back in the Heaven Room. People surrounded me. I blinked another few times and looked around, only to discover I was lying down on a bed.

"Peyton, you all right?" Lovie asked as she studied me.

"What? What happened?" I asked.

"You passed out," Ryan answered as I realized he was holding my hand. "You took one step into this room an' then fainted."

"So we put ya on the bed," Hannah added.

"Did you make contact?" Lovie asked as my attention returned to her. I nodded and remembered the spirit I'd met. My heart felt heavy. "What did the spirits tell ya, Peyton?" Lovie continued.

I sighed, suddenly feeling drained and exhausted. "She told me that in order to stop this demon, the Axeman, from killing many people in New Orleans on Tuesday, I have to go back to the beginning and make sure he never escapes into the present." Of course the woman had also foreseen my own death but that was a detail I didn't want to share with anyone, mainly because I didn't want to put that weight on Ryan's shoulders. I didn't think it would be fair or right to saddle him with information he could do nothing about. I wanted to spare him the pain because I loved him.

"What does that even mean?" Ryan demanded.

"It means," Christopher answered. "That we need to pay another visit to Guarda."

"Guarda?" I repeated, my stomach dropping. "Why?"

Lovie nodded. "Because she's the only one I know o' who can weave a spell that would allow Peyton ta return ta the year 1919 an' stop the Axeman once an' fer all."

Chapter 14

It started to rain by the time we reached Guarda's hovel. It seemed like whenever a visit to Guarda was in the cards, the heavens themselves wept. I didn't know why, exactly, but the thought of Guarda always gave me a sinking feeling in the pit of my stomach. The depth of my distrust and dislike for her didn't really make a lot of sense, because it wasn't as though she'd injured me in any way. If anything, she'd only helped us. So why was it, I wondered, that I couldn't get rid of the bad taste Guarda left in my mouth?

"Je suis profondément préoccupé," Drake started. "*I am deeply concerned, ma minette. I do not know what to make of our visit to LaLaurie.*"

"*What to make of it?*" I responded in a patronizing tone. "*I know exactly what to make of it! Tuesday will mean not only my death, but also the deaths of who knows how many people in this city!*"

"*Oui,*" Drake replied as he cleared his throat. I could just see him giving me that frown that meant he didn't appreciate my sarcastic tone. "*It is also a well-known fact, mon chaton, that spirits usually tend to exaggerate and many can be accused of outright lying.*"

"*Well, in this instance, I think it's better to err on the safe side and suppose the spirit from the LaLaurie Mansion was telling us the truth,*" I replied, figuring there was really no other alternative. As far as I was concerned, disregarding the spirit's advice might result in our own peril.

"*Oui,*" Drake said again. "*I believe we are stuck between the proverbial rock and a hard place, mon chaton. I do not know which direction we should turn.*"

"*I think we're going in the right direction,*" I answered, and sincerely hoped I was right. "*Now I have to focus, Drake,*" I finished as I glanced around the darkness of Guarda's house, trying to avoid getting creeped out by it.

"*Oui,*" he responded.

As to Guarda's, the one thing that provided some relief was that I wasn't alone—Ryan and Lovie came with me. Lovie insisted that Christopher remain in Ryan's truck, apparently because she worried Guarda wouldn't help us if Christopher was present. I made a mental note to myself to ask Lovie just what the situation was between the hostile warlock and Guarda. For now, though, my attention was reserved for more impending subjects.

For one, I found it uncanny and off-putting that Guarda's attention hadn't shifted from Ryan once since he'd walked through her front door. Lovie and I might as well not have been there for the amount of attention she paid us.

"Ahem," Ryan cleared his throat, obviously uncomfortable with Guarda's scrutiny. We'd just finished telling her about our trip to the LaLaurie Mansion, and the ensuing trouble that was predicted on Tuesday.

"Tell Guarda the rest o' what the spirit tol' ya, honey," Lovie suggested.

"Um," I started, finding it difficult to engage Guarda while she was so blatantly staring at Ryan. "The spirit said that New Orleans would be a river of blood on Tuesday if we failed to go back to 1919 and stop the Axeman demon. Apparently, he needs to be destroyed or exorcised, or whatever it is you do to a demon to permanently eradicate it. And all of it must happen back in 1919, before he can travel to present times," I explained, shaking my head, not even really comprehending what my words meant. Time travel? I didn't even know how that was possible, even with voodoo hoodoo magic.

Guarda nodded although she continued to watch Ryan. For someone who didn't appreciate strangers, she could've fooled me. "You gotta name?" she asked him at last, eyeing him directly. Apparently, everything I just said went in one ear and out the other without so much as a nod of acknowledgment.

"Kelly, ma'am. Ryan Kelly," he answered with a hesitant smile as he held out his hand to her in his true Southern, genteel way.

Guarda glanced at his large hand and took it, but did not shake it. Instead, she ran the pads of her fingers over his palm as she closed her eyes and her mouth twitched. Ryan swallowed hard and glanced over at me with a dumbfounded expression at which I just shrugged, as if to say I didn't have any answers for him. Meanwhile, Guarda ran her fingers up his wrist and farther still until she reached the junction where his lower arm met his upper one.

"Yes, you'll do," she said, and Ryan frowned at her, obviously not comprehending her meaning. "Ya got the blood o' the South in yer veins," she continued, lisping since both her front teeth were missing.

Ryan looked down at her and nodded as he eluded her grip and she dropped her arm back to her side. "I'm born an' raised in N'awlins," he said as he came to stand beside me.

Lovie cleared her throat and shifted her weight from one hip to the other, obviously uncomfortable with the bizarre situation. "Guarda, did ya hear what Peyton said?" she asked hurriedly.

Guarda threw Lovie a scowl. "'Course I heard! Mah ears are workin' fine, woman!" Then she faced Ryan again and studied him, her cloudy eyes narrowing. "How ya feel 'bout 'nother man bein' inside yer woman?"

I could hear Drake's chuckle inside my head as my mouth dropped open. I watched Ryan's eyebrows meet in the middle and it occurred to me that Guarda must have been referring to Drake. "I, uh, I think she's talking about Drake," I said quickly, afraid Ryan's temper was about to emerge.

"What does that have to do—" Ryan started, shaking his head with a perturbed expression.

"Jist answer the question," Guarda interrupted as she crossed her arms over her flat chest.

"I don't like it," Ryan said with a tight jaw before he settled his eyes on her. "Now can we move on to the reason we're here?"

Guarda just stared at him for a few more seconds before she sighed and dropped her attention to her hands, nodding. She glanced up at me and her eyes seemed to harden. "You gonna be dead come Tuesday."

"What?" Ryan yelled as he took a few steps toward her, his anger evident in his voice. I immediately stepped in front of him and held my palm against his chest, trying to calm him. I hadn't exactly told him everything the spirit woman at the LaLaurie Mansion had told me concerning what awaited us on Tuesday. Now it was coming back to bite me in the ass, thanks to Guarda.

"Maybe, but maybe not," I said, taking a deep breath as I faced Ryan. "Yes, Tuesday is going to be unpleasant," I started. Ryan frowned at my use of the word "unpleasant." "Unless I can return to 1919 and get rid of the Axeman first."

"Is that what the spirit told you?" Ryan demanded in a hushed tone, his eyes begging me to refute the information. I just nodded.

"Riddin' yerself of a demon ain't no easy feat," Guarda announced.

"We need yer help," Lovie said, taking a few steps toward the older woman. "Whateva payment you got in mind," she started.

"I already got mah payment," Guarda lashed out as she turned to face me before her gaze rested on Ryan again. I didn't know why but I had the distinct feeling that Ryan was of much interest to Guarda. Yes, she appeared to be taken with him but there was something more to it than that. She was looking at him like I imagined the witch had looked at Hansel and Gretel.

"Okay," I said, as I reached over and took Ryan's hand, feeling strangely protective of him. As to Guarda mentioning payment, I was confused. Hopefully she simply meant that Lovie had already paid her more than enough cash, something which I was more than sure I would be billed for later. I could only hope, however, it was as simple as that.

"I haven't paid ya anythin', Guarda," Lovie said suspiciously.

"I been paid in other ways," Guarda snapped as her lips parted into something that almost resembled a smile—aimed at Ryan. "I helps ya."

"I still don't understand what all this talk about returnin' to 1919 is all about," Ryan started, alternating his gaze between Lovie and me. Apparently, Drake and I weren't the only ones who were confused. "That sounds like crazy talk."

"The last time 'fore now that the demon made hisself known was 1919. It was the last time he spilt blood," Guarda said with a shrug, like the answer was obvious.

"It's not possible to go back in time," I said, recoiling at my own words even as I uttered them.

"Ain't nothin' impossible in the spirit world," Guarda retorted as she turned her back on us and hobbled into her kitchen. She started opening her cabinets and pulling items out that I couldn't see, given how dark her house was.

"The spirit world doesn't recanize time," Lovie explained. "Time doesn't exist in the spiritual plane like in our world. Time simply stands still, which is how spirits can exist in our time an' think they're back in their own time. As far as they know, their world is unchanged—everythin' remains as it always was ta them."

I nodded, thinking that part made sense. But I still wasn't sure how my going back in time could work because I wasn't in the spiritual world. Then something occurred to me. "Am I able to manipulate time because part of me is Drake's spirit?" I asked.

"*Ah,* très vrai," Drake said. "*Very true, mon chaton.*"

Lovie nodded. "Somethin' like that, yes."

"So how does this work?" I continued, putting aside my understanding, or lack thereof, of the specifics of time travel. The other questions I had seemed more pertinent at this point. "Will I actually be back in the year 1919? Or will I just be dreaming or hallucinating or something?"

"As far as yer concerned, you will be in 1919," Lovie answered with a shrug. "I dunno fer sure how it all works but—"

"Yesss," Guarda hissed as she stumbled back into the living room and handed me a plastic bag of what looked like sticks of incense. "Yer gonna be in 1919." I couldn't say my attention was on the contents of the bag, though. Instead, I watched as Guarda hobbled over to the wall of skulls and pulled the closest one down, handing it to me. I was reluctant to touch it. "Go on," she said as she shoved the thing toward me.

"*Do not touch it, ma minette!*" Drake said, sounding panicked. "*I do not trust this woman! Perhaps the hideous thing is charmed?*"

"*What could be her reason for charming it?*" I thought back as I accepted the skull and my skin began to crawl at the thought of how perfectly smooth the cranium was.

"Is that a real human skull?" Ryan asked as he studied it with a shocked look that quickly turned to revulsion.

"'Course," Guarda responded as she busied herself at a table in the far corner of her living room. It was concealed by a red tablecloth and covered with all sorts of vials, candles, dolls, and other things that defied categorization. She picked up the various vials and studied them for a few seconds before putting them down again and moving on to the next.

"Is it legal ta own human skulls?" Ryan inquired, his posture uptight and uncomfortable.

Guarda glanced back at him and smiled a toothless, gummy smile. "Everyfin' I does is legal."

Not wanting her to elaborate, I changed the subject. "Going back to this whole time travel thing . . ." I took a deep breath. I tried to make sense of something that, by its very nature, defied logic. "If I really am going to be in 1919, how will I know where to go or what to do? How am I going to even find the Axeman?" I took a breath. "What day will I go back to, exactly?"

"*Will I be there as well?*" Drake piped up. "*Or will I still possess your body?*"

"And would Drake be alive then? Or would he still be inside me?" I asked, cringing at my word choice as soon as the last sentence left my mouth. I glanced up at Ryan and smiled sheepishly in apology.

"I don't want you doin' this alone, Pey," Ryan said, his expression seeming harder.

"She ain't got no choice. She gots ta do it alone," Guarda answered as she apparently found whatever vial she was looking for and carried it over to a cabinet beside the table. She set the vial down on the edge of the table and opened the cabinet, reaching for a large decanter of clear liquid. She pulled the top off the decanter and uncorked the vial, pouring maybe two ounces of the clear stuff into the vial, which already contained about an ounce of a light-blue liquid. She recapped the vial after putting the decanter back into the cabinet. After she shook the vial for a few seconds, she studied it before nodding with contentment.

"What do you mean?" I asked.

"You's the only one wif a direct connection ta the spirit world, since you got a spirit in ya. So you's the only one can bridge the gap 'tween this world an' that one," Guarda answered as she handed the vial to me. Realizing my hands were already full with the skull and the bag of incense, Ryan accepted the vial for me.

"What is all this stuff anyway?" he asked as he inspected everything she'd just handed us.

"Three sticks o' incense," Guarda said as she gestured to the plastic bag in my hands. "Frankincense fer summonin' spirits. Aloeswood ta dispel evil spirits." I assumed that was to help me get rid of the demon of the Axeman, a task that required further clarification. "Myrrh fer protection an', co-in-cidentally, it also known fer stimulatin' sex-u-al-i-ty," Guarda finished with another gappy smile directed at Ryan.

"Why—" he started, but I shook my head.

"Don't ask," I warned as I offered him a little smile that he returned.

"The skull is fer travelin' from this world ta the spiritual one," Guarda continued. "It's yer guide," she said to me. "An' ya gonna drink the contents o' that vial ta git there." Then she reached for a coiled snake candle, which was sitting on top of the table beside her and handed it to me. "Burn this an' this one too," she said as she handed me a red candle that was in the shape of the devil. Lovie accepted them both for me, looking at each of them quizzically as she did so. I wasn't sure why, but the snake candle seemed somehow familiar to me, like I'd seen it before. I brushed off the feeling of déjà vu and figured I could have seen the candle on the last visit we'd made to Guarda's. Or maybe I'd seen something similar at Lovie's store.

"Ta answer yer questions," Guarda continued as she worked her way back into the living room. She sat down in the only chair that stood in the corner of the room, beside the wall of skulls. "Once ya drink mah tonic, it'll put ya inta a trance-like sleep. When ya wake up, you'll be in 1919, in the same spot ya went ta sleep in. An' ya ain't gonna hafta go far ta find the Axeman. He already lookin' fer ya." She took a shallow, raspy breath. "He been lookin' fer ya all along. You an' he got some unfinished bidness 'tween the twos o' ya. I dunno nothin' mo' 'bout it than that."

I swallowed hard, but decided not to press her on that point. Instead, I recalled the other questions that required answers. "How will I know what day it is when I wake up?"

"You gonna hafta go back jist befo' the Axeman's last kill," Guarda answered.

"What does that mean?" I demanded. "A day before? An hour before? What?"

Guarda narrowed her eyes. "No mo' than a day 'fore the Axeman kills 'gain. An' don't be thinkin' yer gonna be no hero an' try ta stop 'im from killin'. It ain't up ta us ta change the course o' history."

I wasn't sure how that information sat with me but I left it alone for the time being, paying attention to the logistics instead. "How do I pinpoint the date so I make sure I go back on the right one?" I asked.

"You gonna keep the date in yer mind when ya do yer ritual," Guarda responded. "Yer will is what's gonna make things happen." Then she silently eyed me for a few seconds.

I nodded, figuring the whole thing followed the same lines whenever I dealt with the spirit world in general—thinking things to make them happen, or not happen, as the case may be.

"Will her corporeal body be sent back to 1919?" Ryan asked.

Guarda and Lovie both shook their heads, but it was Guarda who responded and, surprisingly, looked at me, rather than Ryan. "Yer body gonna be here, on this plane, the whole time. But ya ain't gonna be awake. People not knowin' better would think ya was in a deep sleep."

Hmm, so maybe it was just my spirit that would go back to 1919? "Can I die then?" I inquired.

"'Course," Guarda answered, shaking her head like I was stupid for asking the question in the first place. "If yo' mind thinks yer dead, yer as good as."

Fear began to well up inside me. I just couldn't seem to accept knowing that my life was on the line. "And what about Drake?" I asked, detecting his impatience as it swelled up inside me.

"What 'bout 'im?" Guarda asked.

"Will he be alive in 1919? Or still possessing me?" I answered, hearing the tremor in my voice.

"He be alive jist as he once was," Guarda said, sounding bored.

"Will he know who I am?" I continued.

"Ya jist touch 'im an' he'll know who ye be," Guarda answered. Then she stood up and started for the door. "Now all's ya gotta do is burn dem candles an' incense an' drink half that tonic. Put the skull in yer lap durin' the ritual an' you be on yer way." She sighed for a few seconds and had to stabilize herself against a nearby chair when she started to waver a bit. "By some miracle, if'n you is able ta exorcise that demon, ya jist drink t'other half o' that tonic an' next thing ya knows, y'all be wakin' up in yer own bed."

"But how do I defeat the Axeman?" I asked, my voice cracking because it seemed like Guarda was rushing us and I still had a myriad of unanswered questions floating through my mind.

"Only you can answer that question fo' yerself," Guarda replied.

"What do you mean?" I demanded as my stomach flip-flopped on itself and I started to feel nauseous. "I know nothing about defeating demons!"

"Y'ull know what ta do when the time comes," Guarda responded stoically. "Ain't nothin' mo' I can say on the subject." Then she walked to the front door and opened it, to signify that we'd worn out our welcome.

“I’m not sure what game Guarda is playin’,” Lovie said as she sat down beside me on my bed later that evening. She studied the red candle, which was shaped like the devil. Christopher nodded, but didn’t say anything. He just continued staring out of my bedroom window as if he was half expecting someone to walk up my driveway.

As for me, I was so overcome by the shock of what I was about to do—time traveling—that I felt completely numb. I didn’t really comprehend how I would dispel a demon, which I was in no way prepared for. When I questioned Lovie about it, she supplied me with an arsenal of exorcism implements: a red candle for Saint Michael; a small bowl meant for holy water; a vial of holy water; a small bowl of kosher salt; a swinging incense censer; a purification blend of incense made up of frankincense, myrrh, and benzoin; a dagger made of iron, and tied with a red thread knotted nine times (a ward against dark powers); and a spirit bell. “You really think I’ll be able to bring all this stuff with me?” I asked, even though I knew the answer was no. As far as I could tell, all of the time travel accoutrements would purely exist in my head.

Lovie nodded as she handed me a folded sheet of paper, on which she’d written down precise instructions. They said how to carry out the exorcism ordeal and what, exactly, I needed to repeat and when. “Here’s your instructions, honey,” she said as she tucked the sheet into the bag containing the implements of exorcism. Apparently, like me, she didn’t buy into Guarda’s whole notion that I would know how to rid myself of the demon when the time came.

“What did you mean when you said you didn’t know what game Guarda was playin’?” Ryan asked from where he stood in the doorway as he watched us both. He leaned against the doorjamb with his arms crossed against his chest and one leg over the other. With his dark-blue jeans and green-and-blue-plaid, flannel shirt, he looked like he stepped straight out of an L.L.Bean catalog.

Lovie shook her head and picked up the silver candle shaped like a coiled snake. "A candle shaped like a snake is used in rituals where the outcome is ta bind or control someone," she said as she looked at the red candle in the shape of the devil. "An' this candle is used fer commandin' lust." She took a deep breath. "Red is the color fer courage an' victory. So ya put the two together, this candle is sure ta control someone's lustful appetite."

"Huh?" I asked, already confused. "Why would Guarda be interested in controlling my sex life?"

"I dunno," Lovie answered with a frown as she studied both candles that Guarda had given me. She shook her head as if to say she was at a complete loss. Putting the devil candle on top of my bed, she gave her full attention to the snake candle. "I'm mo' concerned with this one," she said after a protracted silence. "Silver is the color o' moon magic, goddess magic."

"What does that mean?" Ryan demanded.

"It means that the candle calls on the magic of the moon, which is an incredibly powerful being," Christopher answered from where he stood in solemn silence by the window. "It strengthens the power of the snake candle." He sighed. "And, yes, I too am concerned by this."

"Why?" Ryan asked, spearing both Lovie and Christopher with his gaze.

Lovie shrugged. "It could be nothin', but I find it a little odd that Guarda is requestin' us ta burn a candle laced with magic that allows one person ta control another."

"Maybe it's for me to be able to control the Axeman?" I asked, not intending to be the devil's advocate, but there it was.

Lovie nodded at the same time that Christopher cocked his head to the side, as if he was just now considering that angle. "That could very well be," Lovie admitted as Christopher nodded. "But the part that makes me scratch ma head is that both you an' me cain't remember a thing that happened ta us when we was at Guarda's gittin' yer block removed."

"A very strange happening indeed," Christopher agreed. "It makes one wonder what Guarda felt she needed to cover up."

"Right," I said before realizing I wasn't really following the conversation at all, and shook my head. "Wait, what do you mean?"

"Mind scrapin' is standard procedure when someone don't want someone else ta know what's been goin' on," Lovie answered.

"Why didn't you mention this to us earlier?" Ryan asked Lovie as he folded his hands across his chest and looked irritated. "That sounds like important information."

"At first, I didn't think nothin' of it," Lovie answered. "It isn't so uncommon fer this sort o' thing ta happen after a major episode o' magic. I figured Guarda's magic was so intense when she was removin' Peyton's block that it naturally scrambled our memories." She took a deep breath. "But now, seein' these candles, I'm startin' ta rethink that angle."

"But why would Guarda want to control Peyton, Lovie?" Christopher asked. He might as well have substituted my name for "chopped liver."

Lovie shrugged. "Why does anyone want ta control anyone else? An' further, who am I ta say what dark thoughts haunt that woman's mind?" Christopher nodded, apparently satisfied with her response. "My question is, just what is Guarda coverin' up?" Lovie continued.

"That could be a mystery we might never solve," Christopher answered.

"So we just don't burn those two candles," Ryan said as he pointed to the snake and devil candles with a shrug. "End of story, right?"

Lovie shook her head. "If we don't do everythin' as Guarda tol' us, it could mean the spell won't work just right." She sighed as Christopher nodded.

"It could be that the snake candle is part of the magical net Guarda wove for you, Peyton," he said.

"Yep, we gotta do it jist how Guarda tol' us to, otherwise we takin' too big a chance," Lovie concurred. "But that isn't ta say we cain't work in our own magic ta thwart evil intentions," she finished. She reached inside her fabric bag where it sat on my bed beside her and pulled out a white candle. "I planned fer this," she announced. "I anointed this candle with clarity oil an' Abre Camino herbs."

"What is clarity oil?" I asked, watching her set the candle on a piece of what looked like charcoal on top of my bedside table.

"This candle is designed ta give clarity to a situation an', in its way, ta break through the artifice created by magic," Lovie answered.

"Um, what?" I asked, none too eloquently.

"The purpose of the clarity candle is to break any spells of control or compulsion which might have been placed on you," Christopher answered, rolling his eyes like I was slow.

"Oh," I said as I faced Lovie, who was busily lighting the white clarity candle.

"Now, Peyton, I'm goin' ta repeat Psalm 134 eight times, an' while I'm doin' that, ya need ta hold in yer head the idea that any ties or binds from Guarda ta you are done away wif, ya understand?"

I nodded and closed my eyes, finding it easier to concentrate without the distraction of everyone surrounding me. Seeing only the darkness of my eyelids, I imagined all ties to Guarda dissolving away as Lovie began reciting the psalm.

"Praise the Lord, all you servants o' the Lord who minister by night in the house o' the Lord. Lift up yer hands in the sanctuary an' praise the Lord. May the Lord bless ya from Zion, he who is Maker o' heaven an' earth."

She repeated the psalm another seven times as I did my damndest to concentrate even harder until I was pretty sure that any claim Guarda previously had on me was now done away with.

"We should be okay now," Christopher announced as I opened my eyes.

"*Ma minette,*" Drake piped up suddenly, and I realized he'd been strangely quiet for the last few minutes. "*I am fearful for you,*" he started. "*I know your mind is made up, so I will not attempt to talk you out of it.*"

"*Drake, you know what's going to happen Tuesday if we don't go through with this,*" I replied.

"*Oui, oui,*" he answered hurriedly. "*That is why I am not going to attempt to change your mind. I just . . . I want you to know, mon chaton, how much I care about you.*" He was quiet for a few seconds before making the sound of clearing his throat. "*I wish you much luck, mon amour,*" he finished, and I was left with the distinct impression that he hadn't said everything that was on his mind.

"*Thank you, Drake. I'll see you soon,*" I said, trying to sound as happy about it as I could.

Sighing, I faced Lovie, who nodded at me before looking at Christopher. She motioned to the skull, which was sitting on the floor of my bedroom. I didn't like the idea of putting it on my bed or my bedside table, so I relegated it to the floor and did my best not to look at it. Christopher reached for it and carried it between both of his palms with his arms extended out in front of him, looking odd, to say the least.

"It needs to go in your lap," he said, offering the skull to me.

"I know," I responded as I begrudgingly accepted it, placing it on my lap before I faced Lovie and sighed. "So this is the part where we send me back?" I asked, even though the question was a rhetorical one. Knowing we'd done everything we needed to do up to this point, I took a deep breath as I brought my eyes to Ryan only to find his eyes were already riveted on me.

"Could we have a few minutes, please?" Ryan asked Lovie and Christopher. They both nodded and left the room as Ryan walked from the doorway to my bed and sat down beside me. He took my hand and closed my fingers into my palm as he covered my hand in his. "I'm not goin' to pretend to understand what's goin' on here," he started as I lost myself in the depths of his amber eyes. "But I am goin' to tell you that I'll stay right here with you the whole time, Pey."

"Thank you," I said with a bittersweet smile as I felt the sting of tears burning my eyes. I blinked them back furiously, chiding myself that Ryan needed my strength right now, not my fear. Maybe, more truthfully, I needed my own strength.

Ryan leaned into me and held my cheeks between his hands. "I know you can do this, Peyton," he whispered. "I've got all the faith in the world in you."

I couldn't say anything, so I just nodded and closed my eyes tightly once I felt them growing wet. I took a deep breath and forced all melancholy thoughts from my mind so I wouldn't start crying.

"I love you, Peyton," Ryan said softly as I opened my eyes. He leaned into me and the feel of his lips on mine was pure bliss.

"I love you too," I said as I pulled away from him and shook my head, not liking the territory this conversation was headed into. I wasn't prepared to say good-bye to him. I wouldn't allow myself to even comprehend that possibility. "We aren't saying good-bye," I announced sternly. "This isn't good-bye, Ryan."

"No, this isn't good-bye," he answered with a haunted smile as he nodded and sighed. "I will never say good-bye to you, Pey, not when we've only just found each other. No, this isn't good-bye."

I smiled up at him and forced the tears back from my eyes because I was more than aware that this moment could very well be the last time I ever saw him. I wasn't able to speak as I allowed my eyes to gaze on his masculine beauty, to outline the square angle of his jaw and the way his cheekbones were so pronounced when he smiled. His eyes were so warm and with the sad smile on his face, I wanted nothing more than to hold him and promise him that everything was going to be all right.

But as wonderful as that fantasy was, I knew I couldn't bring myself to say those words. Not when my future was cloudy at best.

"This isn't good-bye," Ryan repeated again, bringing his index finger to my cheek as he traced the side of my face.

"Then please tell Lovie and Christopher to come back in," I said in a hollow voice as I closed my eyes and blinked back tears. I would not allow myself to cry. I was strong and capable and I intended to best the Axeman at his own game.

I opened my eyes and found Ryan still gazing at me. He smiled and patted my thigh as he stood up and approached the hallway. As he walked away from me, I thought how incredibly strong and powerful he was. His body was so large, yet sculpted so beautifully with ropey, sinewy muscles. Ryan was a stunning example of a man. I smiled as I realized how absolutely lucky I was to have earned his love. Knowing he would be here, waiting for me, somehow gave me inner strength, and reinforced my resolve to get on with my mission.

I watched Ryan walk through my bedroom door with Lovie and Christopher in tow. I turned to Lovie and nodded, suddenly feeling strangely invigorated and ready. "Let's get this over and done with," I said.

Lovie placed the snake and devil candles on my table and lit both of them. Then she lit the incense sticks and faced me. "Now all ya gotta do is drink half o' the tonic," she said as she fished the tonic from her bag and handed it to me. "An' keep in yer mind the date of October 25, 1919."

On October 26, 1919, Mike Pepitone had been attacked by the Axeman. He was the last known victim to die from the blows of the

Axeman's axe. I figured by going a day before the attack was destined to happen, I could find Drake and persuade him that I knew the Axeman was going to attack again. My hope was that we could take the Axeman into custody together, at which time I could perform the exorcism on him, and release him from the demon's possession.

I wasn't sure how good of a plan it was, but it was the only one I had, so I intended to go with it. I accepted the tonic, but made no motion to pull the top off the vial. "What's the worst that can happen to me if this doesn't go as planned?" I inquired.

Lovie glanced over at Christopher, who shrugged. Then she faced me again. "Well . . ." she started.

"Give it to me straight, Lovie," I demanded.

She cleared her throat. "Put it this way, it cain't be any worse than what's already waitin' fer us on Tuesday."

I nodded, agreeing with her; she had a good point. I removed the cork from the vial of tonic and felt like my stomach was rising up into my throat. The opaque liquid smelled of earth somehow—not an offensive smell, but it didn't exactly make me want to drink it.

I held the vial up to my lips and gripped the handles of Lovie's bag full of exorcism implements. I looked at Ryan, who watched me with doleful eyes. I smiled at him as best as I could, loving him with all my being. Then, I opened my mouth and downed half of the tonic.

Chapter 15

I was swimming in darkness, but it felt balmy and warm. There was a bitter taste deep in the back of my throat that somehow reminded me of what I supposed soil would taste like. Heady and raw, I could only describe the flavor as rainwater after it drips off the branches of pine trees and soaks into the ground below.

Suddenly, the darkness was broken by the smallest speck of white dust. As I gazed at the speck, it grew larger, becoming an amorphous shape. Continuing its expansion, the former speck transformed into a torso with legs, arms, and a head. It began to increasingly resemble a man. The more I studied the strange entity, the more delineated he grew until I could recognize him. "I know you," I said, but my voice sounded foreign and very odd, almost like I was talking underwater.

"'Course you do, baby!" the man replied as his skeletal face contorted into a smile. He was dressed in a black top hat and a matching tuxedo. The circles of his dark glasses kept rotating around and around. Staring at them, I nearly succumbed to the hypnotic cycling.

"Who are you again?" I asked when it became clear that I couldn't remember his name.

The man laughed, but I couldn't understand how that was possible because his mouth never moved. His mouth must have been good for something, however, because he was smoking a fat cigar, which his barely-there lips clamped tightly. The cotton plugs sticking out of his nostrils completely threw me. "I'm the Loa o' the dead," the man said. "An' you, mah pretty little creature, was 'sposed ta visit me in the land o' the dead. We had us a deal or did ya already fergit it?"

"We had a deal?" I repeated, utterly lost. The man drew on his stubby cigar and the smoke poured out from behind his glasses, surrounding me in a smoky hug. I breathed in deeply, and relished the taste of the smoke as it filled me up with its warmth. Suddenly, I had an undeniable yearning and urge to touch the Loa, to know him. But before I had the chance, he began to fade right before my eyes, along with the smoke that emptied from behind his glasses. In fact, it looked as if the smoke itself was erasing him as it wafted and circled over him. The visual of a graveyard, with aboveground tombs reminiscent of Lafayette Cemetery, flashed into my mind.

"Ya needed mah protection, sweet baby," the Loa's voice continued even though he was nowhere to be seen anymore. "An' if'n ya needs mah protection, ya gots ta pay tribute in mah own land."

"The graveyard?" I inquired as his words began to make a little sense to me. "I know! You're Baron Samedi," I announced when it eventually dawned on me.

"An' she hits it right on the nose!" he said with another laugh before unexpectedly blinking back into sight. He dropped his chin and looked at me over his dark lenses, and his eyes glowed white when he took another puff of his cigar.

"I would have come to visit you," I started, shaking my head, "but Guarda made me forget everything you and I talked about."

The all-knowing Loa of the dead nodded and appeared somewhat pensive for a moment or two. "You be careful wif that one, mon chaton," he said, his voice suddenly adopting Drake's accent and tone. It vanished as instantly as it appeared. "An' you come an' visit me real soon, ya hear? I don't like gittin' lonely."

I nodded and Baron Samedi beamed another frightening smile at me before vanishing as if he'd never been there at all. I was left in the void and darkness once again. As I grew more accustomed to the pitch-blackness, it felt like I was starting to sink, dropping through the vast emptiness that had previously engulfed me. My heart rate increased as fear began to flow through me and my breathing quickened. My body began to feel heavier and more substantial, no longer buoyant. I fought hard to stay aloft and to avoid being sucked into the darkness, but no matter how I struggled against it and tried to resist its force, I could feel myself slipping helplessly. I was falling fast.

When I felt my butt hit something hard, I sat up, pulling my legs into my stomach. Blinking against a blackness that wasn't quite so black now, I tried to open my eyes all the way so they could adjust to the brighter atmosphere. I dropped my hands to the ground below me and realized I was sitting on a hardwood floor. I could barely make out the rays of moonlight as they streamed through the floor-to-ceiling windows and illuminated the gold accents of the most magnificent grand piano I'd ever seen.

On wobbly legs, it took me a second to stand up. Once I felt like I could manage, I righted myself, using the piano to lean on. Looking down, I discovered I was wearing a tubular-shaped, very *un*fitted dress in an array of pleats, the hem of which ended just below my knees. The material was a champagne-colored silk, so far as I could see in the moonlight. My feet wore delicate shoes that quite resembled ballet slippers and matched the hue of my dress.

Taking a cleansing breath, I glanced up and noticed an ornate, Louis XIV gold gilt mirror, which hung on the wall beside the piano and reflected the elegance of the piano's three gold legs. I started to take a few steps toward the mirror, but felt uneasy and light-headed as I made my way. When I reached it and saw my reflection, I recognized my own face looking back at me, except my hair was pulled tightly behind my ears and a close-fitting, round hat hugged my head.

"I'm actually here!" I whispered to myself as the revelation dawned on me. "I did it!" My shocked voice could not contain all the wonder and awe that was pumping through me. Fear, anticipation, excitement, and triumph all took turns pounding through me as I realized I'd just accomplished the impossible. I turned on my toes so fast I had to brace myself against the wall before I lost my balance. Once I caught my breath, I took in every detail of Drake's music room as it appeared in 1919. My heart pounding through my chest, I realized the room looked exactly as it did in my dream visit with Drake only a week or so earlier.

I gulped when my eyes settled on the twin leather club chairs that were the color of milk chocolate. Between them, I saw the same table with the same tray holding the same decanter of whiskey, but now, only one glass was present. Still feeling light-headed and slightly nauseous, I took a few strides forward and tried to decide what to do next. Hopefully Drake was home—I figured that would be my first task at hand, to discover where "Frenchy" was.

I closed my eyes as I inhaled deeply and prayed I wouldn't pass out. I just couldn't seem to shake the vertigo that kept returning. I opened my eyes again once I felt better, and took another step, but suddenly my toe bounced off something cold and hard.

"Shitballs!" I said under my breath as I heard the shattering of glass. Looking down at the ground, I realized I had just kicked the other glass of whiskey, which was now all over the floor in an intoxicating puddle of glass shards and alcohol. Why someone would so stupidly put a glass on the floor in the first place was anyone's guess.

My heartbeat started pounding through my head, and I looked around, trying to find something to clean up the mess. But finding nothing, I remembered my hat. Yanking it off, I leaned down and used it to mop up the whiskey while delicately sweeping up the broken glass. "Double shitballs," I said as I winced at the sharp pain on the end of my pinky finger, which told me a stray shard of glass had just found its way into my flesh. I dropped the hat and brought my finger up to eye level, trying to inspect it, just as I saw shadows suddenly move across the walls. It felt like my heart leapt into my throat, and I swallowed it down and forced myself to focus on the shadows. Choking on my own fear wouldn't do me any good. Tracing the shadows to their source, I realized they were coming from a tall, oil-burning floor lamp, which stood in the corner of the room. And standing next to that was Drake, with a pistol aimed at me. Any relief I felt upon recognizing Drake instantly fled, replaced with concern once I focused on the barrel of his gun.

"*Quelle surprise!*" he said in a tone that sounded more amused than angry. "Either you are an ill-timed birthday present, or quite an inept thief," he finished, with his signature engaging grin.

"Drake!" I exclaimed in astonishment. Seeing him now, in the flesh, was an incredible experience. He looked just as he did whenever I saw him in my mind's eye, but there was something slightly different about him. I couldn't quite put my finger on it, though. He was just as handsome as always with his clean-shaven face, square jaw, high cheekbones, and penetrating, dark eyes. But now there was something more youthful about him, a certain adolescence I never noticed in my dream visits with him.

"And how do you know my name, mon amour?" Drake demanded. Although his tone remained playful, there was something in his eyes that told me he was anything but.

Impulsively, I took a step forward only to hear the crunching of glass underfoot, before I felt a sharp piercing as a shard of glass penetrated the bottom of my shoe and deposited itself into the ball of my foot. "Fuck!" I yelled out as I hopped over to the piano to stabilize myself. I attempted to remove my shoe and assess the damage.

"I must say, my mysterious guest possesses quite the potty mouth!" he remarked with a devilish smirk. "Have we already met, mon amour?" he asked as he lowered the pistol to his side and walked toward me. He was wearing only a pair of white, cotton pajama bottoms, and even though my foot and my hand ached like mad, I still noticed Drake's delectable physique. Ahem, a *very* delectable physique.

"*Have we met?*" I repeated in an irritated tone. I momentarily forgot that to him, we had not met because back in 1919, I was not yet even a twinkle in my great-grandparents' eyes. "Yes," I answered, "we have met." I was still wincing from the pain that radiated from my foot and my little finger. "I promise to explain everything as soon as you put that gun away and help me. Please?" He didn't make any motion to put the gun away or to help me. Instead, he just stood there, as though he were admiring me, albeit amusedly. "And, despite what it looks like, I'm not a thief," I added quickly.

"Oui, I can see that much for myself," he said with a smile as he placed the gun on a side table beside the door. "But my question of what you *are* doing here still remains unanswered, and more importantly, how did you manage to get in? I generally keep all of my windows and doors locked at all times."

With a frown, I raised my eyebrows at him. "And is it customary to allow a young woman to bleed to death in your music room without offering her any help or assistance at all?"

"Perhaps, when said *femme* resorts to breaking and entering? And into a peace officer's home, nonetheless . . ." he replied. Seeing that damned flirtatious smile of his, I assumed he no longer deemed me a threat. He approached me.

"I told you," I started, concentrating on removing the offending piece of glass, which turned out to be quite a small one. "We'll get to introductions in just a second. As you can see, I'm a little preoccupied at the moment." Remembering Guarda's instructions, that I only needed to touch Drake for him to remember me, I figured our introductions would be a relatively quick and easy process.

"And no apology for breaking one of my best drinking glasses?" Drake said as he shook his head and clicked his tongue against the top of his mouth in mock disappointment. Coming to stand right next to me, he reached down for my foot. As soon as he touched me, I felt a jolt of energy shoot straight up my foot and into my legs, which dispersed once it reached the center of my body. It was so unexpected, I gasped. "You have very little pain tolerance, don't you?" he asked with a grin, apparently still unaware of my identity. I would've thought his expression might change after learning who I was, at the very least. "This flesh wound of yours is nothing more than a mere abrasion of the skin," he continued, inspecting my foot curiously.

"Don't you recognize me now?" I asked, wondering why he didn't seem to.

"Now that I've held your foot?" he scoffed with a chuckle. Then he shook his head as he sighed. "*Quelle honte*, what a shame."

"What's a shame?" I demanded.

"That you are so stunning," he said as his attention moved from my head to my chest. "With lovely, large, round breasts," he continued, unwilling to conceal his obvious appreciation for my feminine assets. "I do so abhor these modern female fashions which favor a prepubescent, almost boyish figure," he said as an aside, still shaking his head. He smiled when his eyes found mine again and it became painfully obvious why Drake was always so popular with the ladies. More than just a lady-killer, he had charm, grace, and an endearing sense of humor. "But here you are, your body just begging for me to pleasure it, and yet I fear you have completely lost your sanity," he finished. I frowned at him and wondered if I could get a refund from Guarda.

"I haven't lost my sanity, thank you," I started, my nose pointing up in the air as his expression told me he begged to differ. Fortunately, rather than argue with me, he chose to remove the small shard of glass from the ball of my foot. He then gently lowered my foot back onto the floor and held up the miniscule sliver of glass. It was maybe a quarter of an inch long. I could barely see it in the low light of the room.

"I believe I have recovered the offending piece of glass, mon amour," Drake said with another practiced smile, his expression hinting to the fact that I was completely overreacting because my "flesh wound" could hardly even be considered a wound in the first place. Apparently my slipper shoe had absorbed the majority of the damage. "Perhaps you would like me to bandage your foot now?"

"Yes, please," I answered as I placed my hand in front of his face. "Oh, and I cut my finger too."

"Very well, I shall bandage that too," he said, chuckling softly as he reached for my finger. When he took it, there was still no sign of any recognition on his part. "Perhaps now you will reveal to me how you and I are acquainted?"

We started for the hallway. When we reached the table with the gun, he grabbed it, carefully tucking it into the waist of his pajama bottoms. At the base of the long flight of stairs, he paused and eyed me skeptically. "Given the state of your foot, climbing these stairs might prove something of an obstacle," he said with a lascivious smile, suddenly hoisting me into his arms. It was more than obvious that he was looking for any excuse to do so because he'd made it more than clear that the wound on my foot was anything but concerning.

"I can walk!" I started to protest, but quickly looped my arms around his neck when he pretended to trip. "Smooth, Drake, real smooth," I muttered as I caught him gazing at my breasts again, now barely constrained inside the loosely flowing fabric of my dress.

"The bandages are in my bedchamber," he said with a shrug, as if it weren't his fault they were located there. When we reached the top of the stairs, he didn't set me down on the ground, but continued to carry me into the master bedroom, the same room where I first heard his ghostly footsteps, albeit in the twenty-first century. The thought made me a little nostalgic for the relationship that Drake and I shared in modern times.

I wondered why Drake didn't seem to recognize me, even though we'd touched one another repeatedly. I didn't know how in the world I could convince him that a previous friendship really did exist between us. There was no way I could persuade him that I was possessed by his spirit in my own time, and returned to the past in order to defeat a demon by the name of the Axeman! Nope, he'd sooner have me booked on the closest train to Looneyville.

He kicked open the door to his bedroom and carefully set me down on top of his bed. The room's light source was an oil-burning floor lamp that matched the one I saw in the music room. Then it dawned on me that in 1919, electricity could not have been standard in every home. I looked around and immediately recognized the bedroom from my dream visits with Drake. The dark walnut floors, the three floor-to-ceiling windows overlooking a view I knew so well. I recalled the navy-blue curtains on either side of the windows as well as the charcoal-gray walls. I even recognized the spicy scent in the room, an aroma that uniquely belonged to Drake.

Drake disappeared into the adjoining bathroom and returned moments later with a black, circular tin, which read in white cursive letters, "B&B Adhesive Plaster Tape." "There now, mon chaton, we will have you all mended in a hurry!"

"Mon chaton?" I repeated, wondering if he used the familiar pet name because he now remembered who I was.

"Ah, excuse me, mademoiselle," he started with a shake of his head and an embarrassed chuckle. "In English, I was calling you my kitten."

"I know," I answered immediately, disappointed that he still had no clue of my identity.

"Perhaps you could enlighten me as to our association, mon amour?" he asked, glancing down at me with a raised brow. It was almost as if he was bored being the well-mannered host and wanted to get down to the real nitty-gritty.

I sighed, knowing I couldn't tell him the truth, not if I wanted him to think I was still in control of all my faculties. "Drake, look at me," I said, hoping my tactic would work, but doubting it all the same. He faced me curiously. "Look at my face and deeply into my eyes and then tell me you don't know who I am," I said.

He looked at me. Then he stared at me. Then we both stared at each other. But there was still no spark of recognition in his eyes at all. However, something was certainly sparking in me. And it had nothing to do with time travel recognition. I was completely consumed with the burning urge to taste him. I wanted to touch his lips with mine and feel the wetness of his tongue and mouth. Then, as if turning on the light switch to my libido, I instantly hungered for him, in a desperately ravenous way. The thought occurred to me that this could simply be the work of Guarda and her blasted red devil candle.

"I'm sorry, mon amour; though I will repeat that I find you quite lovely, I cannot place your face," Drake said with a sigh. "Please do not blame me for it, though, as I am certain our time together was definitely worth it."

I frowned. "What time together?"

He unwrapped the bandage, picked up my foot, and studied it for a moment before securing the "plaster tape" on top of my wound. Then he faced me again. "Yes, whatever magical evening we spent together, I am certain was . . . well worth it."

What? Did he think I was just another chick he'd had drunken sex with, and now couldn't remember my name? Great, just great. "I'll have you know," I began my tirade, then inexplicably lost my train of thought. I had the irresistible urge—or was it need?—to kiss him. I grasped the bed linens and shut my eyes to avoid dealing with the passionate force that was growing inside of me.

"You'll have me know?" Drake continued.

"I'll, uh, I'll have you know," I repeated as I opened my eyes, but failed to restrain my sexual feelings from resurfacing. Drake placed my foot back on the bed and, even though it was probably the worst thing he could have done, he came closer to me. He studied me with undisguised curiosity before leaning down and reaching for my wounded finger, which he lifted up to inspect.

"It appears to be merely a tiny sliver, mon amour," he said, in a deep, husky voice.

"Okay," I answered hesitantly as my urge to lick his body almost overwhelmed me. "Then, uh, then you, uh, you don't have to put a Band-Aid on it," I said, gritting my teeth as I tried to remain on the bed. It probably looked like I was struggling to control a serious bout with gas.

He raised a brow in my direction and closed his hand over mine, bringing my fingers to his lips. He gently kissed them while intently staring at me. Guessing his ploy—to lure me into having sex with him—I might have laughed at his blatant attempt had I possessed my wits. As it was, fueled by a passion that burned even more furiously, before I could stop myself, I lurched out toward him. I grabbed the back of his neck, and pulled him down on top of me, while planting my lips onto his.

He melted into me as our lips met. I felt him gyrating his lower body against mine, right before he suddenly went stock-still, and an instant later, pulled away from me. I sat up and, completely against my better judgment, grabbed him by the upper arms. I pulled him back down toward me with great difficulty because he abjectly resisted, while vigorously shaking his head. Since I refused to be ignored, he pinned me down on the bed as he faced me with an expression that revealed shock as well as recognition.

"Ma minette?" he asked with a frown, and both of his eyebrows furrowed in the middle of his forehead.

"You remember me?" I asked, wondering if it was our kiss that had done the trick. I was momentarily relieved that the sexual feelings inside me instantly subdued themselves. Hopefully for a long time.

He shook his head. "*Non*," he started with a sigh. "That is the problem. I do not remember you, though I am overcome by many memories of you and the uncanny feeling that I know you well . . . intimately well."

"Well, we actually don't know each other *intimately well*," I started, even as I realized I was well on my way to knowing him intimately, and the thought didn't exactly thrill me. I attempted to move, but his manacle-like grip on my wrists disabled me. "I think I'm okay now," I said as I blushed from the roots of my hair down to my feet. "I mean, I'm not going to try to seduce you again," I corrected myself, hoping he got my gist.

He frowned, seemingly still worried that I might try to bed him again. But when I returned the frown and even looked slightly ticked off and impatient, he let up. Taking a deep breath, I was relieved to no longer feel that insatiable sexual yearning inside me. Sitting up, I rubbed the life back into my wrists and felt the weight of his stare now upon me.

"How could I not know you and yet possess a myriad of memories, that insist that I do?" he demanded as he stood up and took a seat on the boudoir chair beside his bed.

Scratching the top of my head, I tried to figure out the best way to explain something that, at best, sounded impossible. "Because we know each other from a different span of time," I said.

"A different span of time?" he repeated, frowning at me.

Hmm, so my current explanation wasn't exactly comprehensible. Time to change gears. "Do you believe in magic, Drake?" I asked, hoping to hear an emphatic "yes!"

He laughed. "One cannot live in this city and *not* believe in magic, ma minette," he answered, becoming visibly uncomfortable with the pet name he called me. He shook his head. "I do not understand these feelings I know I harbor for you. When I touched your lips, I seemed to unlock something inside me that makes me believe I care . . . very deeply for you." His eyes dropped down to his hands and he extended his long fingers while continuing to shake his head. "It is not a feeling I understand. I know I have never seen you before, even though I now possess new memories, for which I cannot account. How could I care so deeply for someone I have never met?"

"Magic," I said with a shrug. I also silently gave a prayer of thanks that Guarda's magic finally decided to pull its head out of its . . . "You and I *are* very close, Drake, although not in a way that you might expect."

"Why is it that I feel part of you somehow?" he asked as his eyes pored over me. Apparently, his memories weren't too exact because he obviously didn't realize he had been in possession of my body. And it wasn't like I looked forward to telling him any time soon. I didn't think he would respond well to learning he was a ghost haunting my, er, *our* house.

"Some things are too difficult to explain." I shook my head. "Suffice to say you and I are very close and I've traveled to hell and back to find you, because I need your help."

"*Mon aide*?" he said before shaking his head and apparently realizing he was speaking in French. "My help?"

I nodded. "Yes, Drake, something terrible is happening in this city, something demonic in nature."

He nodded, but didn't look at all surprised. "I am aware," he answered stoically. I guessed his memories were intact enough that this wasn't exactly breaking news. "The demon is the Axeman," he continued in a monotone. "Although I should consider this news, my memories have informed me otherwise."

"Yes," I answered immediately. "Drake, we must catch the Axeman and when we do, we must exorcise the demon inside him and send it back to wherever the hell it came from." And then I realized I had another problem. "Shit!" I said and sighed, realizing my hunch about Lovie's exorcism tools had been spot on. "Lovie's exorcism tools didn't make it here with me!" I said, facing Drake as I realized what that meant. The rest of the tonic that was supposed to get me out of 1919 and back to the present was also in Lovie's bag . . .

"Do not fret, mon chaton," Drake said as he shook his head. "The old woman must have had a reason for telling you that you would know how to deal with the Axeman when the time came." He shook his head again and sighed. "I do not understand how I am even in possession of this information."

I nodded, figuring that he'd somehow accessed my memories about Guarda because as far as I remembered, Drake had been absent through most of my interactions with her. As to the missing bag, I would just have to exorcise the demon without it. I didn't have a choice. "Then you will help me?" I asked him optimistically.

He chuckled and stretched his arms above his head as he sighed. "I do not know if I look for trouble, or if trouble just finds me, ma minette."

"What does that mean?" I demanded, feeling the minutes falling through my fingers like grains of sand.

He smirked a devilish grin. "It means that I am not a man who would ignore the request of a damsel in distress."

Chapter 16

I couldn't sleep all night; but it wasn't really like I expected to, not when there was so much riding on the next day. Regardless, I continued to toss and turn, listening to the chiming of each hour as it pealed from a grandfather clock. The clock stood beside the wall in one of Drake's guest bedrooms, which happened to be on the third floor, next to his bedroom.

After our kiss, which had reinstated Drake's memories, he became very quiet and I figured he was pretty much stunned by the whole ordeal. He politely escorted me to the guest bedroom before retiring to his own bedroom, claiming to have a headache. But, after hearing him pacing in his room all night, I knew a headache wasn't the culprit. Figuring Drake probably needed some time to himself, if only to work through the mess of his thoughts, I left him alone and focused, instead, on the mess of my own thoughts.

A stream of light pierced through the white plantation-style shutters covering the windows and aimed itself right into my eye. I rolled over, hoping and wishing that my exhaustion would finally claim me, because it was imperative that I got some sleep. Exorcising demons without any exorcism implements was hard enough, but to compound that by doing so without any sleep? I didn't think my current condition of fatigue would yield a very happy result.

"Ma minette?" Drake's voice sounded at the door at the same time that I heard his timid knock. "Are you awake?"

"Yep!" I called out, with no inkling of morning voice. "Just give me a second!" I sat up and remembered taking off my shapeless, tubular dress in order to sleep more comfortably in my undergarments. Those undergarments were a pair of short boxer-looking bottoms, which extended to my lower thighs and were a rosy beige color, fringed with beige lace. The matching top was actually cute. Constructed from the same fabric and lace, it looked like a loose-fitting blouse with spaghetti straps. The silk failed miserably at hiding my nipples, though, so it was definitely out of the question for me to receive Drake when dressed in only that.

"*Bien sûr*," Drake called back. "Of course, mon chaton, take your time."

I stood up and retrieved the bizarre dress, which was nowhere near as cute as I imagined 1920s fashions should be. I pulled it down over my head, being careful to smooth my bobbed hair back in place behind my ears. After I was decent, I started for the door and pulled it open, pasting a big smile on my face. "Good morning!"

Drake immediately smiled while taking stock of me from head to toe—making it more than obvious that he appreciated the female shape, even when his mind should have been on other subjects. "Good morning, mon amour," he started, his gaze resting on my breasts for a few seconds before he looked me in the eyes again. "I trust you slept well?"

"I didn't sleep at all," I answered with a shrug, as if to say it wasn't a big deal.

He nodded, frowning. He was wearing dark-gray pants that were nicely tailored, along with a long-sleeved, white-collared shirt, which was tucked into the pants. A navy-blue tie complemented the brown buckskin of his leather shoes. Topping it off with a newsboy cap, he looked ever so charming and handsome. "Oui. Neither did I, mon amour. My mind was much too clouded with questions and concerns that persisted in plaguing me all evening."

"I'm sorry to hear that," I said. I smiled apologetically and shrugged as if to say there wasn't anything either of us could do about our situation.

"Oui, well, it is a trivial point, really," he finished. Then he cleared his throat and took a deep breath. "I washed the whiskey and the glass shards from your hat, ma minette, and left it to dry in the kitchen."

"Thank you," I started, surprised that he would have bothered with such a task. I'd actually completely forgotten about my hat, the whiskey, and the broken glass.

Drake rolled his eyes as if to say laundering my hat wasn't a big deal. "As to your outfit," he said, while looking me up and down again, "you will need something heavier and warmer to wear if we are to spend our evening awaiting the Axeman. I daresay we shall spend a good portion of our evening outside."

"Yes," I answered, further lamenting my bad luck because I'd written the address for Mike Pepitone, the Axeman's final victim, on a piece of paper that I'd securely placed inside Lovie's bag of tricks. "Do you happen to know a man named Mike Pepitone? Or more importantly, where Mike Pepitone lives?" I asked, bracing myself for him to reply in the negative.

Drake shook his head. "But I can search our police records for any and all Pepitones in New Orleans." He inhaled deeply. "Do you know any details about him that might aid us in our quest?"

I nodded as I tried to recall the various articles I remembered reading from the *Times-Picayune* newspaper archives. "He lived at the rear of his grocery store, and if I remember correctly, was in his middle to late thirties." I squeezed my eyes shut and tried to recall the address I'd written down on the white sheet of paper, but the only thing I could remember probably wouldn't do much good. "I know he lived on the corner of two streets. I just can't recall what those two streets were."

"More information is better than less," Drake said with a sigh as he ran his hands through his shiny, soft-looking hair. "I have debated and argued with myself for hours regarding what should be done this evening," he said with another sigh. "Although I would prefer to alert all of the officers at the station, I cannot do so because everyone will question our knowledge, and probably not believe our story. Even though New Orleans as a whole is understanding of ghostly activity, I cannot say the police are." He took a long breath. "Or, worse yet, they might accuse us of conspiring with the Axeman, since we are in possession of information we should not know."

I nodded and agreed, thinking his line of reasoning made total sense. "Right. Telling anyone about it probably wouldn't be very smart."

"Oui," Drake said, rubbing the back of his neck as if he was frustrated or overwhelmed by his thoughts. "Oui, oui," he repeated as his voice started to fade. He began chewing on his lower lip and zoned out on the floor. After a few seconds, he faced me again. "This means we will only have ourselves to rely on."

"Right," I said again, wondering why it was taking him so long to reach this conclusion. For myself, even though I'd figured such was going to be the case, I couldn't say I felt good about it. Instead, my stomach was in knots and my heart was beating so fast, I was afraid I might have a heart attack.

"I cannot, in good conscience, allow you to risk your life, ma minette," he stated as he set his jaw in stubborn defiance.

I started shaking my head immediately and worry soured my stomach. If Drake didn't allow me to come with him, I'd never be able to do what I'd come to do. "I have to go with you, Drake," I insisted. "If I don't expel the demon and send it back to wherever it should be, all hell will break loose on Tuesday!"

Drake nodded that he understood, but didn't look convinced.

"So I'm going with you," I insisted, straightening my posture and daring him to argue with me. "End of story."

"*Mon Dieu, tu es une poignée!*" Drake exclaimed, throwing his hands up in the air like I was a lost cause.

"And just what's that supposed to mean?" I demanded.

"It means you are quite a handful!" he replied. I could only smile because it appeared I'd won the argument.

"Regardless," I started, dropping my hands from my hips, and inspecting my pinky finger. I wanted to see if the cut had reopened because it had begun to sting like an SOB. "What's our plan for today going to be?"

Drake nodded and started rubbing the back of his neck again. He was quiet for a few seconds before he cleared his throat and his eyes found mine. "We find you a new pair of shoes and some warmer clothes," he started, and I bobbed my head in eager agreement. "Then, I pay a visit to the police station to look up Mike Pepitone's address."

"And where do I go?" I asked.

"You, mon chaton, can take a walk or perhaps you would like to busy yourself by enjoying a meal?" He wrapped his arm around me and started escorting me down the hallway to the stairwell. "You will have to keep yourself otherwise preoccupied."

"Why can't I just come to the police station with you?" I asked.

He immediately shook his head. "I do not want us seen together, ma minette. I do not know what the aftermath of this situation will be; and I do not want to endanger you."

I figured it was a good point because I didn't really know how long I was going to be stuck in 1919 since I didn't have the remainder of Guarda's tonic to return home. That thought only brought me unbearable grief, so I immediately pushed it into the back of my mind. I had more important things to focus on. "Okay," I said in a softer tone.

"First things first, mademoiselle," Drake continued. "As I said, we must get you some warmer clothes and new shoes." Then he pointed to my shoes, which he'd placed beside the front door. Even though I spotted a slice in the sole of one of them, I didn't have any other shoes, so I guessed I was SOL until we could buy a new pair. Then something occurred to me.

"Um, Drake, I don't have any money," I blurted out, realizing the only thing I did have were the clothes on my back.

"Unimportant," he answered while shaking his head. "Leave the finances to me."

"But . . ." I started.

Drake chuckled. "I am certain you will find a way to pay me back," he said with another devilish smile, his eyes twinkling. "Or perhaps you will allow me the chance to choose your payback method?"

I shook my head as he opened the front door for me and we walked outside into the brightness of Prytania Street. As soon as I saw the scenery surrounding me, I felt my stomach flip. The view was so familiar and yet, so different. The street was still lined with the same oak trees, but they weren't as large as those I knew. And the walkways weren't quite as torn up by their invasive roots.

Once outside, my attention turned to the various automobiles parked on the street. They looked pre-industrial age to my untrained eye, like something you'd see from an old black-and-white movie about Bugsy Siegel. As I stared at them, openmouthed, Drake hurried past me and approached a shiny, four-door number, which was painted a dark forest-green. It appeared to be a convertible, and the black rubber top was pulled down behind the second row of seats. The wheels and tires were so thin, they reminded me of bicycle tires. The front of the car had a long hood, which ended in an iron grille, flanked by two round headlights. Smaller headlights also appeared on either side of the windshield.

"Mademoiselle," Drake said as he opened the passenger door for me. The only windowpane was the one above the dashboard. Other than that, the car was completely open and subject to the elements.

"Thanks," I said, plopping myself down onto the black, plush, couch-like seat. The front seat, like the back, was long and continuous, similar to a loveseat rather than the usual bucket seats I was familiar with. The back was raised a bit higher than the front seat was. "What kind of car is this anyway?" I asked, as I ran my hand over the metal dashboard.

"An Overland," Drake replied as he patted the steering wheel in a proud sort of way. "I purchased it last year." Then he turned on the ignition and smiled at me. "Isn't she a beaut?"

I laughed, finding it funny to hear Drake use slang. Ordinarily, he sounded so prim and proper. He put the Overland into gear and we were off, bouncing down the street in a series of uncomfortable and jarring bumps as the narrow tires traversed the road.

As we drove down Prytania Street, I couldn't keep my eyes from bugging out as I observed my surroundings. Drake hung a left on Seventh Street and then we reached St. Charles Avenue. People meandered this way and that, dressed in suits and ties, bowler hats, and nondescript, unflattering dresses, such as the one I was wearing.

I glanced up at the buildings as we drove by, reading the signs that hung above them. "Imperial Shoe Store."

"Oui, mon chaton, and that is our stop." Drake pulled the Overland up to the curb and parked it, before turning off the ignition. He exited the driver's side quickly to open my door for me. "Mademoiselle," Drake said as he smiled down at me and offered me his hand. I gratefully took it and couldn't help loving how real he felt to me, so warm now, and so three-dimensional. It suddenly occurred to me that if Drake and I had lived in the same time period, maybe something special could have existed between us. As it was, I continued having a hard time remembering that everything surrounding me wasn't reality, and I would hopefully be returning to my own time soon enough.

We walked into the Imperial Shoe Store, arm in arm, and Drake immediately started for the women's section, which was located at the front of the store. There, countless pairs of shoes lined the shelves on the walls—some dressy and some not so dressy, but all looking antiquated and archaic. I never hoped to see a pair of Nike tennies more than right then. "I can't walk or run in any of these shoes, Drake," I said.

"*Pourquoi pas*, ma minette? Why not?"

I shrugged. "Because there's a good chance I'll need to be quick on my feet tonight, and that's something I can't accomplish in heels!"

"I do not believe you have much choice in the matter, mon chaton," Drake said, and I sighed, resigning my poor feet to a terrible fate as I searched for the shoe that looked the least confining. I reached for a pair of boots that resembled an extra-rigid white sock that had been mounted onto black high heels. The leather boot featured sixteen white pearlescent buttons down the front.

"This is our balmoral cut, with a button closure and a straight fly," a man announced from behind us. I figured he must be a salesman.

"They'll do," I said, sighing as I wondered if I could even walk more than a few yards in them.

"Your size, miss?" The salesman inquired.

Instantly at a loss, I wondered how shoe sizes were determined in the 1900s and figured I was about to find out. "Um, I don't really know," I answered sheepishly.

"You don't know?" the man repeated as he sighed, without saying anything more. He looked at my foot for a few seconds while frowning as he scratched the side of his head. "I believe you must be a size eight," he mentally calculated.

Silently, he disappeared into the rear of the store while Drake looked at me with raised eyebrows. "*Quels grands pieds*, mon amour!

You should pray your feet grow no larger as I do not believe size nine even exists!"

"Ha-ha, funny!" I grumbled as he continued to chuckle. I pretended to punch him in the stomach, which only resulted in louder chuckles. Then, apparently feeling sorry for me, he draped his arm around me, as if to apologize. The salesman returned from the rear of the shoe store with a shoebox under one arm. Pulling out the shoes from the box, he knelt down and removed my ballet flats. He slipped the boots onto my feet and then forcibly yanked them up my calves. He started buttoning them, which seemed to take an eternity. When he was finished, he placed my feet on the floor and I walked a few paces forward. "They fit," I said, although I refused to lie and say they were comfortable.

"Very well," Drake said with a smile as he reached into his pocket and retrieved his black leather wallet. He handed the man a bill and then faced me again. "Our next stop is the dress shop, right next door," he announced as we started for the front door. The salesman met us in the front of the store, handing Drake his change.

When we walked outside, we swung a left. We entered a store called Bromley-Shepard Co. The first thing I noticed was the large assortment of dress coats on mannequins at the very front of the store. "You will require a proper coat as the evenings get quite chilly, ma minette," Drake advised me as he stopped walking. Silently taking stock of each coat, he narrowed his eyes as he studied every one of them.

"Are they all fur?" I asked, the tone of my voice suggesting I wasn't exactly thrilled with the concept.

"Yes, of course," the salesman answered as he came up behind us unexpectedly. The thought crossed my mind that 1919 salespeople had a lot in common with stealthy ninjas.

"Oh, mon chaton, I like this one," Drake said as he reached for the sleeve of a reddish-brown jacket.

"You have very good taste, sir," the salesman said, nodding. He cleared his throat and smiled, revealing teeth that looked like someone had stuffed his mouth full of Cracker Jack. "This is our best selection of very fine coats. This particular coat is made completely of wool, trimmed with genuine beaver pelt, and lined in silk. Again, this is the finest coat made, sir."

Drake agreed as he looked over at me with his eyebrows raised. "Well, mon amour?"

I shrugged and leaned forward, glancing at the price tag that hung from it. "Forty-nine ninety-five!" I said, aghast. I frowned while trying to figure out what the coat would have cost in my own time, adjusting for the inflation rate. But lacking a calculator, and not knowing what the rate was, I just figured it cost a lot. "Drake, we really don't have to get the most expensive coat in the store," I argued, shaking my head.

"*Non-sens*, mon chaton! We will take it," Drake told the salesman, ignoring me and facing him. The salesman simply nodded and pulled the coat from the mannequin, draping it over one of his arms.

"Very good, sir," the salesman said as he smiled gratefully at Drake. He boxed up the coat and wrapped it with brown paper.

When the transaction was completed, Drake offered me his arm and we started for St. Charles Avenue again.

"You didn't have to spend so much money, Drake," I said after he had me comfortably seated in the Overland. He placed my coat in the rear seat before opening his door and sitting down beside me.

With a charming grin, he said, "I am aware of that, ma minette," and started the engine. As we pulled into the street, he revved the engine and downshifted, smiling at me boyishly. He took the curves in the road a little too recklessly, which made me suspect he enjoyed driving fast. Luckily for him, as an officer, he could probably talk his way out of a speeding ticket if he ever got one. I could just imagine what he would have done behind the wheel of a Ferrari or Lamborghini.

"I am fortunate that money is no object," he announced. "And, besides, I enjoy spoiling you, I must admit."

"Well, thanks," I said as the feeling of the wind in my hair made me smile. Glancing out of my window, and seeing the quaint city, I thought perhaps it really wouldn't be that bad to live in New Orleans in 1919. Then I remembered Prohibition, and the fact that women couldn't vote, and then it didn't seem quite so great.

"I must go to the police station now to search for the address of Mike Pepitone, mon chaton," Drake informed me as we came to a stop sign. "Would you like to return to my home, or would you prefer to busy yourself by shopping in town?" Feeling my nerves on high alert and not exactly thrilled with sightseeing on my own, I opted to return to our house so I could attempt a little rest and relaxation. I figured I could use all the rest I could get, given the fact that I had no idea what awaited me this evening.

Chapter 17

It was ten minutes to eleven and Drake and I were just on our way out of his house and headed to Mike Pepitone's home. "Here, ma minette," Drake said as he paused just before the front door. He reached beneath his uniform jacket and produced a gun, which he then handed to me.

"What?" I hesitated, looking down at the gun but making no motion to accept it. Having never shot a firearm in my life, I wasn't particularly thrilled with the prospect of shooting one now.

"I would prefer you to be prepared, ma minette, should trouble come our way." He answered and thrust the gun at me again. This time, I gripped the handle and held it so that the muzzle was facing the floor. "That is a thirty-two caliber revolver," he informed me.

"Where did you get it?" I asked, unable to keep my nervousness from my voice. "From the police station?"

"*Non*," he replied with a chuckle. "As I said earlier, I am attempting to keep a low profile where you are concerned, mon chaton. The firearm is from my own collection."

Whether the gun was his or not really wasn't the problem. The problem was that I had no idea how to shoot it. And, furthermore, I wasn't convinced it would do me any good anyway. I glanced up at him and shook my head. "What good is a gun going to do us in the first place?" I asked as I found his mirthful eyes already focused on me. "We're hunting demons, remember?"

Drake cocked his head to the side and nodded. "Oui, I have not forgotten, mon amour. But demons must occupy a host, correct?" I nodded, immediately glomming on to where he was going with his line of reasoning. "Correct," he answered his own question. "And a mere human can be killed by a bullet, ma minette."

"Okay, point taken," I grumbled. "So where's your gun?"

He pulled his police jacket to the side where I spied a holster wrapped around his waist, the butt of a pistol resting alongside his left hip. "Thirty-eight caliber Colt Police Positive double-action revolver," he said, and, from his tone, he sounded impressed.

"Okay," I repeated as I inhaled deeply. "This might come as a surprise but I have no idea how to shoot one of these things."

Drake shook his head, playfully sighing like I was a nuisance. But then he stood behind me and, gripping each of my arms, held them out straight in front of me. "Use both hands to grip the handle," he started. I did as instructed and couldn't help the surging feeling of giddiness that attacked me as soon as I felt his warm breath against my neck. I could only imagine that Guarda's sex candle was still at work. "Once you have a firm grip on the firearm, hold your arms out straight in front of you. Lock your elbows, mon chaton. Doing so will stop most of the recoil when you fire."

"Okay," I whispered, doing my best to pay attention to his instructions and not the feel of his large hands on my upper arms.

"Now you simply aim," he continued, apparently completely unaware that my breath was coming fast and it was all I could do to force myself not to drop the silly gun in order to turn around and kiss him. Yep, this had to be Guarda's magic at work because I couldn't imagine I would naturally be so stupid as to be having sexual thoughts about Drake when my life could come to an end that very evening.

"I aim," I said resolutely, forcing my thoughts back to the task at hand. Nothing like thoughts of my own death to ground me.

"Oui, mademoiselle. Aim the firearm at your target and then slowly apply pressure to the trigger. You must be careful not to lower the gun, unlock your elbows, or make any sudden movements as you will most certainly miss your target if you do."

"Okay," I said softly and focused the barrel of the gun on a picture of a landscape that was hanging directly across the room from me.

"If you need to take the shot, mon chaton, you would do so by pulling back the hammer, which is this little wing at the rear of the gun, before you shoot the gun. For every shot, you will need to first pull this hammer back." Then he released me and faced me with a handsome smile. "Do you understand, ma minette?"

I nodded and then sighed, wondering if I would remember everything he'd just said. "I think so," I answered.

"Very good," he said and then opened the front door, holding it for me as I walked into the dark and cold night. Drake hurried past me, opened the passenger door to the Overland, and once I was seated comfortably, sat beside me, turned the engine on, and started down the road. Neither of us said anything as we drove from Prytania Street to Ulloa Street. The Pepitone family grocery store was located on the corners of Ulloa and South Scott Streets.

Drake parked the Overland on Ulloa Street, maybe five houses from the Pepitone's. He checked his pocket watch and announced that it was now midnight. Because I couldn't recall the exact time of early morning when the Axeman was supposed to strike Mike Pepitone, our plan was to simply wait him out.

"Mike Pepitone and his wife, Rose, are immigrants from Italy," Drake said as he played with the buttons of his police uniform jacket. He tried to pretend that he wasn't getting cold even though we both kept blankets over our laps. I, myself, was actually quite grateful for the beaver coat Drake had purchased for me because it did a good job of keeping me toasty in the frigid air.

Because this was police business, Drake insisted on looking the part, although he neglected to wear his uniform hat because he didn't want to be too obvious, just in case someone spotted us from the street. We were trying to stay incognito, which was why Drake took the Overland rather than a police squad car. He'd put the convertible top up and parked under a large oak tree to further shield us from curious eyes.

"From what I remember of the attacks, it seems the Axeman was mostly interested in targeting women," I remarked as I watched Drake pull out his gold pocket watch yet again. "Five past midnight," he announced with a sigh. There wasn't a thing going on outside. "Oui, ma minette, most of the Axeman's victims have been women. The youngest was merely nineteen years old."

"Sarah Laumann," I answered immediately, already aware that she had been the Axeman's youngest victim.

"Oui," Drake said as he looked at me, and his handsome face took on a wistful, sad smile. "I visited her at Charity Hospital numerous times." He shook his head like the whole thing was a hapless shame. "She was ever so frail and slight, but she possessed such a lovely face, even with the bandages that covered her head."

"She was or is my great grandmother," I announced flatly as he turned and faced me with widened eyes. Then he began to nod as if it wasn't such a huge surprise after all. Maybe he was becoming so accustomed to surprises now that they didn't really register as anything extraordinary to bother mentioning.

"Oui, *bien sûr*," he started. "I can see the similarity between the two of you in your eyes and perhaps also your mouths." Then he chuckled and shook his head again. "Though Miss Laumann possessed none of your . . . fire, shall we call it?"

"Ha!" I said with a mock frown as he grinned at me. It was fairly obvious that Drake liked teasing me.

The grin soon vanished a few seconds later and was replaced with a thoughtful and pensive expression as he stared straight ahead. "I cannot help wondering how it is possible that I am sitting beside the great granddaughter of a nineteen-year-old woman." Then he turned toward me quickly. "And I do not actually wish to know how it is possible, so please, do not enlighten me."

"Okay," I said, never planning to tell him anyway. In general, I tried to avoid relating stories that would hint to or directly involve his death. So I just smiled at him and changed the subject. "Tell me more about Sarah."

He shrugged and began tapping his fingers against the steering wheel, as if keeping up with the beat of a song only known to him. "Miss Laumann lived alone and was mercilessly attacked in the night by a man wielding an axe."

"The Axeman," I interjected.

Drake nodded. "She sustained wounds to her head and until recently, she was recovering at Charity Hospital."

"Was she able to tell you anything about the Axeman?"

Drake shook his head and exhaled slowly. "*Non*. When I questioned her as to the nature of her attacker, she could only tell me that he came in the dark and was no more than a blurry shadow." He continued shaking his head and I could tell he was frustrated that he couldn't uncover the identity of the Axeman. He resumed bopping his fingers against the steering wheel as his attention returned to the street in front of us. "At any rate, I located the blood-stained axe *le bâtard* attacked her with in the yard of her modest abode."

"Hmm," I said, realizing there was information that I hadn't yet shared with Drake.

"The reason the Axeman wants me is chiefly because I am related to Sarah. It got angry when she didn't die from her wounds." I inhaled as my omnipresent fear started to flutter through me again. "I guess you could say it wants to finish the job."

Drake's jaw went tight as his eyes narrowed. "I will not allow this entity to harm a hair on your lovely head, ma minette," he announced in a steely tone. Then he diverted his attention to a car that suddenly meandered down the street. I felt my heart freeze up in my chest. But the car continued, passing through the stop sign at the end of the street and disappearing around the bend in the road. Drake sighed and leaned back into his seat again. I could see the frustration playing out over his face. It wasn't easy just to sit here and wait.

"Tell me more about your association with Sarah," I said. I liked learning about my lineage, and, at the same time, I wanted to keep Drake's attention engaged. Regarding my own family history, my mother had died when I was young and had rarely mentioned her side of the family. She'd left home at a very early age, and, as far as I could tell, she hadn't been close to any of her family members.

Drake cocked his head to the side and smiled. "I do not know Sarah Laumann that well, ma minette. I have only visited her a handful of times."

"In Charity Hospital?"

"Yes and in her new accommodations too."

"Hmm, sounds like you know her pretty well then?" I asked, eyeing him intently and wondering why he wouldn't just come out with it and tell me what the real situation was with her. I was convinced they'd become more than just friends, and I wasn't sure why, but I wanted to hear the truth from Drake's mouth.

"We enjoy one another's company," he answered matter-of-factly and shrugged. His nonchalance regarding his association with her failed miserably, however, and I suspected he was keeping some juicy details from me.

When I remembered talking with Drake in my dreams, when he'd still been haunting my house, he had made it sound like there was more than just a superficial acquaintance between my great-grandmother and him. "Are you positive you and she aren't more of an item?" I asked, shaking my head as I scrutinized him. "I seem to remember you saying you have a special sort of relationship with her?"

Drake shook his head again. "I would not term what we have as that kind of relationship, ma minette. Perhaps I visited her more often than I recollect. Sometimes, if I am in the area, I stop in to check on her and make sure she does not succumb to depression. After the attack, she was quite traumatized and downhearted, as you can probably imagine." He cleared his throat uncomfortably. "Our association reflects a mutual fondness for each other."

Of course she was "fond" of him. How could she not be? How could any woman not be incredibly fond of so handsome and charming a man? In fact, at nineteen years old, Sarah was probably head over heels in love with Drake. The mystery of how she wound up purchasing his house, which she left to my great aunt, Myra, who then willed the house to me, was still up in the air. But I guessed I couldn't learn the answer to that tonight.

"What time is it?" I asked after I couldn't take the silence in the car any longer. Drake fished his watch from his pocket and checked it again.

"Ten minutes to one," he answered as he stifled a yawn with his fist. I nodded and tried to resist yawning as I searched for another subject to talk about. Shivering in the cold night air, I wrapped my arms snugly around myself. "Ma minette, take my blanket," Drake said. He started to peel the blanket off his lap to give to me, but I shook my head.

"I'm fine and I know you're cold, so you keep it."

"Mon chaton," he started with a frown, but on this point, I insisted.

"I mean it, I'm fine," I repeated, pushing the blanket back at him. He shook his head and frowned, but replaced the blanket on his lap as I faced him, eager to begin a new topic of conversation. "You know, Drake, you didn't have to spend all that money on me today. I could have just made do with a new pair of shoes and one of your jackets."

He shook his head, and there was a strange expression on his face. It seemed like a blend of pensiveness and melancholy, but when I noticed the slight lift at the ends of his lips, it seemed to be a sweet melancholy. I watched Drake's gaze settle on the street ahead of us as the silence in the car persisted for a few more seconds. "According to these foreign memories of mine," he started in a voice that was deep and raw. Then he laughed and seemed almost embarrassed. "I have never told you, but . . ." He cleared his throat and looked extremely uncomfortable. When he turned to face me, his expression was kind, but serious. "I care deeply for you, mon chaton. Again, it is difficult for me to understand these feelings. As far as I am aware, you and I have only just met, but I feel something for you that, I daresay, quite resembles love."

I didn't know how to answer that so I reached for his hand. He covered my hand with his, looked over at me, and the bittersweet smile returned to his lips.

"I know it sounds absurd," he continued as he looked down at our fingers, which were now intertwined. "You and I are an absolute impossibility as decades of time separate us." He was silent for a few seconds. When he spoke, he brought his eyes back to mine. "Even so, I am unable to deny the feelings flowing through me, ma minette." He smiled sadly. "I do not know what might happen this evening," he continued, and sighed. "My memories fail me with regards to this evening, but whatever fate awaits us, I must tell you that when I look upon your face, I am consumed by the passion I feel for you."

I could feel tears welling up in my eyes as I smiled at him and tightened my grip around his hand. "Thank you, Drake," I said, knowing there really wasn't much more I could say. "If our situations were only different . . ." I started.

But Drake immediately shook his head vigorously and offered me a smile of consolation. "Things are as they must be," he said. "Fate has delivered us and now we must live according to our stars, ma minette."

Just as I was about to respond, Drake's expression changed. His eyes grew wide with surprise, and a moment later, he tore the blanket off his lap and reached for his Colt revolver, which he'd stashed on the floor of the Overland.

"He has arrived," Drake calmly announced as I looked at the Pepitone grocery store and noticed a shadow lurking in front of one of the side windows on South Scott Street.

"Drake, you can't stop him until after he's committed the crime!" I reminded him, reaching out and gripping his arm when it seemed he was already preparing to go after the Axeman. "Remember what Guarda told me!" I insisted. "We can't tamper with history! Whatever happened is meant to happen. We can't stop it!"

Drake took a deep breath as he sat back against the seat, but I could see a sheen of sweat breaking out across his forehead. "*L'horrible ironie!*" he said, slamming his hand into the bottom of the steering wheel as he turned to face me. "It is not an easy feat for me, as a sworn protector of the people, to allow that man to forcibly enter the house without doing anything about it, ma minette," he finished with visible restraint.

"I know, Drake, I know," I said as I tried to console him. Inside me, though, was another story: I was scared to death. "Mike Pepitone is the only one who gets attacked, strangely enough," I said, remembering the articles I read on the incident. "The children and his wife will be left alone." I hoped that information would be of some relief to him. I couldn't be sure, though, because as soon as the Axeman broke the window, Drake's posture turned rigid and I could see his breath coming in short spurts. "Drake," I started.

"I understand," he barked back at me, and I could see it was taking all his will to remain in the car. He fished out his pocket watch and checked the time again. "It is ten past one," he announced monotonously. I didn't respond. Instead, I watched the Axeman clear the broken glass from the window as he reached inside and threw the latch, raising the window as far up as it would go. Because the window was located on the ground floor, it took little effort for him to hoist himself through it, and, seconds later, he disappeared inside the house.

Drake reached for the .32 caliber Colt, which was sitting between us, and handed it to me with one hand. He started to open his door with the other. "Will you be able to pull the trigger if need be, ma minette?" he asked after I accepted the gun and held it tightly gripped in my shaking hand.

"Yes," I answered, my voice filled with fear.

Drake pushed his door open and didn't seem to notice the blanket when it fell from his lap and landed on the ground outside the Overland. Holding his .38 caliber in one hand, he reached for my hand with the other. I dropped the blanket from my lap onto the floor of the car and slid over to the driver's side, allowing him to assist me. Once outside, I could feel the cold night air as it wrapped itself around my legs. I wasn't sure if the goose bumps covering my body were from the freezing air or my own unmitigated dread.

"He'll make his escape through the children's room, which is on the opposite side of the house," I said, remembering the detail from the *Times-Picayune* articles.

Drake nodded and started up Ulloa Street with me right beside him. He held his gun with both hands, his arms straight out before him, but the barrel of the gun was aimed at the ground. He explained that this was the best way to hold the gun until one was ready to aim it at a target. I followed suit, but the grip of the Colt felt really heavy and cold in my hands.

Just before we reached South Scott Street, Drake cut across the sidewalk, being sure to stay hidden in the shadows provided by the trees. I followed him into the rear of the Pepitone's home, which was just behind their grocery store. We passed by the window where the Axeman had made his entry. Drake scaled the wall of the house and paused just before it ended, keeping his back up against the side of the one-story house. I stood next to him, shivering at the coldness of the wooden façade. Drake peeked his head around the corner, and moments later, faced straight ahead again.

"He hasn't tried to escape yet," he whispered.

It was strange, but I couldn't hear any sounds coming from the house at all. It was eerily quiet. As soon as the thought crossed my mind, though, a woman's startled scream pierced the air before it was utterly silent again. A few seconds later, I could hear the sound of heavy footfalls on a wooden floor. It sounded like someone was running. The Axeman was making his escape and from where we stood now, I thought only the thin wall separated him from us.

"He's nearly to the door," Drake whispered as he held his revolver up higher in front of him. I clutched the grip of my gun more tightly and tried to ignore my increased heartbeat as it pounded through me. I was so scared my mind went blank. It was almost as if I no longer had possession of my own body.

The heavy footsteps slowed and I heard the sound of the doorknob turning. Then the door jerked open violently as the sound of window shades hitting the door's glass window accosted my ears. I blinked and observed Drake launching himself forward, with his revolver aimed straight out in front of him.

Chapter 18

Do not move!" Drake commanded the dark figure looming before us. I came up behind Drake and went to his side, holding my gun out in front of me as well. I could see the shadowy form of a man who stood maybe ten feet in front of us, his back toward us. He was wearing a long, dark overcoat and a fedora. He was hunched over, and when he slowly turned around to face us, I couldn't believe his immense height and girth. He had to be at least six foot three or so, with substantially broad shoulders and a barrel of a chest. I didn't imagine he would be easy to take down. I couldn't see his face, but I had the uncanny feeling that his attention was completely focused on me. I could practically feel the weight of his eyes and was also keenly aware that this man, or creature, knew me.

"Put your hands on the top of your head!" Drake yelled, but the man made no attempt to obey him. He continued to evoke the strangest feeling that he was smiling, no, leering at me.

"You brought her to me," the Axeman said, but his voice sounded distant, low, and grumbly. He took a step toward us as Drake moved in front of me, protecting me with his body.

"I said, put your hands on top of your head!" he demanded, but the Axeman just continued walking toward us, as if Drake were of no consequence to him at all. "If you do not stop walking, I will shoot you!" Drake warned him.

The Axeman stopped advancing when he was perhaps four feet from us. I still couldn't make out his face. He just stood there, his chest rising and falling with his rapid breathing. I could still feel the penetration of his gaze, even though Drake stood directly in front of me, with the barrel of his revolver aimed at the Axeman, the demon. I was so scared I couldn't even think, couldn't even breathe.

"Now, very slowly, put your hands on top of your head," Drake said again, but he didn't yell this time.

The Axeman brought his arms up to his sides and propped one hand on his head. He raised his other arm in Drake's direction and swatted it through the air as if he were shooing a bothersome flying insect. I watched in utter disbelief as Drake became airborne and then was thrown forcibly backward, as if by invisible hands.

"Drake!" I shouted as I watched him land a good ten feet away from me. He groaned as he bounced against a tree before dropping to the ground. He released the gun and it fell down beside him. Shaking his head, he instantly found his feet and stood up, swiftly retrieving the revolver.

"Shoot him!" Drake yelled as I brought my eyes back to the Axeman. But it was too late. He was already rushing me. He pushed against me and I fell backward, away from him. As soon as I hit the ground, the Colt flew from my hands. Trying to catch my breath, but also realizing time was of the essence, I craned my head in the direction that the gun had fallen and watched it land in a patchy stretch of grass about ten feet away from me. I started to get up, but realized I couldn't. It was as if my body suddenly refused to obey my mind. I attempted to shift my arms and move my legs, but they were frozen still. Meanwhile, the Axeman ambled closer until he stood directly over me.

"What are you?" I demanded when I saw that even up close, I still couldn't find his face. He appeared simply as a dark shadow. He didn't respond, but dropped down on his knees and straddled me.

He held his hands about four inches above my face and I could see darkness pouring from them, blurring the delineation of his fingers until it looked like his coat sleeves terminated in black smoke.

All of a sudden, I felt my neck and head rising up off the ground. It was as if I were responding to his hands, which he held directly over my face. My mouth opened by itself, not voluntarily, and it suddenly felt as if a great wind blew throughout my entire body. The wind died down unexpectedly and was replaced by intense agony. It felt as if my insides were being ripped apart. I squeezed my eyes shut tightly against the pain and tried to resist the intensity of the creature's hold on me.

"Leave her alone!" Drake screamed. I opened my eyes and saw him coming up behind the Axeman. Drake aimed his revolver at the man's head, and, without wasting another second, pulled the trigger. The Axeman fell over instantly, and the indescribable pain I'd been experiencing suddenly vanished. I immediately sat up and caught my breath, while bringing my hand up to my throat. I tried to massage away the residual pain, which still lingered there.

"Drake!" I screamed as soon as my eyes met his. I watched his body as it suddenly lifted into the air directly in front of me. His feet dangled helplessly as if he were hanging by his neck. I looked up at his face and saw him turning white as if he couldn't breathe. It looked like an invisible cord was choking the life out of him. Black smoke began pouring out of the Axeman, enveloping him in a dark cloud. The smoke wafted in a single line directly around Drake, surrounding him in its nightmarish web. Slowly, the darkness began diffusing into him.

I watched Drake lift his hand, which still clutched the revolver. He painstakingly brought the revolver to his temple. "Drake, no!" I cried out as soon as I realized what he intended to do.

The demon was in the process of taking possession of Drake. That much was as obvious as the black smoke now filled his body.

And what was worse, Drake had to know that he would soon be rendered completely powerless against the demon's control.

"I'm sorry, ma minette," he managed to say in a tortured voice. I shook my head as tears stung my eyes and began rolling down my cheeks.

"Please don't do it, Drake," I begged before he shook his head and pulled the trigger. A jolt traveled through his body and he suddenly collapsed onto the ground. The smoke that was dissolving into him began billowing out of him, fleeing his body at an accelerated pace. The darkness coagulated in the air, just above Drake's now-prone body. It began to float away from Drake, traveling through the air like a giant, black cloud.

That was when I saw it was approaching me. It was as if a huge army of airborne black ants suddenly combined to charge me as one, swooping down over me in a blast of blackness. I scrambled to get away from the cloud, but my body was stricken immobile. I collapsed against the ground before I was lifted into the air, as if by invisible hands. The blackness surrounded me. I could feel my skin prickling and stretching as the darkness began to engulf me, absorbing into my skin as it did so.

Panicking, my mind instantly went blank.

Was this how I was meant to die? I asked myself. The darkness was continuing to consume me, eating up everything that was Peyton Clark as its ugliness took control of me. I could feel my spirit weakening, lessening as an unbelievably powerful entity claimed my body as its own.

As the obscurity continued to fill me, knowledge began to grow within me, awareness. It wasn't a knowledge that I'd previously possessed, however, but the knowledge of experience—and experiences, memories that weren't my own. I realized, with horror, that as the demon was forcing its way into my body—and in the process, forcing me out—its memories and experiences were beginning to implant themselves inside me.

I was overcome with the understanding of what this demon was and where it had come from.

Images of days long gone began to infiltrate my head. I could see New Orleans as it would have been in the early twentieth century, the archaic automobiles offering a clue. I could feel myself running through the dark streets of New Orleans, hungry and thirsting for something I didn't understand. I could hear my own heavy breathing and the uneven sounds of my footsteps against the pavement, even as I realized this wasn't really me, this wasn't Peyton Clark. It was merely the imprinting of the demon's memories as it staked its claim on my body.

The image of the dark streets of New Orleans was then replaced with images of contorted and screaming faces I didn't recognize. Moments later I remembered them. They were victims . . . my victims. With the memory came the tangible feeling of an axe in my hands. I noticed the blood dripping off the end of the blade. I glanced back at the faces of those I'd attacked and noticed they were bludgeoned, bloody, and unrecognizable. Although I knew I should've been appalled by the images revealing themselves in front of my eyes, there was a growing part of me that thirsted for the violence, thrived on it. Demanded more.

The images of the killings dimmed away and were replaced with a memory of how I'd taken form, how I'd come to travel from Guinee, the spirit plane, to this earthly one in the twentieth century. I was overcome with the feeling that I'd been called to the earthly plane, forced here through voodoo magic.

In my mind's eye, I saw a mortal woman, hunched over a myriad of candles as she stood in the darkness of a ramshackle structure. Her long gray hair fell over her face, but I could still see her lips moving.

She chanted words, incantations that begged for my return, uprooting me from my sleeping place and forcing me into the mortal world. Her eyes danced behind the screen of her eyelids. I could feel my power growing with every word she said. Moments later, I burst through the void separating Guinee from the earthly plane and captured the body of a large and burly man, forcing his essence out.

But this wasn't the circumstance of the demon's original birth, and 1918 wasn't the first time he'd visited the mortal plane. No, I could feel the fact that this entity was much older. As soon as that thought birthed itself, I was overcome with memories of a time before 1918. The recollections surged into me, confusing me as they became my own. I fought to separate myself from the memories, to maintain my own independence, but I failed. It was a sure sign that the demon was winning in the fight to take control of me.

I saw the circumstance of the demon's first appearance on the earthly plane. It had taken the body of a slave woman in New Orleans. She'd summoned it through her voodoo, begged for it to use her body as a vessel, to exact revenge for her and her people. So it had. The entity had destroyed the entire household, the woman's master and mistress as well as their children. But it hadn't stopped there. The thirst for violence, for bloodshed, was deep within the demon and it couldn't discern between those to kill and those not to kill. So it had murdered them all, every last person in the household, slave or slave owner.

Then the demon had started to hunt for more victims. The thirst, the hunger, was never ending. After a killing spree that lasted months, it was finally forced back to the spirit plane at the hands of a practiced voodoo priestess. But though the demon was gone, it hadn't been forgotten. No, the entity had left its mark on the mortal plane and those who were in the know realized how powerful this demon was. And that information, when in the hands of the wrong practitioners, meant that the demon would continue to be called upon. It would appear, wreak its havoc on the mortal world, only to be exorcised back to Guinee by those who were strong enough to attempt it.

Until now . . .

Now it had captured my body and I was dying. And once my soul departed, that meant the demon would be free to use my body as a vessel in its murderous rampages.

Help me! I cried out in my mind to no one in particular.

And then I realized what I needed to do, to whom I needed to appeal. There was only one person, one spirit, who had the power and the ability to help me. I had to call for help from the Loa of the dead. Baron Samedi was the only entity I knew who could free me from the demon's hold and send it back to the spiritual realm. I clenched my eyes shut tightly, burning with the feeling of the darkness as it infiltrated me. I could feel my whole identity being swallowed up by it.

Baron Samedi, I thought to myself. *Please hear me, Loa of the dead! Baron Samedi, I need your help!*

The black fog continued to encircle me, keeping me aloft as it fed from my life's energy. The haze surrounding me began diminishing little by little as it continued to fill me up.

Baron Samedi, please hear me! I called out again. *You promised me protection once! I need your protection now! Please help me!*

Then I saw him. I wasn't sure if he simply existed in my mind's eye, or if I was seeing him in person, but I could breathe in his presence as well. The smell of his cigar filled my nostrils. I opened my eyes and found him standing alongside me, studying me curiously.

"Please, Loa," I said, my voice strained.

"Please what, baby?" he responded. "I need ta hear yer request 'fore I can do anythin' 'bout it."

"Please send this demon back to wherever it came from!" I screamed, unable to resist being filled up by the foreign entity. My own power and life force was rapidly fading away. I was growing weaker by the second as the entity's strength continued to build.

Baron Samedi laughed and took another puff of his cigar as I realized I wasn't witnessing him from my mind's eye. He was here with me, in the flesh.

"I'm not in the business o' helpin' without the favor bein' returned, baby," he said calmly, languidly, as if he wasn't concerned that my life was dissipating right before his eyes.

"Whatever you want," I whispered against the pain.

He smiled and shook his head. "That's a big risk yer takin' there, baby. Makin' promises 'fore ya know what the consequences could be."

The air filling my lungs was hot, like I was inhaling smoldering embers. I couldn't lift my head off the ground and my appendages had long since grown numb. I was nearly dead. Whatever I had to do to repay Baron was worth it, as far as I could see. "Anything," I whispered. "I'll owe you whatever you want," I continued before something occurred to me. "With the exception of my soul. I'd rather die than owe you that."

Baron laughed and the sound reminded me of rolling thunder. "I ain't interested in yer soul, baby." Then he looked me up and down as if to say just what it was that he was interested in.

"Okay," I managed, my voice starting to sound like a mouse squeaking. "Then we have a deal?"

"We have us a bone-if-fied deal, baby," he answered, removing the cigar from his mouth and dropping it to the ground before stepping on it and putting it out. He disappeared into thin air, only to reappear directly above me, his face mere inches from mine. Then he did something I'd never seen him do before. He opened his mouth. He opened it into a wide circle and a bright, white light emerged from it, reminding me of a beacon of light at the end of a long and dark tunnel. Slowly, the Loa of the dead began to inhale. He opened his mouth even wider and sucked in a deep, powerful breath. I glanced down at myself and noticed the darkness of the entity being pulled away from me. It looked like a film reel of black ink thrown on me, only in reverse, the droplets of pitch-blackness pulling away from me as they were sucked into the maelstrom of light inside Baron Samedi's mouth.

I could feel the demon trying to retain its grip on me, clinging as hard as it could to avoid being sucked into the vacuum of the Loa's mouth. But Baron Samedi just kept inhaling more deeply until he sucked every last drop of darkness right out of me. Relief started to make itself known little by little as the numbness began leaving my fingers and toes. I could feel heat returning to my cheeks and my breathing began to grow more even as my vitality was restored. Baron Samedi took one final breath before closing his mouth and swallowing the demon.

I felt myself drifting back down to the ground, and once I touched the cold, dewy earth below me, I sat up, taking a deep breath. I felt dizzy. "Thank you," I said as I looked up at him, panting.

Baron Samedi just smiled at me and held up his hand as a cigar magically appeared between his fingers. He plopped the lit stogie into his mouth and inhaled deeply, while the smoke wafted out from behind his dark, round glasses. "No problem, baby," he replied. "You jist remember we made ourselves a deal."

I nodded and took another deep breath, trying to focus on inhaling and exhaling in the hopes that the dizziness in my head would let up. "I won't forget," I managed.

"I look forward ta our next meetin', mortal," Baron Samedi said and then smirked broadly at me, as if he was privy to information that I wasn't. Then, in a blink, he was gone.

I took another deep breath before I stood up, with my legs still wobbling. After a few hesitant steps, I could bear my own weight, and I hurried over to Drake. I knelt down and tried not to stare at the bullet hole in his temple where the blood had already pooled and was running down his face. His body still felt warm to the touch. His hair was matted with blood, but I couldn't stop my fingers from running through it. I couldn't resist my inexplicable need to touch him. My ceaseless tears splashed against his beautiful skin, and some of them washed away his blood.

"*Ma minette,*" his voice sounded in my head. "*I shall always love you.*"

More tears filled my eyes as something caught in my throat and I choked back my grief. The realization that I loved Drake suddenly dawned on me, overwhelmed me. "I will always love you, Drake," I whispered softly, stinging inside with the weight of the realization. And then it struck me that I had always loved Drake. Even though our situation had made it impossible for us to be together, that didn't mean that I cared about him any less. The truth was that Drake had been my confidant and my friend from the time I'd moved into our house and he'd made his presence known.

"Please don't leave me," I whispered as I ran my fingers over his cheeks and wiped the tears from my eyes. Glancing down at him, I suddenly noticed my fingers growing more and more transparent. Blaming my blurry vision, I tried to stop crying. I wiped the tears from my eyes and then glanced back at my hands. They were disappearing, growing translucent just like my fingers had. Looking down at the rest of my body, I realized I was fading right before my eyes. It was almost as if someone were erasing me.

"What's happening?" I asked, panicking as my voice wavered and I suddenly found myself consumed by darkness that was inky black, but felt balmy and warm.

"Peyton!" I heard a man's voice cry out and I tried to swim through the black void of my mind, searching for a doorway that could lead me to the familiar voice.

"Peyton, wake up!"

Opening my eyes, I saw the face of an angel staring back at me. I blinked a few times, trying to focus my watery vision. His face was ever so handsome and his golden hair fell into his eyes, which were the warmest amber I'd ever seen. His rosy, plump lips parted into a smile of relief as he ran his fingers softly down the side of my face. "Peyton," he whispered.

"Ryan?" I asked, taking a deep breath and sitting up to discover I was in my guest bedroom. Lovie and Christopher stood beside Ryan, each of them staring at me with unmasked relief. "What-What happened?" I asked in a groggy voice.

"We brought ya back," Lovie answered with a warm smile.

I shook my head, fully lost and confused. I didn't understand how I'd just been kneeling beside Drake in the freezing cold and now I was in my guest bedroom. "Drake is dead!" I cried out as the memory of his passing jolted through my mind. In response, tears burst from my tired eyes and I felt my entire stomach drop with the weight of my sorrow.

Lovie simply nodded with a sad expression, but then she smiled down at me. "He's not gone, Peyton," she said. "Talk ta him."

At first I didn't understand what she meant. I couldn't bridge the gap that I'd watched Drake die right in front of me and yet Lovie was telling me he wasn't gone and that I could talk to him. I started to shake my head before I remembered where I was. I was back in my own century, and then I understood. "*Drake,*" I thought in my mind.

"*Oui, ma minette,*" came his reply, and I immediately closed my eyes.

I could see him again. He was standing in his living room, dressed in his immaculate police uniform. It was as if no time at all had passed between us. He smiled that handsome grin at me and suddenly feeling buoyantly happy, I threw my arms around him. Burying my head against his warm chest, I inhaled his familiar scent and let my tears flood my eyes.

"Ma minette," he said with a little chuckle. "Do not be upset, mon petit chaton. I do not like to see you cry."

I wiped the tears away, wishing I could clear the frog from my throat. I pulled away from him and tried to smile as I beheld his beautiful face and sensuous, endearing smile. The thing that struck me most, however, was that Drake didn't seem at all surprised. Because after experiencing everything that we'd just endured, shock and intense sorrow seemed to be my only feelings. But not Drake.

"You knew," I said to him, as the realization continued to dawn on me. "All along, you knew how this was going to end, didn't you?"

He nodded sadly, that melancholic yet nostalgic smile of his still in place. "*Bien sûr*, mon chaton, of course I knew."

Without another word, I brought my hands to his face so I could run my fingers down his cheeks. I loved being able to touch him—and how real he felt. Finally. He seemed just as real to me as he had in 1919.

"Peyton?" I heard Ryan's voice.

I didn't say anything to Drake, but he just nodded as if he understood that I had to leave him . . . temporarily. "Go," he said as he bounced his finger off the end of my nose. "We will have plenty of time to visit later."

"Thank you," I whispered. "Thank you for . . . everything."

"Do not thank me, ma minette," Drake responded, his eyes revealing the fact that he regretted nothing. "I did only what I had to do . . . because I love you."

I felt my heart break at the same time because I loved Drake too. What was more, I knew I needed to tell Drake the truth regarding how I felt about him. "I love you too, Drake, and you will always have a special place in my heart. I can't tell you how fortunate I feel to have been able to see you in real life in 1919, to have been able to experience what it would have been like for us to be together." But then I realized what also needed to be said, what had to be made crystal clear. "I do care about you very much, Drake, but . . . you and I also know that we can never be anything other than two ships passing in the night."

"Oui, ma minette, I understand," Drake said, his voice sounding dejected. "Though I have tried to convince myself that we could love one another in dreams or that strange yet lovely place that exists when you close your eyes . . ."

"It isn't real, Drake. You and I could never be anything other than what we are right now because only one of us is alive. You know that," I said and paused for a moment because it was a thought that had occurred to me as well. But when it came down to it, Drake was a spirit and I was alive, with a vibrant and exciting life ahead of me that I had to experience, that I wanted to experience. I couldn't live the rest of my years in my head or in my dreams. I had to live in the moment, in the now.

"Oui," he responded and then sighed. "Oui. Much though it pains me to admit this, mon chaton, le barbare is good for you. He is . . . a good man. And, what is more, I can see his love for you."

I smiled and, figuring there wasn't anything more I could say, I opened my eyes.

I found Ryan gazing down at me. I was suddenly so happy and relieved at the sight of his beautiful face that I couldn't hold back another bout of tears. I looped my arms around his neck, needing to feel him closer to me, and aching to feel his warmth.

"It's okay, Pey," he crooned into my ear as he ran his hands through my hair. "Everything's gonna be all right now."

Although his words soothed me, I didn't understand how everything could be all right. I pulled away from him and addressed Lovie. "How?" I started. "How did I get back here when your bag with the tonic and all the exorcism tools in it stayed here and never traveled back with me to 1919?"

Lovie smiled and patted my arm with tenderness and care. "Y'all have Samuel ta thank fer that," she said. As soon as she mentioned him, the strange little creature blinked into existence, and I spotted him where he sat on Lovie's lap. "Samuel's block was removed," Lovie continued, "an' as soon as it was, he warned me that ya needed help gittin' back here."

I nodded as the puzzle pieces started to fall in place. "Samuel's block must have been removed when Baron Samedi swallowed the demon," I said as Lovie nodded. "But how did you get me back here?"

Lovie smiled wider as she reached down and started petting Samuel. Apparently, now she could see him again. "I relied on mah sixth sense, Peyton," she answered. "Once Samuel's block was removed, I was able ta witness everythin' you was experiencin' through my connection with Samuel. Once I understood ya needed help gittin' back ta yer own time, I simply fed ya the tonic, little by little, while you was sleepin'."

So Lovie managed to bring me back by making me drink the tonic in the present time. Interesting . . . I inhaled deeply and heaved a sigh as I remembered Baron Samedi was the one who had forced the demon out of me and exiled it into the land of the dead. Now it remained to be seen what his payment would be. Somehow I wasn't worried about it though. Maybe it was foolish, but I had a feeling that Baron Samedi wanted me to succeed. I didn't know why but I felt as though he was on my team, rooting me on.

The memory of the Loa of the dead inhaling the demon of the Axeman suddenly hit me like a great gust of wind from a previous life. I felt my entire stomach drop as worry began infusing me. I faced Lovie with widened eyes. "Do you think the demon is gone for good?" I asked.

She nodded immediately. "Oh, he definitely gone." Then she eyed me curiously. "An' once ya gits ta feelin' betta, I gots me some questions ta ask ya." I was pretty sure her questions centered on Baron Samedi, but I didn't say anything; I just nodded.

Lovie stood up and took Christopher's hand. "We gonna give y'all some time now ta be alone with each other," she said as she started for the door, dragging Christopher with her. I watched them leave the room before my eyes fell back on Ryan.

"Are you okay?" he asked with a warm smile.

"I think so," I said, heaving a dramatic sigh of relief. I thought long and hard about my adventure, and how I'd made it back to my own time. I knew I would never forget my time with Drake, nor how he threw his own life down to protect mine. I took a lot of comfort in knowing he was still in possession of my body, and as such, he was still a substantial part of me. I smiled up at the breathtakingly handsome man who had captured my heart. "Actually, I'm better than okay."

Chapter 19

TUESDAY, APRIL 22, 2014

It was five minutes to midnight on Monday, April 21. It was five minutes before the truth would be revealed about whether or not the Axeman really had been defeated.

"Are you nervous?" Ryan asked me as he reached over and grasped my hand in his much larger one. We were sitting on my bed in my guest bedroom. The television was on, although I didn't have a clue what program was playing. Instead, my attention was riveted outside. The full moon reflected against the bare branches of a nearby tree, which swayed this way and that, subject to the strength of the wind. A light rain had started up only an hour or so earlier and now the wind blew the drops against the window until they sounded like fingers drumming against the glass, punctuated by the occasional scraping of the branches.

"Yes, I am nervous," I answered, seeing no point in pretending otherwise.

Ryan pulled me into his broad and warm chest, wrapping both of his arms around me as he kissed the top of my head. I rested my head against him and tried to take comfort in the fact that he was there with me, that I wasn't alone. I glanced at the clock and noticed two minutes remained before midnight.

"There's nothin' to worry about, Pey," Ryan crooned into my ear. "I'm here with you an' I'm not goin' to let anythin' happen to you."

I smiled up at him but didn't say anything. Instead, I brought my attention back to the clock and started the count down in my mind. Fifty-five seconds remained.

I'd turned Drake off in my mind, seeing as how he didn't exactly appreciate my more intimate moments with Ryan. Regarding my ghostly friend, I didn't really know what the future held for us. I figured it made the most sense to exorcise Drake from my body and put him back into our house or, better yet, free him so he could move on to greener pastures in the unknown. But the idea of losing him left me nothing but cold. The truth was that Drake had become a part of me, a part of me that I didn't want to do without.

I glanced at the clock again.

Thirty-five seconds.

Whatever happened with Drake would remain to be seen. It would be a long and involved conversation that I would have to think about another day . . . well, that is, if midnight didn't bring with it the end of everything I knew.

Twenty-five seconds.

"Everythin' is goin' to be fine, Pey," Ryan whispered into my ear again as he held me even more tightly.

Fifteen seconds.

Suddenly the television flashed as static took over, the sound deafening in my small room. I felt my stomach drop to my toes as my heart started beating frantically. "What—?" I started as I sat up from where I'd been leaning against my headboard. I was suddenly on high alert. "What just happened?"

Five seconds.

Ryan jumped up and started for the television at the same time that the rain seemed to increase tenfold, the wind blowing even more frantically, throwing the rain into the windows until it sounded like someone was trying to break through the glass.

I glanced at the clock again.

One second.

When the clock struck midnight, the static on the television blinked away and we were faced with an attractive woman talking about the benefits of Tide Plus Bleach. Ryan turned around to face me and smiled widely. “See? Everythin’ is just fine,” he whispered as I swallowed down my own fear. “Must have just been a power line or somethin’ that freaked out for a bit,” he finished. He patted the top of the television and continued to smile at me. “Nothin’ to worry about, Pey.” He reached over and turned the television off.

I was still holding my breath as I peered around the room, my senses finely tuned to . . . I didn’t even know what. I started to inhale as I realized nothing was happening. The room was just as quiet as it had been and the wind and the rain outside continued to pelt the glass with the same intensity as they had only moments earlier. There were no sounds of screaming or back panels of doors being chiseled out. There were no sounds of windows shattering or axes meeting flesh and bone. There was only the sound of my own breathing in time with the beating of my heart.

Ryan walked back toward me and reached for both of my hands, gently pulling me up until I was standing directly in front of him. He leaned down and tilted my chin up, his warm lips brushing mine as I felt his tongue suddenly enter my mouth. I closed my eyes and melted into him, loving the feel of his hands as they played with my hair. His hands traveled down my back, and farther south still, until they finally rested on my bottom. He cupped each of my cheeks and pulled me against him, allowing me to feel his stirring excitement.

After another few seconds, he pulled away and smiled down at me again, his grin salacious and laced with hunger.

"I made you a promise," he whispered. "You will always have mah protection."

I started to smile and thank him but the smile and the words faltered on my lips. As the milky rays of the moonlight hit his stunningly handsome face, I could swear that the irises of his eyes were glowing white.

Or maybe it was just a trick of the light.

Acknowledgments

To my family: Thank you for all your support!

To my editors at Montlake: Thank you for making this book so much stronger!

To my agent, Jane Dystel: Thanks for being awesome!

To New Orleans: Thank you for being such a magical city!

About the Author

A *New York Times* bestselling author, H.P. Mallory began her writing career as a self-published author. She's a huge fan of anything paranormal, and anything ghost or vampire related will always attract her attention. Her interests are varied, but aside from writing, she's most excited about traveling. She's very fortunate to have lived in England and Scotland, both places really having a profound effect on her books. H.P. lives in Southern California where she is busily working on her next book! Please find H.P. on the web at www.hpmallory.com